Kate's Journey

LELA JEAN CLENDANIEL

WESTBOW
PRESS®
A DIVISION OF THOMAS NELSON
& ZONDERVAN

THE HOLY BIBLE, NEW INTERNATIONAL VERSION®, NIV® Copyright © 1973, 1978, 1984, 2011 by Biblica, Inc.® Used by permission. All rights reserved worldwide.

This is a work of fiction. All of the characters, names, incidents, organizations, and dialogue in this novel are either the products of the author's imagination or are used fictitiously.

WestBow Press books may be ordered through booksellers or by contacting:

WestBow Press
A Division of Thomas Nelson & Zondervan
1663 Liberty Drive
Bloomington, IN 47403
www.westbowpress.com
1 (866) 928-1240

Because of the dynamic nature of the Internet, any web addresses or links contained in this book may have changed since publication and may no longer be valid. The views expressed in this work are solely those of the author and do not necessarily reflect the views of the publisher, and the publisher hereby disclaims any responsibility for them.

Any people depicted in stock imagery provided by Getty Images are models, and such images are being used for illustrative purposes only.
Certain stock imagery © Getty Images.

ISBN: 978-1-9736-4477-4 (sc)
ISBN: 978-1-9736-4476-7 (hc)
ISBN: 978-1-9736-4478-1 (e)

Library of Congress Control Number: 2018913431

Print information available on the last page.

WestBow Press rev. date: 1/4/2019

To my very special family, all seventeen of them, and to all my
friends and neighbors who have encouraged me to keep on writing

Bear with each other and forgive whatever grievances you may have against one another. Forgive as the Lord forgave you. And over all these virtues put on love, which binds them all together in perfect unity.

—Colossians 3:13–14

Chapter 1

The holidays are now over, and a raw, whistling wind can be heard screaming around the tall, bare oak trees. The once-manicured lawn is saturated from the previous night's heavy rain, and dark, foreboding clouds lie heavy in the windblown sky. It is a typical, miserable January Monday morning in rural Cecil County, Maryland.

Kate Remington stands in the kitchen, bundled up in a fluffy bathrobe, silently staring out the window, as Jake, her husband, comes quietly up behind her. A brimming cup of hot coffee awaits him on the kitchen counter as he puts his arm around her waist and nuzzles her neck. A lone tear can be seen in the corner of her eye.

He takes a sip of the coffee and looks at her intently. "A penny for your thoughts. Why such a solemn and faraway look so early in the morning?"

Kate drops her gaze and turns her head. "I keep having that recurring dream with a partial memory of the beating I took at the hands of those two thugs, and I can't seem to get it out of my mind. It's one of the things I seem to remember of that awful day. Sometimes the pain actually comes back, goes up my neck, and settles on the top of my head. Those two Goth-like characters erased my whole memory of my previous life of forty-two years. That brutal attack left me with this head injury, a neck scar, and this stubborn amnesia."

Kate sounds exasperated and sighs. "It was that crash to the cement garage floor that really rattled my brain. I just hate them!" The tear rolls down her face. Jake rubs her shoulder and puts his coffee down.

Kate says, "I wish I could have those years back again. I get so emotional when I try to recollect what really happened in our garage five years ago. I guess I'm still bitter, and I can't let that part of my life go. I just hate what I went through. And then on top of that, Pastor Perry preached on the subject of forgiveness yesterday. How am I supposed to forgive those two criminals who did that to me?"

Kate sniffles and wipes her face on the dishtowel. "I despise them!" She slams her fist down on the counter. "I'll never forgive those two characters." Her face is red, and tiny beads of sweat appear across her forehead. She is trembling.

Jake steps back and gently turns her around, face-to-face now. "Kate, your anger and temper are justified, but you have got to deal with this and let some of this go. I know it is not an easy thing to do, but the police did catch the guys who attacked and kidnapped you. In fact, one of them is serving life in prison, while the other one died in that weird attempt to escape in a garbage truck. I don't like seeing you this way." Jake rubs her shoulders and massages her neck. He can see the turmoil and pain in her face.

"I don't even know who I am anymore," Kate says. "I couldn't even recognize some of our old friends at Angie's wedding. I am tired of pretending to know people when I don't have the slightest idea of who they are. Maybe I should go back to Wyoming. At least my life started over out there, and I knew who I was talking to."

Kate stops, looks down at her left hand, and sees her gold wedding band. Jake catches her glance as she takes a deep breath. Her cheeks become red again, and she wonders, *Oh, now what have I said? I don't want to hurt Jake with talk of Wyoming, but I felt so safe and free there. My life started over out there.*

Jake steps back. Now it is his turn to stare out the frosty window and wonder. "Kate, these past four years, I have tried to make your transition home as easy on you as I could, but this talk of Wyoming and your time out there has got to end," he says, clearly irritated. "I cannot compete with your constant talk of those memories or even of your changed life out there as Rose on that ranch or your feelings for Brad Crawford. I know you have had a hard time adjusting to your old life here, but please remember, this is where you belong—right here as a mother to Matt and Angie, and as my wife. Don't forget I spent a whole year trying to find you. Even the FBI tried to track you down. It was like you disappeared into thin air."

Jake's voice becomes softer. "I am still amazed by how you managed to travel clear out to Wyoming with those truckers you didn't even know. The

Lord was watching over you. Kate, the whole time you were gone for that year, Matt and Angie and I prayed earnestly for your protection. We almost had a memorial service for you, but I felt you were out there somewhere, surviving. It really made us grow stronger as a family, renew our faith, and place all our fears and everything in the Lord's hands. He has a plan for our lives, and I have come to believe that God is in control of our family, no matter what happens. Forgiveness is a choice. We may question many things that happen to us in our lifetimes, but we have to allow the Lord to guide us and mold us for his glory, not ours."

Jake sounds more sympathetic and deeper. He smiles and cocks his head, saying, "Our lives have not been the same since you returned. I feel like I am married to a completely different woman. You don't even cook the same meals anymore. In fact, little things seem to distract you. I guess I never realized how much I took you for granted until you were gone for that whole year. Kate, we will work this out together. I still love you, and no matter what happens, I'm sure—with your stubbornness and tenacity—you will survive. That's one of the things I have always admired about you. Just knowing how you crawled out of that half-submerged van in a flooded stream and then managed to gather your wits and survive is one for the books." Jake smiles now and musses her hair with the flip of his hand. "We will make this marriage work."

Kate pauses and wants to change the subject. "But if you and Matt were not by my side at Angie's wedding, I would have embarrassed our daughter terribly. I felt so inadequate meeting all those people again. They seemed to know me, but as hard as I tried, I couldn't place them or even remember half of their names."

Jake replies, "You have to remember I did not know some of the people either because they were from Dan's side of the family. I think people understood, and besides, you did just fine."

"I miss Angie so much every day," Kate says. "We really bonded while we were making her wedding plans. I felt like I was her best friend and not her mother. We found we had so much in common, especially since she is working at the same county hospital where I worked. I almost wish I could go back to nursing again, but I've forgotten so much, and there have been many changes for nurses. I guess I should be content with helping out at big brother Richard's veterinarian clinic. Then there is Matt." She looks at Jake with a deep sigh. The tears are gone. "He seems so distant at times. What do you think?"

Jake shakes his head and finishes his coffee. "All these pent-up feelings are going to put a wall between you and not just Matt but with me as well. Kate, you are home now, safe and sound. Please relax. I am going to be late for work. Look at the clock!"

Jake sounds impatient. He kisses her on the cheek and heads for the coat closet. "We can talk some more when I get home, I promise. Matt will be here too. Talk to him. You two need to sit down and talk over your concerns. He and Angie are two different personalities. Angie has always been more open and direct. Matthew is not as gabby as Angie, and he holds his feelings in close to his chest. You know he loves to eat, so the best way to get to him is through his stomach."

Jake hopes that brings a smile to her face. "That should be easy for you since you brought back a dozen new recipes from your diner friend, Dolly, in Wyoming."

Kate says, "Matt's been a great help in bringing me up to date on our computer in this electronic age. I'm sorry, but sometimes I just feel like I don't know what to do or where I'm supposed to be. I feel like I am just going through the motions of being a wife and a mother. I've tried to adjust and put that year behind me, but I can't help but blame God for not protecting me from those two attackers. I guess that sermon hit a raw nerve with me. How can I forgive those people when I have come to hate them more and more every day? Sometimes that is all I think about." Her voice sounds angry again.

"Kate, I knew this conversation would come up again because I could see you becoming listless and restless," Jake says. "Do you really want to go back to that ranch in Wyoming? You were working almost as hard as one of Brad's hired hands. They grew to depend on you. You were feeding all those cowpokes and taking care of Mary. Or is it Brad Crawford you are longing to see?"

Kate's face turns red, and she stops sniffling. She steps back from Jake, stares at him, and looks straight into his eyes while shaking her head. "I made my decision on that snowy trip home with you, and I'll stick with that decision. This is where I belong. As for Brad Crawford, there is still a soft spot in my heart for him too. It's just that I feel like I am two separate people—Kate to you in Maryland and Rose to my friends in Wyoming. I feel like I am letting you down when you have been so encouraging and loving to me. I know in my heart I should be here with you. You are my husband, and Matt and Angie are my responsibility too. As for Brad, we did have an understanding, but he knew that when I found out my true identity and my past, and who I really was, I would be leaving the ranch forever."

Kate sighs. "It's just that Angie is married to Dan now, Matt is off to college, and you are off to work every day. These cold, gray days of January make me feel like I am not needed anymore. I guess I'm feeling a little sorry for myself. I have come to really depend on you too, and I don't want anything to happen to you. What would I do without you to lean on?"

She turns and gazes out the window again. The wind still sounds raspy as the old dead leaves are blown across the wet lawn. The rain drizzles down as the gray clouds march across the sky. She wipes another tear from her eye and sighs.

"I know you still keep in contact with Brad's mother, Mary, through your emails. How is she?" Jake turns toward her and steps back. He begins reluctantly to pull on his overcoat.

"Yes, she keeps me up on ranch news. She hardly says anything about Brad. You know, I have never mentioned to Matt or Angie about what could have happened between Brad and me. They have only heard me mention some of the people's names who helped me and protected me. I guess that is our secret. You knew, since you talked to him out in the stable that day. He wanted to marry me and keep me there as Rose. That was all he knew of me until you showed up to claim me as your long-lost wife, then proceeded to cart me home in that pickup truck. I guess the realization of having two kids at home and a reminder of that responsibility really settled it for me."

A smile crosses her lips. "I remember the confrontation between you two. I was afraid Brad and you would come to blows that day in the stable over me. I do remember that conversation as plain as day. I was caught in the middle. My feelings were a jumbled mess. There was a lot of confusion and anger from both of you. I believe the picture album you brought with you made Brad stop and think too. That sealed the deal."

"Kate, we can finish this conversation when I get home. I love you no matter who you think you are." He smiles. "If anything happens to me, you will be taken care of, I promise. So don't worry. We can work this out."

"I know we can, and I love you for putting up with me and all my crazy moods, my stubborn amnesia, and accepting me as a changed wife. I'll see you after work, and please be careful. It is miserable out there."

He blows her a kiss as he buttons his coat and heads out the door. A blast of cold air rushes in and causes Kate to shiver. The door is pulled shut with a bang, and Kate is left standing in the middle of the kitchen, wiping her face on her sleeve.

She turns again and gazes out the frosty window as Jake's car pulls out of the driveway. *What would I really do without Jake? He never gave up looking for me during that whole year I went missing. He searched and prayed for me. He has brought me both sanity and security in my mixed-up world. He's such a stable and reliable guy, and I love him for that. He and Brad are so much alike.*

Despite the howling wind outside, her thoughts now return to the warmer summer days of last June. Winter can be such a boring time. She begins to relax as a smile parts her lips. Kate's thoughts return to the events of Angie's June wedding day. *Angie was such a pretty bride—and Dan, the handsome groom. It was such a nice outdoor wedding and a perfectly warm summer day.*

Kate smiles as she remembers the decorative lights and lanterns that swayed in the breeze from the tall maple trees. Then suddenly someone gasped, and a crash was heard. Angie and Jake were ready to step out, proud father and beautiful daughter, arm in arm, down the white-carpeted aisle to the altar. Everyone was in place. A colorful plastic lantern came loose from the tree and fell on Dan's dear old Aunt Betsy's head with a clatter.

There was a gasp and then a sudden silence, and all heads turned to see what had happened. The wedding music stopped. Aunt Betsy's hat flew off and was now on the ground. She looked around at all the surprised faces. There were little chuckles heard here and there. She then just so nonchalantly picked up her bonnet, grinned sheepishly, and plopped it back on her head, backward of course. She didn't care. She was just glad to be there. Everyone just smiled.

Then George, one of the ushers, hurriedly ran to pick up the lantern, only to trip over one of extension cards. He crashed into some of the empty chairs. What a sight! He was so embarrassed. Poor George! His tan tuxedo knee had a smudge of grass stain with a little dirt on it, and his shirttail now hung out beneath his suit coat. It was just like he was sliding into home plate at the ballpark. Matt rushed over to straighten the chairs while George was getting up. George just kept smiling and apologizing to everyone. It was really comical.

A smile crosses Kate face. *I guess everyone will remember that wedding! Poor, lovable Aunt Betsy! She is such a dear.*

Matt, the big brother, was soon ushering more people to their seats and then rechecked the video equipment. He wanted everything to go well for his sister's big day. He was taking charge. After the wedding, vows were finally spoken, Angie's beaming father gave her away, and a final kiss was smooched. Pastor Perry took a deep breath and looked around. The ceremony was quietly performed, and things seemed to have settled down. Matt hurried around to make sure nothing else could go wrong. The wedding guests soon began to mingle and congratulate the couple.

Richard's backyard for the sixty guests was just the right size for the festivities and had just enough room on the patio for the caterer to serve the hors d'oeuvres, sandwiches, and cake. Everyone seemed to enjoy the relaxed sunny day. Angie was now Mrs. Daniel McCallister. They made such a good-looking, happy couple.

Kate sighs. *With his job in the hospital pharmacy and Angie's nursing position, they should have a good life together. They will do fine.*

She yawns, looks at the clock, and comes back to reality. *Oh, my! I really got up early this morning. It's no wonder I'm tired. At least Jake and I had a good talk this morning. I hope our little discussion didn't make him late. I hope he is not irritated with me. Maybe I can catch a nap later today. I hope he can sneak by his boss and into his office without being seen. He's done that before. Oh well...................*

Jake arrives early at the plant while it is still a little dusky and gray outside. He parks his car in his reserved parking spot and proceeds to walk toward the long, wooden, red-and-white gate arms of the plant entrance. The wind whips his long overcoat around his knees. A light mist of cold rain hits him in the face.

Jake pulls his collar up around his neck and stuffs his right hand into his pocket. He hears a truck motor start up in the background but ignores it. He continues to walk at a brisk pace.

An old, dark-colored pickup truck is parked on the wet grassy area behind some flimsy bushes. The young attendant in the small guard shack sees Jake approaching, recognizes him, and waves him in. It's the night guard, Ricky Appleby. He appears half asleep and yawns noisily.

Suddenly the noise of a revving motor shatters the quiet early morning. Spinning tires can be heard against the loose gravel as a quick gear shift puts the truck into second, then third gear. Its lights are dimmed, and a small squirrely figure is bent low behind the steering wheel of the dented pickup.

It picks up speed and comes barreling through the gates, spewing bits of gravel beneath its wheels. Jake hears it and turns, then tries to step aside as it breaks through the gate's wooden arms.

Too late! It rams Jake squarely in his back and throws his body in the air, tossing it against the nearby oak tree. Jake's body lies deathly still, crumpled around the cold, wet tree trunk.

The guard crawls on the ground outside the guard house, where a piece of the wooden gate arm came smashing through its small window. Ricky's glasses were thrown off his face as he tried to duck away from the flying debris. His broken lens leaves a gash across his nose.

Dazed by the impact, he tries to get up and manages to stumble to his feet as he squints to focus on the accident. He sees a blurry, dark pickup turning around and heading toward him as he dives back down into the muddy gutter. It stops short, and a dark figure jumps out.

The man hurries over to Jake's crumpled body and turns him over. He quickly searches Jake's pockets and snatches something from his pants pocket. He then whirls around and jumps back into the truck. He revs the motor, steps on the gas, and aims the truck through the broken gates. A dark, dirty blur passes in front of the guard's eyes as he scrambles around on his hands and knees, searching through the dirt and grass, trying to find his Coke-bottle glasses.

Ricky is stunned. He can't believe what just happened. "Where is Mr. Remington?" he mumbles. Looking around in the dim daylight, he tries to focus on the situation. He manages to make out a crumpled mass, a body next to the gnarled oak tree. He stumbles upon something a bit shiny.

"My glasses," he exclaims. Trying to put them across his nose, he realizes one lens is gone. "I've got to call this in." Limping into the guard shack, he dials 911.

A sleepy responder answers. "Yes, may I help you all?" the polite southern voice says.

"Yes, please send an ambulance and the police to the front gate of the plant immediately and please hurry. A man has been badly hurt. Please hurry!" Ricky drops the phone. He can hardly breathe as he returns to the crumpled body.

"Oh, no, Mr. Remington! Who was that idiot?" He leans against the tree trunk and mumbles something to Jake.

Ricky shakes Jake's shoulder. There is no response. He fears the worse. Ricky knows Jake won't respond.

He slides down to the ground to the wet dirt, holding his head in his hands and tries to remember. "Where have I seen that battered pickup before? This is like a bad dream."

Chapter 2

The sirens are shrill as the noise and flashing lights pierce the morning mist. The ambulance and police arrive together at the front gate. A small group of night shift onlookers run toward the crash site. The news of the crash travels fast.

The EMTs jump out of the ambulance, and CPR is attempted on Jake but to no avail. They silently lift Jake's broken body onto a stretcher. Their faces are grim, and their heads nod back and forth.

Ricky can't believe what he has just witnessed as he slowly makes his way back to the guard shack in shock, unable to think clearly. The splintered arms of the gate are strewn across the bare ground, and tire tracks can be seen on the dark paved area. "I can't believe what just happened. I can't believe this."

The ambulance sirens are turned on again as the ambulance speeds to the county hospital. A lone police officer makes his way to Ricky and puts his arm around him. "Come with me. I will need a statement from you as to what really happened. Let's go to the hospital." Ricky nods and appears numb. He stumbles after the state trooper.

The EMTs alert the emergency room crew that an accident victim is arriving. Dr. Perez and the charge nurse meet the ambulance at the ER door. After opening the ambulance's door and seeing their grim faces, everyone steps back and allows the stretcher to be pushed through the electric doors and into exam room number one. There is a deathly silence as Dr. Perez listens for a heartbeat and gets no response. He merely shakes his head and reviews the shape of the twisted body.

Jake's broken body is transferred to another gurney and covered with a sheet. The grim look on Dr. Perez's face says it all. Finally, he speaks.

"This man did not have a chance. Try to find out his identity and contact the next of kin as soon as possible. How did this happen?"

Karen Kennedy, the charge nurse, starts for the phone to call the plant. Before anyone can answer, she sees an unsteady guy in a guard's blue outfit come through the door, escorted by one serious-looking, tall state trooper, Corporal Keith Madison.

"Can I help you? Are you with the accident victim?" she asks while hanging up the phone. Ricky tries not to stutter as he starts to answer. Resetting his broken glasses across his sore nose, he tries to focus with only one lens.

"Yes, yes," he repeats. "We followed the ambulance here, and we figured someone might need some information. Poor Mr. Remington." Ricky stops and takes a big breath. "I'm a little shaky, but I, yes, I was there." He pauses. "I was there when the accident happened." Ricky trembles, trying to remember.

The state trooper takes a tablet from his pocket and starts to take notes.

"My name is Ricky Appleby, and I was the guard on duty at the gate when some idiot crashed through it and hit poor Mr. Remington squarely in the back. The impact of the truck threw his body against a tree. It was horrible, just terrible! I still can't believe it. He's dead, isn't he?"

Nurse Kennedy nods. The trooper removes his hat and pats Ricky on the shoulder. He nods hopelessly at the nurse.

"Let's go into this other room where it is private and get some more information." Nurse Kennedy picks up a chart as she pulls a pen from her uniform pocket. "Someone will have to notify the next of kin. Do you know anything about his family, address, or phone number?"

Ricky gulps and tries to talk. "I believe he lives out in the country, near Fair Hill. I know he has a wife and a couple of kids. Her name and picture were in the paper a few years ago. She was the one who was kidnapped and beaten and was lost for over a year. I think her name is Kate."

Ricky takes a deep breath and pushes his sandy hair across his pale forehead. "Our boss, Jim Watson, the plant manager, has been notified and should be calling or coming real soon. You can get more information from him too. This is such a tragedy. Jake was such a nice guy. Who would run somebody down like this? He was liked by everybody."

Ricky is still shaking and wringing his hands. Miss Kennedy pats him on the shoulder. The trooper busily takes notes. Ricky rocks back and forth in his chair.

"Are you going to be all right, or do you need to see the doctor too? Do you need something for your nerves? I can see you are quite upset." She repeats the question again. "Are you going to be okay?" The nurse casts a worried look to the state trooper. "Would you like something to drink?" The nurse's hand is on his shoulder. "You have witnessed a terrible accident, and something like this will shake anyone up."

"I'm not sure what I need right now, maybe just a cup of coffee, a strong black cup of coffee." Ricky's hands are still trembling. His eyes are downcast.

"I'll see what I can get." Miss Kennedy motions to the ward clerk for the cup of coffee. "It'll be a few minutes," she says as she turns to go back to her desk.

"Apparently, someone had it in for him," interjects Trooper Madison. "Did you recognize the truck or anything about this person?"

"I sort of remember something about that truck, but my glasses flew off, and everything was a bit blurry. I did see what looked like the guy go over to the tree where Jake's body lay and pick something up from Jake's body. Maybe it was his wallet or something. I'm not sure."

"There was no identification on his body, according to the EMTs. Maybe he did snatch his wallet and ID. I'm wondering if he took his credit cards with his money too. That's another worry. We'll have to talk to his wife."

As the corporal finishes, he looks up, and a big, harried man comes bustling around the corner to the conference room. His jacket is unbuttoned, and his tie is slung over his shoulder. His tight white shirt shows a large protruding belly. A stern look is on his face.

"What in the world happened? How's Jake? Ricky, they say you saw the whole thing. What's going on?" It is the plant manager, big Jim Watson.

Ricky's eyes drop, his hands still trembling. Tears fill his eyes as the ward clerk hands him a cup of steaming coffee in a Styrofoam cup. Ricky tries to sip it while tears stain his cheeks. He can barely talk, and he clears his throat. He shifts his weight in his squeaky conference chair.

"I'm so sorry, boss, but I didn't see it coming. Some dude smashed right through the gates and ran into Mr. Remington. His body was thrown into that big old oak tree by the front gate. It was awful, just awful. He's dead, sir. I know he is. No one could survive that impact."

"I can't believe this! Nothing in all my years as plant manager has ever happened like this. Who was this guy? Did you get a good look at him? What was he driving?"

"Sir, my glasses flew off when I hit the dirt and the mud, and now one lens is gone. I think I've seen that old pickup in the plant before, but I'm not sure. As for the guy who was driving it, everything was just a blur. I couldn't make out who he was. I'm so sorry. boss. Mr. Remington was such a nice guy."

"It's not your fault, son. Just take it easy now." Jim Watson scratches his head and plops down beside Ricky in the empty chair beside him. The chair groans under his weight, and there is an uneasy quiet. He finally speaks. "Who would do such a thing? It's certainly not your fault Ricky," he repeats.

He pats Ricky on the shoulder. "Take the rest of the day off. I'll drive you home. I'll check with some of the other workers and see if Jake had any disputes with anybody. I wonder if this had anything to do with the guy we fired last week. I heard that that guy left to go back down south somewhere. I'll have to look into this. This is really a sorry day." He looks over at the state trooper.

"Sir," the trooper interrupts, "I'll need to follow up with this too. How about if I head back to the plant and get some more information on this victim? By the way, someone will have to notify his wife." He looks directly at Jim Watson.

"Sure, anything. I'll drop Ricky off at his house, and I'll meet you back at the plant. I'll try to contact his wife and then run out and see her. This is such a tragedy."

"Ricky, if you remember anything more, please give me a call," the trooper Madison interjects. "Here's my card. It's the number of the state police barracks. Just ask for me, Keith."

The trio stands and then quietly leaves the small counseling room. They head for the exit doors. Ricky's shoulders are bent forward, and a quiet sniffling is heard. A motionless body covered with a white sheet can be seen through the half-open exam room door. The trooper turns and stops by the nursing desk, quietly speaking to the charge nurse.

She nods and sees them off. "This is no way to start off a Monday morning. The poor guy," she whispers. "Have a member of the family stop in to identify him."

Chapter 3

Kate is methodically cleaning the kitchen counters and then remembers she promised her brother, Richard, to help out today at his vet clinic. Monday mornings are always a busy day over there. It's like a pediatrician's office when a mother calls the first thing in the morning about her kid, who has been sick all weekend; only this time it is all about their sick animals.

Kate begins to hurry, dresses, and gives a quick look in the mirror. *Oh, my hair is a mess, but so is this rainy weather. Those sick animals won't care what I look like.* She grabs her coat and heads out the door and into the garage. The sky is still misting a little rain, but there is a patch of blue sky in the west. *Maybe this will clear off and be a nice, quiet day after all.*

She looks around and shivers. *This is where my nightmare began. Jake did a great job of cleaning up my blood from the floor. Those two hoodlums must have carried me out unconscious to their stolen van. They say I put up quite a fight.*

Kate settles in her car and turns on the motor. She backs out of the garage and turns the windshield wipers on. *Oh, how I hate those two guys, and then Pastor Perry preaches on forgiveness. I know I'm bitter, but I have every right to be.* She feels a tightening in her chest as her hands grip the steering wheel. *Someday I'm going to go and see that one in jail and give him a piece of my mind, if I don't strangle him first.*

The rain lets up as she heads down the road. Time gradually passes, and soon she turns into Richard's vet clinic. It is eight o'clock, and already there are cars parked out front. She can hear a few *yip yips* as she enters the clinic door. She sees her brother through the exam door's window, signaling for her to hurry up. It's a busy day already. She grabs her lab coat and stashes her purse under the desk counter.

Richard is having a hard time holding onto a small puppy. It looks like the puppy may have swallowed something unusual. He is trying to hold its mouth open with one hand while trying to probe its mouth using his other hand's fingers. The puppy slides across the shiny exam table. Liz Brown, the owner, is still in her flannel pajamas and old worn housecoat. She nervously looks on at her squirming pup, wanting to help.

Kate steps up and manages to secure the little terrier's legs as Richard tries to free the penny from the dog's back teeth. A clink is heard on the floor as the coin pops out. Liz gives a nervous sigh of relief.

"Welcome to a bit of chaos so bright and early this morning," whispers Richard. Liz hugs her puppy and pats his furry head. Feeling much relieved, she sighs heavily and hugs Richard too.

"Oh, thank you so much, Doc, for seeing me right away. I am so grateful. This puppy—I call him Newt—means so much to me, and he almost choked to death."

Richard smiles knowingly.

"My husband gave him to me before he passed away. Newt is so special." She turns and then hurriedly follows Kate out to the full waiting room and the desk. Liz pulls a checkbook out, writes down the office visit amount, and hurries out the door, carrying the carrier in one hand and poor Newt under her other. A little *yip yip* is heard as he tries to squirm loose out of her tight clutch.

Richard goes to the door and signals Kate to send the next patient in. "I think I can handle this tabby cat. He only needs his shots updated," he says as he gently takes him out of his carrier.

Kate settles down at the desk as "clients" yip and meow in their cages. It's a typical Monday morning. The routine settles her as she begins to think of all the good things she remembers with her renewed life in Cecil County.

I have two great children; one is now married and doing well. Yes, dear Matt is still a little undecided about his future. He loves baseball and computers. If it wasn't for him, I would know nothing about the Internet, cell phones, emails, or even the latest news. Matt will be graduating from college soon, but there's no real love interest yet. Oh well! Time will tell.

The morning hours fly by, and Kate decides to run home for an early lunch break. The office is quiet now. Richard decides to make a farm visit to see a pony down with forage poisoning.

Turning into her driveway, Kate is glad to be home for a quick lunch. She can put a load of clothes in her washer and begin to think about what to prepare for supper. Opening the kitchen door, she hears the phone ringing. She reaches for it and hears Jake's boss say, "Kate is that you? I've been trying to get you all morning! I've got to see you right away. I'm on my way out to your house right now. Jake has been hurt really bad. I've been trying to contact you all morning." He sounds breathless.

"Sure, I'll be here. What is wrong with Jake? Tell me. Tell me!" Her voice is demanding now, and her hands close tighter around the phone. "What's wrong?"

The voice goes silent, and the phone clicks off. Kate slumps down on a kitchen chair, the phone still in her hand.

This must be quite serious. He wouldn't tell me over the phone. Why would he be coming here right now? Where is Jake? I'll call Angie. She might know something if Jake was taken to the hospital.

Before she can make the call, she hears a car coming into the driveway. It looks like Angie's car. She puts the phone down. *What is she doing coming out here? What is happening?*

Kate meets her at the door. Angie is there with tears streaming down her cheeks, still wearing her ICU scrub outfit. Her pockets are bulging full of pens and pads.

"Angie, what is going on? What has happened to your father?"

"You don't know, Mom?" Angie grabs her mother and buries her tear-stained cheeks in her mother's neck. She gulps. "It's just awful. It's Dad! Dad is gone! He has been run down and killed by some lunatic at work. It's awful!"

There is a sudden unbelieving pause as Kate chokes back tears. Her eyes stare through Angie. Kate's body stiffens as she drops down into the kitchen chair.

"He was run over by some maniac at the plant in a pickup truck. They brought him into the emergency room this morning, and I just found about it about a half hour ago. I had to go down there and identify him and give the ER all his information. They have sent his body to the morgue. Seeing him like that was just awful, just awful, Mom."

Tears stream down her cheeks. "I guess they didn't know where you were or how to contact you. Someone must have told his boss that I worked in the ICU, so then he called the state police, and a trooper came and notified me. Jim Watson, dad's boss, has been trying to find you. He contacted me, and I told him you might be at the vet clinic. I guess they just missed you there. What a nightmare!"

"This can't be happening! Why is this happening to us? Who is this so-called maniac? What am I going to do without your father?" Kate is sobbing and breathless. "Do they know who did this?"

"Mom, the only thing I know right now is that someone crashed through the entrance gate and plowed right into Dad. His boss thinks it might be the guy they fired last week. He said he was a little odd and has a history of having a bad temper. The state police are investigating this right now as we speak."

Turning toward the sound of another car entering the driveway, they see a late-model tan car stopping out front. Big Jim Watson awkwardly gets out of the car. They meet him at the kitchen door. His face is drawn in a serious grimace, and his huge shoulders are slumped forward. He glances at Angie, then stares at Kate.

"Kate, I couldn't tell you this over the phone, but there has been a very serious accident at the plant. Some idiot smashed through the front gate and hit your husband squarely in the back, which tossed him up against a tree. He must have died on impact. We rushed him to the hospital, but there was nothing anyone could do. I'm so sorry, Kate! Oh, Kate. I am so very sorry. Nothing has ever happened like this before. Oh Kate. I am so sorry!"

Kate and Angie appear ashen and numb. No one speaks.

Jim steps back and started to wring his hands. Beads of sweat stand out on his forehead. "I've never had to deliver this kind of news to anyone in my whole life. I'm just so sorry. Jake was my right-hand man. I loved him like a brother. I could count on him to do anything and everything and to do it always right." He stops and takes a breath. "The only person that comes to mind that might have done this terrible thing is some guy Jake fired last week on my orders. The police are trying to track this guy down now."

"Mom, we have got to call Matt before somebody tells him. I'll try his cell phone number. What time are his Monday classes over?"

"I don't know, but he usually gets home about four p.m. on Mondays and stays for supper. I can't even think."

Angie pulls out her cell phone from her purse and punches in his number. She listens. She nods. There is no answer. She leaves a voice message to call home.

"I wish I could stay, but I've got to get back to the plant," Jim says. "A state policeman is there, and he might need some more information about this character." He seems a little uneasy as he puts his hand out to reach for the doorknob. "Ricky, the gate guard, was there when it happened, but his glasses flew off and broke, so everything he saw was a bit blurry. He doesn't think he can identify anyone. I took him home and told him to take the rest of the day and night off. Poor guy! He's a basket case."

He stands there, motionless, one hand in his pocket, shaking his head. "I must be going," he says softly. "I'm so very sorry for you both. I'll talk to you again. Let me know if I can do anything for you, anything at all." He opens the door, closes it quietly, and heads to his car.

The shock and horror of these moments can still be felt in the kitchen as the two women clutch each other and sob into each other's arms. It seems like an eternity before Kate's low, soft sobbing voice can be heard.

"Why? Why, Lord, why?"

Angie releases her mother and tries wiping her tears away. A wave of nausea engulfs Angie as she turns toward the sink. She pats her stomach.

Kate drops down again on the kitchen chair, still wiping tears away with her trembling fingers. She looks over at Angie. "Now what do we do?"

The sun begins to peek through the clouds, and a ray of sunshine begins to fill the country kitchen. The rain has stopped, and there is a sudden stillness in the air. It is a rather eerie stillness.

"Mom," Angie says, trying to speak, "Dad would want us to cling together and get through this as a family. That's the way we managed when those two brutes took you away for a year. We did a lot of praying too. That seemed to hold us together."

"Sometimes God feels so far away," Kate whispers. "I feel like I can't take another thing. This family has been through so much already. There must be a reason for all of this, but I just can't see it. I feel so angry at God. At this point I don't feel very forgiving at all. How can I forgive such a maniac who kills your husband? I hope they catch that character, lock him up, and throw away the key!"

"Mom, I don't have any more tears to cry. I am cried out. My head is pounding, and I feel sick to my stomach. How about I fix a cup of tea?" She begins to fill a couple of mugs and then puts them in the microwave. A tea bag bobs up and down. The nausea subsides.

"I did come home for an early lunch, and so far I haven't had a bite to eat. I know I should try to eat something or at least sip on something. I think a cup of tea would be good for both of us. I have a headache too. I just can't believe your father will never be coming home again." Tears trickle down Kate's cheek. She chokes down a sob. "Should we take a trip into town to the ER?"

"Let's wait for Matt to call." Angie tries to stay calm and think things through. She doesn't like the thoughts and images racing through her mind. "I really don't think you want to see him like that. You don't need to go right now. Maybe we should remember him as he was the last time you saw him, so handsome and fun loving. I called Dan before I left to come out here, and he said he may be stopping by as soon as he can get some help in the hospital pharmacy. He sometimes has to work over until the temporary pharmacist can get in."

Kate sips her tea and stares down at her wedding ring. "We never finished our conversation from this morning. He was almost late for work. We had so much to talk over."

The phone rings, and Angie answers. "It's probably Matt." She lifts the receiver. "Hello."

"Hey, Angie," Matt says. "What's up? I got your message. Is everything okay? You sounded a little upset. Is Mom all right?"

"Matt, it's Dad! There has been a terrible accident at work, and well, Matt, it's this way. Dad was killed in some bizarre accident. I'm here with Mom, and neither of us is doing real well right now. Where are you? Can you come home?"

There is a sudden gasp from Matt. "What? Angie, I don't believe it. This can't be true!" He pauses. "Let me think. I'm done with my class for today. I'll be right home. I don't believe it. Was it an explosion at the plant?"

"No nothing like that, Matt. Some nut ran Dad down at the front gate, and the impact threw his body up against a tree. We are still in a state of shock. Just come home. I'm so sorry to give this news to you over the phone." Angie can hear sniffles through the phone.

A coarse voice replies while choking back tears. "I'm on my way."

Kate and Angie move about the kitchen like zombies, neither knowing what to do or say. Their faces are drawn and pale, with no more tears left to shed. The numbness shows in their legs as they stumble about, trying to do something, anything. to keep their hands busy. They wash their mugs and remove the clean dishes from the dishwasher.

Hours pass. The rain stops, and the sun casts a quiet glow through the windows. Kate and Angie stare silently out the back window. A tall basketball net on an aluminum pole sways in the breeze. "That's where Matt and I used to play a game of 'donkey' against Dad while we waited for supper," as Angie continues. "This is Dad's chair where he always sat to eat."

A car door slams shut in the garage. "It must be Matt." Kate and Angie glance at each other.

Mother and daughter turn as Matt enters the kitchen. His eyes are teary, and a look of disbelief shows across his face. No one speaks. The trio embraces as quiet sobs fill the room.

Chapter 4

The mood is somber as the organist softly plays "Amazing Grace" in the sanctuary of the local Bible church. The line of friends and neighbors finally dwindles as they file down the aisle to pay their last respects to Kate, Angie, and Matt. Dan quietly sits in the front pew. Pastor Perry moves slowly to the podium as a hush comes over the congregation. Angie finds her seat beside Dan as Matt and Kate follow. Kate sits and stares straight ahead. Her back is rigid. Matt puts his arm around his mother.

The music fades away. Pastor Perry glances at Kate and begins. "Thank you all for coming and supporting this family." He bows his head and says, "Let's pray." He begins with the Lord's Prayer. The congregation follows along. "Our father, which art in heaven, hallowed be thy name; your kingdom come, your will be done, on earth as it is in heaven. Give us this day our daily bread. Forgive us our debts, as we also have forgiven our debtors. And lead us not into temptation, but deliver us from evil. For thine is the kingdom and the power and the glory forever. Amen."

The pastor looks at the foursome in the front pew. He speaks about Jake and how loved he was and how he was such a good father and husband, loved by all who knew him. Kate continues to stare ahead, tears staining her cheeks. Sniffling is heard on both sides of her now. Angie reaches for a tissue. Dan's arms go around her shoulders.

Kate is not listening to the flowery words. She sits, unmoving. *Forgiveness, forgiveness. All this talk about forgiveness. I don't feel like forgiving that character.*

The pastor's words continue as Kate sits motionlessly. Angie glances over at her mother as she grasps Kate's hand.

"We'll get through this, Mom," she whispers.

Kate doesn't answer as the memorial service continues. Now it is time for friends and neighbors to respond.

Mike, a coworker, speaks. "It was always a pleasure to work with Jake. He could always figure out the problems at work, and I always knew I could count on him being there. He always had a smile on his face and an easy gentle nature, never sharp and critical. He will be missed."

Next is Joe. "I remember the time Jake brought in that delicious turkey and gravy for our Thanksgiving treat. We kept the turkey warm in one of the curing ovens, but the gravy spilled out all over the floor. We mopped it up, and no one was the wiser. I don't think we have done that since. We all ate dry turkey that day."

There are a few chuckles here and there throughout the congregation. The reminiscing continues, with some funny stories and some serious ones. Soon the eulogies end, and an announcement is made about the church ladies offering some light refreshments in the fellowship hall. It is nearly four o'clock.

Matt, Angie, Dan, and Kate stand as the pastor walks toward them. He can see the tenseness in Kate's tear-stained face.

"I know this has been a terrible week for all of you," he says, "but I know Jake is in a very safe place now with the Lord. I hope that can bring some comfort to you. I'll stop out to see you tomorrow afternoon. You're in my prayers." He gives Kate and Angie a gentle hug. He shakes Matt and Dan's hands. As they turn to leave, Jim Watson quietly approaches them.

"I am so sorry for your loss. He was like a brother to me. I will miss him terribly." He looks earnestly in Kate's eyes. "Could you come into my office tomorrow morning? I really need to talk to you. I have some urgent business that I need to go over with you."

Matt speaks up now, fully in charge. "I'll bring Mother into town tomorrow about ten o'clock. Is that okay?"

"Sure. I'll see you then." Jim Watson turns and proceeds to leave the church. The crowd has finally moved into the fellowship hall, and a waft of strong coffee fills the church. Matt has his arm around his mother.

"I think I'll take Mom home. You and Dan can stay awhile if you like." Matt picks up Dad's picture from the altar table and tucks it under his arm. "We can take the cremation urn to the cemetery another time. I'll see you later."

Matt and Kate move slowly to the side door. Kate continues to grasp Matt's arm. They make their way to his little Mustang, and she awkwardly gets in, bumping her head. She grimaces. All the way home only a few deep sighs are heard. The overcast clouds are finally being blown away as they enter the garage. They walk slowly into the kitchen and look around. There are still some dirty dishes in the sink.

"Matt, I have been so tired this week," she says. "I feel like I have aged twenty years. I really appreciate all the help with all the arrangements you and Angie made this week. I really feel numb. From the sounds of all those people that spoke, we are not the only ones who are missing your dad. I wonder what is so urgent with his boss that he needs to see us in the morning."

"Maybe he just needs to talk to you about some paperwork. I know the state police detectives are combing the town for that maniac. I think they are pretty sure who it was. Now they just have to track him down."

"Well, I'm going get a bite to eat later. It's starting to get dark, and I am so tired. But for now I'd like a nice, hot shower, and maybe I'll go to bed early. Help yourself to some of those leftovers our neighbors brought in. Everyone has been really generous. We have some good cooks on this street. Save some of that cake for your sister. She and Dan may stop by later."

Kate wearily makes her way down the hall and plops down on the bed. As she begins to cast her shoes off and prepare for bed, something white in her closet catches her eye. She takes a closer look and notices her favorite spring jacket, one Jake always said matched her hazel eyes, a jacket she always wore at Easter. There is something white sticking out of its pocket.

Kate reaches in and finds an envelope addressed to her. *I wonder what this is.* Carefully she unseals it and opens it up. She begins to read. It's a letter from Jake, dated a year ago.

> My dearest Kate, I know things have not been easy for you these past years, but I wanted you to know how much I love you. You are truly God's gift to me, and I so admire your strength and wisdom. You are a remarkable woman, and I want you to know if anything happens to me, I want you to be well cared for, happy, contented, and forgiving.

Always remember to follow your heart. You have so much love to give. Much love always, Jake.

Kate chokes back sobs as she holds the note close to her chest. The unreleased tears of the past week finally flow freely down her cheeks. She quietly closes her door, clicks off the light, and curls up under her comforter. Tears continue to flow. Sleep comes finally as she tucks the letter under her tearstained pillow.

Out in the quiet kitchen, Matt grabs some leftover casserole and plops it in the microwave. He sits down at the computer and punches in some keys to retrieve some of Jake's documents. He remembers some things Jake told him regarding some investments, so he opens some folders.

"Wow! What is this and this? Boy is Mom going to be surprised to see all of this." *I wonder if he told her about these stocks, this investment, and this policy.* He ignores the *ding ding* of the microwave as he reads on. "This is a huge insurance policy."

The front door opens, and in walks Angie and Dan. They drop their coats on the kitchen chairs. "Hey Angie, come and look at this." Angie and Dan look over his shoulder. "Some of these stocks have our names on them too. Dad said he wanted to go over a few things with us sometime, but I guess he never had the time. The dates on some of these are from a year ago. Look at this insurance policy with Mom's name on it. I bet she has no idea about this. The only thing she used the computer for was occasional email. Boy, is she going to be surprised."

Angie and Dan gasp. "I bet Mom has no idea he invested this much money," Angie says. "Some of it is probably from that promotion he got a year ago and that big bonus too."

Matt speaks up. "Mom is really bushed now, and I think she is lying down, probably asleep. I'll go over some of this with her in the morning. Dad really was looking out for all of us."

"Speaking of news, Dan and I have some news for her too. Maybe this will cheer her up a little and take her mind off a few things. I was really worried about her during the funeral service. She has been through a lot. First off, what do you think about this? We are looking to buy Dan's grandmother's house, which his dad grew up in. His grandmother, Alice McCallister, has moved into an assisted living facility, and she would like to keep the property in the family. Dan is the oldest grandchild, so we are going to borrow some money to buy it."

"Hey, that's a big step. That's great news. The way you two have been working—it sounds like you both have been putting away quite a bundle. Dad would be proud of you two. By the way, there are some leftovers in the refrigerator if you two are hungry. I think mine is still in the microwave. I'll get it later."

"And number two, we are expecting!" Dan puts his hands across Angie's shoulder and smiles. He kisses her on the cheek.

"I have had a terrible case of morning sickness," Angie says.

"Wow! That's some great news too. Congratulations! That should really perk Mom up! I think this family is ready for some good news finally. Let's get something to eat and celebrate something good for a change. I feel like Dad would like us to do a little celebrating."

Chapter 5

J im Watson is sitting at his desk, shuffling some papers around, when he hears a knock on his office door. It's almost ten o'clock, he notes as he looks at his watch. He then looks up and recognizes the visitors. He beckons for Matt and Kate to come in.

"Come in. I'll be right with you. Have a seat over here."

Matt and Kate approach two wooden-armed office chairs and quietly take their seats. The chairs squeak as they shift their bodies for comfort. The office is cluttered with folders and papers strewn across the desk and file cabinets. The tall bookcase houses a variety of loose-leaf folders and old technical books. A peak around the corner of the desk shows an overflowing wastebasket.

"Can I offer you a cup of coffee? I've got a clean cup around here somewhere." He pushes his dirty coffee mug out of sight. "That was a very nice memorial service yesterday. I only wish it was for someone else. I already miss Jake." He smiles. "Jake would never put up with this mess. His office was always so neat and orderly."

"No thanks for the coffee," Matt says. "We just finished breakfast. What is it you wanted to see Mom about?"

"Oh, yes. Let me see. Here it is right here. I don't know if you know this or not, but my company carries a nice insurance policy for any worker who dies in the line of work. Jake was killed on this property while coming to work on that Monday morning. Since he worked in such a special capacity with me, the dollar figures in this policy are quite substantial. Here, look at this."

Matt and Kate lean forward. "This is a million-dollar policy," Kate says. She and Matt look at each other as they try to absorb the news.

"Mrs. Remington, I would advise you to contact a financial adviser and see that this money is properly invested for you. You should be able to live quite comfortably with this. I know Jake has other investments as well. You need to look into those too. Perhaps Matt can help you with some of this. I have a name of an investor who lives nearby, if you would like." He hands over a small business card to Kate. Matt and Kate continue to stare at the policy form.

Finally, Matt speaks. "You had no idea of this insurance policy, did you, Mom?"

Kate tries to talk and only stutters. "I-I know now what Jake meant by the last conversation we had in the kitchen on that Monday morning. He said if anything ever happened to him, I would be taken care of. This is too much to comprehend right now."

"I'll need you to sign here on the dotted line, and a check will be mailed to you real soon from the main office." He hands Kate a pen and shows her the dotted line. "By the way, the state police and I have been working together to catch this culprit. We think the guy was a certain Buddy Stewart, who was fired over a week ago. He had a nasty temper and almost blew the mixing crew up. He was a real character who was always late for work and never followed orders. Everyone was relieved when he left.

"We now think he headed back to the hills of West Virginia to where his family lives. The police tracked down an old girlfriend, and she gave them a vague description of where he might be. Apparently, he couldn't get along with her either and beat her up once. She left him and is now married to someone else. This is not the first time he has been in trouble."

He pauses and shakes his head. "I'm just sorry we didn't look into his history a little better. We tried to give him a chance, but now we are paying for it. The other two suspects have tight alibis, so the police are focusing their hunt on this guy. Our state police and the West Virginia state police are coordinating their efforts to catch him. They are now headed to the Stewart compound. From what the old girlfriend told them, there is a whole Stewart clan down there. I told them to let me know what they find out and when an arrest is made. Rest assured, they will catch him!"

Matt and Kate settle back in their chairs as Jim Watson folds the papers in an envelope. "I know this has been a really bad week, but maybe this will soften the blow a little. Jake loved you and his family. He talked constantly about you and especially about your rescue from that ranch in Wyoming. You are quite a remarkable woman to have survived that kidnapping and recovery."

Kate nods, still a little stunned, and tries to say something. "I appreciate everything you are doing. I guess I'm still a little numb." She picks up the white envelope and puts it in her purse.

Matt and Kate get up, shake hands with Jim Watson, and proceed out of his office. They quietly close the office door.

On the way home, both are quiet. Then Matt says, "Mom, did they ever find Dad's wallet and credit cards?"

"Now that you mention it, I don't think so. I have forgotten all about that. I wonder if this character, Buddy, has used them. I think I will call the credit card company and have them canceled. He also has his driver's license, so he would probably use that for any identification. That's all I need, a thousand-dollar bill for things I have no use for."

They arrive home and enter the kitchen. "Mom, there are some things on the computer I think you should know about. Come sit down here while I tap into these documents. Dad has another surprise for you." Matt begins to scroll through the information and stops. "Did you know about some of his investments?"

Kate sits wide eyed and tries to take in all she sees. "I know he told me that he had made some money in the stock market, but I figured that was his business, and I knew he liked to keep up on all the ups and downs of the market. I never got real interested in it. He tried to tell me several times, but I never paid much attention to it. Matt, what is all this?"

"Some of these stocks have your name and Angie's name on them. Look at this one. This has my name on it too. I wish I had paid more attention to what he was doing."

"Matt, I guess I'm going to have to contact that financial adviser to sort some of this out. I know your dad had gotten a substantial raise last year and that he paid off the house a few months later. He wanted to buy me a new car too. Whew! Look at all of this! You are going to have to help me navigate through some of this."

"Oh, yes. By the way, Mom, Angie and Dan have some more good news for you too. They will be over later."

"Did they know about these investments and stocks?"

"They were here for a little while last night while you were sleeping.

They know some of this but not about Dad's big insurance policy from work. It's funny, but all of this money still doesn't take the place of Dad. I still wish he was right here."

"I need to make a few phone calls." Kate gets up and heads to the phone. Matt can hear her making an appointment for next week, then another call to the credit card people. She returns to Matt. "Well, there were quite a few extra purchases on my bill. They are canceling the cards. Apparently, this guy went on a buying spree at Walmart and some hardware stores. He ran up a five-thousand-dollar bill. He bought all kinds of tools, two television sets, and a bunch of other stuff. It sounds like he plans to resell some of it and then camp out somewhere. I hope they catch him soon. He's a real nutcase."

She shakes her head. "I'm going to have a hot cup of tea and a sandwich later, and then I'll try to process some of this in my brain. Fix yourself some of those leftovers. There are still some in the refrigerator from what the neighbors brought." Kate moves to the living room and puts her feet up. "I am so tired." Her eyes close, and she dozes off.

Matt's stomach begins to growl, so he ambles to the kitchen and begins to fix a sandwich. A car enters the driveway, and Pastor Perry gets out. Matt goes into the living room and gently nudges his mom.

"Mom, wake up. We have company." There is a knock at the door as Kate comes awake. "He said he might stop by today. I'll let him in." Kate sits up a little straighter as the pastor comes in and sits down beside her.

"How are you feeling? It looks like Matt is taking real good care of you."

"I'm just so tired and a little numb."

"You and your children will get through this, Kate. I don't know why these things happen, but we just have to trust in the Lord."

Kate tries to smile. "I guess I have not been a real trusting soul. Right now, I don't feel like forgiving anybody or even trying to understand this mess. I want that culprit found and put in jail for life or hung from the highest tree! I want justice done. Nothing will bring Jake back. Nothing will be the same." Kate's anger rises as she pushes herself up in the recliner.

Pastor Perry can see the change in her facial expression and looks over at Matt. "Kate, I can understand your feelings and your bitterness, and it will take time to adjust your life around this event. I am here if you need to talk and vent your feelings. I'm sure they will catch this guy and bring him to trial. Let's pray that the Lord will tenderly guide you and your family and bring some peace to you. Let's have a word of prayer." They bow their heads.

Kate's eyes are squeezed shut. Her fists are rolled into a tight ball. Matt puts his hand on her shoulder. There is a tenseness across her back and shoulders. The pastor continues.

Kate barely listens. Her thoughts are far away. He prays for guidance and patience. He prays for divine help and understanding. He prays for forgiveness. Matt can feel her tense shoulder twitch. The prayer ends, and the pastor stands up.

He senses Kate's tenseness and uneasiness. "Kate, I have been a close friend to your family for a long time, and we have shared a lot of good times together, so you know I am here for you if you need me. Remember to come and see me, and we can talk about this again. You are experiencing a lot of real pain right now, and I think if you will let me, I can help." He can see the tenseness in Kate's expression. "Kate, you have been through so much. Time will soften some of these feelings. There are a lot of people praying for you and your family. I hope you let the church family help you too." Kate nods and takes a deep breath. Matt follows him to the door.

"He always is such a forgiving soul. Right now I don't feel like forgiving anybody." There is bitterness in her voice.

"Mom, I don't feel like forgiving that nutcase either, but this hatred that you exhibit has got to change. I can see it in your face. Your whole body is stiff and reacting." Matt pushes his blond hair off his forehead and breathes a deep sigh. "Dad would not like to see you this way either. He is right about time softening some things." He begins to smile. "I think they will catch this guy, and then maybe you will relax a little. I'll call the state police and find out the latest report on this guy."

Matt goes to the phone, and she can hear parts of his conversation. Matt returns and pulls up a chair beside her. "Captain Edwards says that they have located where the Stewart clan lives and are going to see his father, who still seems to have control over the family. They are hoping he can tell them something about his son and maybe tell them where he might be. It's a long shot, but they hope to find him soon. They have found some of the items he charged on the credit card stashed in an old shack in the hills. Apparently, he has taken off in an old pickup he had hidden away. Nobody seems to know his whereabouts. They have brought in extra help and feel they are on the right trail. It's no telling what this nut will do next."

The afternoon passes quietly, and the sun begins to set. Kate doses off and on in Jake's favorite recliner. She can smell Jake's favorite cologne in the smooth leather and feel the worn spots where his arms used to rest. A certain peace flows over her. She nods off.

The kitchen door opens quietly, and Angie and Dan walk in, bringing a takeout box full of hot spaghetti, meatballs, and warm bread. A mixture of greens is found in another bag for an appetizing salad. Matt and Dan arrange the food on the counter as Angie goes in and calls Kate. Kate opens her eyes, smiles, and is surprised to see her and wonders what she smells from the kitchen.

"Time to eat," yells Matt. "Come and get it."

"Mom, come on, wake up. We've got dinner and some good news for you." Angie is really excited. "Come on. Get up, and let's eat before it gets cold. I brought dinner for us all."

Kate manages to slide out of the chair, still a little surprised and anxious. Matt and Dan have begun to fix their plates as Angie and Kate arrive in the kitchen.

"So, what's all this about?" Kate says. "Some good news? I can use some good news about now."

Dan clears his throat. "We are going to buy my grandmother's house and fix it up a little. We have been approved by the bank to borrow some money. Grandmother wants to keep it in the McCallister family, so she's letting us buy it at a real bargain. It's an old stone farmhouse that has about seven acres with some fruit trees and a place for a garden. There is some remodeling that needs to be done in the kitchen, and the garage needs some repair work too. It will take some doing, but we can do it a little at a time. We are real excited. It's located over on Warburton Road."

"Well, that is some good news. I am always ready for some good news for a change. Jake would be real pleased too. That's a big step for you two."

"Now Mom, you had better sit down for the rest of our good news. Guess what?"

Kate looks from face to face. Matt smiles, and Dan moves closer to Angie.

Angie blurts out, "I am pregnant and due in August." Angie blushes, and Dan puts his arm around her shoulders.

"Wow!" Kate first hugs Angie and then extends her arms to Dan. "Maybe this is what I need to get me out of this awful depressed feeling."

She looks across at Matt. His mouth is full of spaghetti. He tries to grin too. For the first time in over a week, there are smiles all around. The future suddenly looks brighter.

Now it is Kate's turn. She glances at Matt. "I have some important news too. I think I can help you two with your loan. Your dad left me with some real good stocks and investments. Some of them have your name on them. I also will be getting a sizable insurance check from the plant because of the accident. I only wish your father was here to enjoy this moment. I'm so proud of you both. I have an appointment with a financial adviser, so with Matt's help, maybe I will be able to learn how to navigate through some of these investments your dad left. I'm a little new at this sort of thing.

"Right now, I am a little worried about that crazy man that hit your father and if they catch him in time before he charges anymore items on the credit card. I've canceled the cards, and the company is going to issue me another one. They seemed real understanding. I guess things like this happen all the time. Apparently, there were a lot of odd things bought from places where we never go."

The phone rings, and Matt answers it. They hear surprise in his voice.

"What? Who? Oh, no!" He covers the phone with his hand. "It's the state police from North Carolina," he whispers. "They want to know if we know where a Jacob Remington lives. There's been a robbery and a shooting down there at a convenience store. A driver's license was dropped at the scene when the gunman pulled the gun out of his pocket. It has Dad's name on it."

He looks at Kate. Her mouth flies open. There is a gasp from Angie and Dan.

"Hello," Matt says, directing his voice into the receiver. "This is his son. His license was stolen over a week ago. The guy that stole it also ran my dad down and killed him and stole his license and credit cards." Matt gulps. "So, I know it wasn't my dad who was there. It's probably the same guy. We think his name is Buddy Stewart from West Virginia. The state police are looking for that guy right now in West Virginia. Maybe you should contact them to verify this." Matt continues to listen and nods. He adds, "Yes, sir. Sure, anything we can do to help. Yes, sir. Thanks. Goodbye."

Dan speaks up. "I thought things were beginning to settle down. I sure hope they catch this guy. He must be on the run. I hope he doesn't show up here again. He must know the police are after him."

"He sounds really dangerous to me," Angie adds. "Maybe we should call our own state police, Captain Edwards, and let them know too. Matt, you're good at this. Give him a call."

Matt finishes his last bite and walks over to the sink. He is deep in thought. He stands quietly by the sink and stares out the window. The setting sun begins to cast a warm glow throughout the kitchen as a heavy feeling of uncertainty begins to set in. *What would Dad do?*

Suddenly, Matt realizes the job that has fallen on his shoulders. The weight on his shoulders feels like a ton as a shiver goes down his spine. *I could never take Dad's place.* He shakes his head and swallows hard. He glances down at his shaking hands. There is a sudden quietness around him. *Oh, Lord, help me!*

Chapter 6

Nervous chatter is soon heard throughout the kitchen as they try to decide what they should do next. Kate looks at Matt. "What else can happen? This is getting to be real scary. Maybe Captain Edwards should contact the West Virginia police right away. That Stewart guy must have really given the police a slip. It must be the same guy."

"Maybe it's because he can't use the credit cards anymore, and he has to rob convenience stores to get money, and then he actually shot someone. He sounds really dangerous." Matt hesitates, then dials the police barracks, and Trooper Keith Madison answers. He introduces himself and proceeds to relate to him the information received from the North Carolina trooper.

"Thanks, Matt. I'm glad you called. I'll give them a call and see what the latest is on this fellow. It shouldn't be too long before they catch him. He must be on the run. Our man in West Virginia interviewed his father, and from the sounds of things, he has always been a hothead and has had several brushes with the law but none this serious."

Matt hangs up and looks at his mother. "I wonder if he will try to double back and come up here again. Well, this guy is now being hunted in three states."

"Do you think he would come back here and do something to us?" Angie nervously asks. "Mom, you could come and stay awhile with Dan and me. Matt could get a dorm room at college, at least part time. We could stop back here from time to time and watch the house. What do you think?"

"I've never thought about that. Do you really think our lives could be in jeopardy with this nut?" Kate asks Matt as she casts a worried look at Dan and Angie.

"Mom, I'm not sure what to think. I'm trying to think of what Dad would do if he was here. I guess we need a plan." All three pairs of eyes are on Matt. Matt begins to nervously shift his weight. He looks down at the floor and pushes his blond hair across his forehead. The responsibilities are piling up.

Just then a car door is heard closing outside. Big Jim Watson gets out and comes to the front door. Matt rushes to meet him.

"Hi, Matt. Glad to see all of you are here." He brushes past Matt and stops in front of Kate. "I just got some bad news that Buddy Stewart eluded the police again, and he might be heading back to Maryland again. The North Carolina state police called me a little while ago to say he may be armed and dangerous. I've got the guards at the plant on alert and just thought I'd drop by and fill you in on the latest."

"We were just talking about that guy. Do you really think he would show his face around here again?" Matt says.

"Matt, I'm not sure what he is liable to do. I just don't want him hurting anyone again."

"Surely the police should be catching him soon," Kate says. "We are not even sure what this nut looks like. Do you have a picture of him we could look at?"

Jim nods. "I'll have the office blow up the one we took when we hired him and have someone drop it off here." He shakes hands all around and turns to go. He pauses at the door and looks back. "Please be careful and keep in touch."

"Thanks for stopping by. We'll be careful." Kate casts a worried look over at Matt. Matt grimaces. "Will this crazy life ever settle down? And to think just over a week ago, your father and I were having breakfast right here in this kitchen and having a very serious talk."

Big Jim nods and pulls open the kitchen door, then steps out into the cool winter air. He pulls his jacket up and around his neck. In a few minutes, his car is headed out the driveway.

Chapter 7

A few quiet weeks pass, and Kate begins to focus on the future. She hears nothing from the state police, and some of her tenseness begins to fade. She sleeps soundly for the first time in many days. It is late morning, and she sits quietly with a warm cup of tea and a buttered bagel. The house is quiet. Outside the gray clouds still march across the winter sky. Matt is sleeping in. His next class isn't until one o'clock.

She begins to think back on the last couple of weeks and the turn of events. *I need to sort some things out. The house is paid for; college costs are now taken care of. I can help with Angie and Dan's purchase of his grandmother's house. I must remember to keep another appointment with the financial adviser.*

Kate takes a sip of tea, then crunches down on her bagel. *The baby, yes, Angie's and Dan's baby. Now that's a bright spot for August. I guess I'd better focus more on that than worry about that maniac turning up here. I hope the police catch that nut soon. They promised to keep us updated and are watching the house.*

She finishes her breakfast and begins to tidy up the kitchen. Matt comes strolling into the kitchen, yawning and stretching. "Hey, Mom. Do you have any of those bagels left?"

"Sure, help yourself, over there by the toaster."

"Mom, I've been thinking. Maybe you need a nice, long vacation just to get away from here for a little while. It's been a little nerve wracking."

"You sound like your father, trying to take care of me." Kate pauses. "Where would I go? And besides, I've got some things to take care of first, and I think I can manage them with a little of your help, but a vacation does sound nice." She smiles. "I want to hang around awhile and help your sister with the remodeling of her new kitchen. I'm sure she'll need all new appliances. Hopefully the wiring and plumbing will be okay. I know Dan said that the old farmhouse has a fairly new roof. This is a real exciting time for them. I'll put my time in at the vet clinic off and on in the mornings with your Uncle Richard, so I'll try and stay busy. Maybe in the spring or this summer, I'll take some time off. Meanwhile, you keep up with your classes and graduate early like you planned. Your dad would be real proud of you."

Matt moves closer to Kate and puts his arm around her shoulders. She feels his strong arms around her, and then he gives her a slight peck on her cheek. "Dad always said you are a survivor." He smiles down at her. "I think this ordeal has brought all of us a bit closer."

"Matt, this is not the way I would want anyone to become closer as a family. These past few weeks have been a nightmare, though I did get a decent night's sleep last night. I hope that murderer gets caught soon. Then I can finally relax." A black-and-gold state police car passes slowly in front of the house. "I see they are quietly keeping an eye on us. There goes a state policeman now. Matt, I've even thought about carrying a gun. I would probably shoot my toes off." Kate smiles. "I'm just kidding. I have you for my protection."

"Seriously, though, isn't Dad's revolver in your bedroom closet? I remember he showed it to me when we had that scare when somebody tried to break in a couple of years ago. Nobody was home, and he tried to break in, but that little chain was across the door. That little chain saved us. I believe they caught the guy. It was somebody roaming through our backwoods."

"Matt, neither you nor I have a permit to carry a weapon. I'd just as soon try to forget about it. I wouldn't know how to load it, much less shoot it."

Matt puts his hands on his hips and smiles. "You know what Dad always said. 'If you shoot 'em, make sure you drag 'em in after you nail him.' You know, shoot first and ask questions later."

"I don't like the way this conversation is going. Go get dressed and get to your class. I'm going to run over to the vet clinic and see if I can help out for a little while. I'll see you later."

Meanwhile back at the plant, big Jim Watson paces the floor. He's out in the hall, talking to his secretary, Wanda. "I just got a call from Captain Edwards, and he thinks our guy, ole Buddy, is back in town. They think he stole another car. Why can't they catch this guy?"

Jim rubs his hand across his forehead. "I don't like that he knows where all the propellant is stored in this plant, and I just bet that's where he is headed. He probably thinks he can get back at us for firing him by blowing something up. I hear too that he shot some poor convenience store clerk in the chest in North Carolina when he was stealing cash from the drawer. This guy is crazy."

He continues to pace. "I've put extra guards on all the buildings around the clock. They don't seem to mind making a lot of overtime. I still have a hard time making any sense of why he hit Jake Remington like he did."

Wanda sits silently and quietly nods in agreement. The phone rings, and Wanda picks it up. "It's for you."

He takes it and exchanges a few words. "What? Oh no! How did that happen? I'll be right over." He hangs up. "Wanda, call the state police. I think our culprit just showed up. Someone busted through the back gate after shooting through the locks."

She can hear some kind of blasting noise in the background. Suddenly their whole office building shakes. A ground-shaking explosion rattles the windows. A cloud of thick black-and-red smoke can be seen through the dusty windowpane where the mixing crew works.

"Call the fire department too and hurry," he says.

"What was that?" Wanda shrieks as she jumps out of her chair. A pencil rolls off her desk and onto the floor. Papers fall to the floor. The whole building shudders.

"A second explosion! Now what? This plant can be a very dangerous place with all that specialized solid rocket fuel. I bet he threw some type of detonator into the storage shed. I hope nobody got hurt. I'm on my way," he shouts back.

Jim Watson runs to the door and hops into one of the green company trucks. The wheels spin, spewing gravel across the muddy parking area. Sharp red flames and dense black smoke billow up and across the back lots, covering the tops of the bare trees. A heavy fog of smoke drops down around the buildings. The tops of some of the buildings are obscured. Choking and coughing can be heard in the distance.

Men in wrinkled blue lab coats run and scramble to their feet across the wet grass, gasping and covering their eyes and ears. High-pitched sirens blare in the distance. State police cars arrive at the plant's front entrance. Alternating sirens scream through the black foggy atmosphere. Fire trucks come around the bend from the front gate. Two speeding ambulances follow the black-and-yellow trooper's cars.

Screeching brakes can be heard as cars come to a halt. Debris has been blasted in the air, and some has landed across the tops of parked cars and on the nearby workshop. The thick grease-like fog descends on the long, narrow blown out buildings. The grass and muddy ruts take on a shiny, slippery, rubber-like appearance.

A late-model blue pickup truck can be seen wedged between two beams and is sitting next to a blown-out door. Hot, dense flames reach toward the clouds. The plant's fire patrol already has their hoses out, trying to squelch the flames. Their faces are covered by gas-like masks. The searing heat keeps curious onlookers huddled behind concrete walls.

It is mayhem as Jim Watson approaches and surveys the ensuing damages. He steps out of the truck and moves toward the perimeter, where the firemen have kept everyone back. Tommy Ryan runs to Watson's side, his face blackened by the smoke.

"Boss, you're not going to believe what just happened. Some nut crashed through the locked back gate and threw something into the mixing building. It exploded, and some of the flames caused an explosion and then caught the next building on fire. I think everyone got out and ran for their lives. Luckily, some of the men were in the break building. They saw some guy jump out of the damaged truck while it was still running and throw something else toward the storage shed.

"That second explosion was from the back storage shed. It was just like the first one. Someone saw the figure of a slight man run out back and climb over that back fence." Tommy is breathless and rubs his stinging eyes. "Who do you think would do such a thing? I thought all of our guards could prevent something like this. Everything happened so fast, boss."

"I think I know the guy. I'll get the police on him right away. You say he headed toward the fence out back?"

"Yep. He was real quick and climbed right over the fence where that pile of stones is. Yep, I think he was the guy. It looks like a piece of his jacket got caught on the fence. I'm going to take a head count and see if everyone is accounted for." Tommy walks back through the perimeter, where the ambulances are parked. He wipes his hands and face on an old blue towel and tries to survey the damages.

The fires are being slowly subdued, but the stench is lingering in the air. Walls of the mixing building have collapsed, and the shed is reduced to ashes. There is a heavy film covering the remaining buildings and a sticky gray material covering the ground. The thick black smoke continues to rise, and a breeze blows it up and around like a gigantic storm cloud. A small white van approaches the gate with large purple initials printed on its side, "WELK News."

Watson sees the van approach. "Great! This is just what I need right now."

A slender, perky brunet jumps out and walks toward him. There is a microphone in her hand, a camera strung around her neck, and a crooked badge pinned to her collar with bright-red letters spelling her name, "Bobbi." Sunglasses are perched on top of her head.

"Boy, bad news travels fast! I've got to make a phone call." He holds up his hands to slow her down as he steps away.

"Hi, I'm Bobbi from WELK News." Her brown eyes dance with excitement as she steps up and thrusts the microphone in his face. "Would you like to make a statement? You are the plant manager, are you not? What happened here?"

"Yes, I am the plant manager, and I'm not sure exactly what happened, and no, I have no comment at this time." There is a certain gruffness and impatience in his voice as he steps away from her. She snaps a few pictures as she follows him. He pulls out his cell phone and dials a number, trying to ignore her. She's right at his elbow. Her ponytail bobs up and down as she turns around and surveys the damage. She snaps a few more pictures, eager to take it all in.

"Wow, what a mess!" she says. "This could be quite a story. Who did all this? The air sure smells funny."

Watson continues to ignore her. He turns away from her and begins to talk into his cell phone. "Wanda, look up the Remingtons' number and give it to me, quick." He waits, then nods. "Okay, I've got it. Thanks." He dials the number and listens. "Great, no one is there. I wonder if she is at the vet office. I've got to warn her. This guy may be looking for her too."

He leaves a voice message, then redials his office. "Wanda, look up the Elkton Vet Clinic's number. I'll wait." He stands there, watching the firefighters and police trying to get information from the workers. Tommy runs back to his side.

The reporter takes notes and tries to manage her camera around her neck. She leans in to listen to the conversation.

"It looks like we have two that are going to need some medical help." Tommy sounds breathless. "Mostly just slight face and hand burns, maybe nothing real serious. Their ears are ringing too. I think we were lucky that no one got killed. Some of the guys are still shaking in their boots. Everyone else is accounted for. Whew! That was a close one!"

Watson nods and takes a pen from his pocket. He begins to write a number down, holding his phone to his ear. "Thanks, Wanda. I'll see if I can contact her." He begins to poke in some numbers on his phone. "Oh, yes, thanks, Tommy. I want to talk to the men too. I need to talk to the trooper over there. I'll walk over with you." The reporter busily takes notes as he leaves her behind.

The phone rings in the clinic, and Kate said, "Hello, Elkton Vet Clinic."

"Hey, Kate. This is Jim Watson out here at the plant. I've got some bad news here. We think Buddy Stewart just detonated a few buildings here and set fire to our mixing building. He climbed over the back fence and is on the loose. It might be a good idea if you stay away from your house for a while. I don't know which direction he is heading, but I know he is familiar with the surrounding area. He might have a friend around here who may loan him a car and help him get away. I am hoping the state police can nab him before he does any more damage. I don't want to alarm you, but this guy is armed and dangerous. I called your house and left a warning message on your phone. I'm glad you are not home. I hope he doesn't know where to find you."

There is a gasp on the other end of the phone. "Really! Thanks, Jim. I'll call the kids too. Matt might be coming home early." She hangs up the phone as Richard sees her worried look. Her hands tremble as she puts the phone down.

"What's going on?"

"Buddy Stewart is on the loose, and he might be traveling out our way. Jim Watson just called me so I wouldn't go home. He said Buddy is armed and dangerous. He detonated some of the buildings at the plant. That must be the black smoke I saw a while ago. This guy is really dangerous. I should alert Matt so he'll know what is going on."

She dials the house number and waits. "He's not there yet, so I left a message on our phone too. He might still be in class." She calls his cell phone and leaves another detailed message. "I don't want him to run into this Buddy character at the house. I told him to come over here."

"Good. You can't go home right now, so stay here awhile. If that guy is still on the loose, we have no idea where or when he might show up. It's twelve o'clock, so let's go up to the house, and Joyce can fix some lunch for us. I've got a gun under the counter. We'll be all right."

He tries to sound reassuring. He takes the pistol out of the lower drawer and begins to tuck it down in his belt in the back. "I haven't fired this in a year, but I see it is still loaded. I guess I'm the one who needs to be careful. The last time I used this was to kill that rabid fox out behind the barn." He grins. "We'll be okay, sis."

"That's just what I need now, a shoot-out! Great! I feel like I am out in the wild, Wild West! Maybe I should know how to handle a gun too." Kate laughs. "Matt says Jake's pistol is in the bedroom closet. I never thought I would ever think about even needing a gun. I need to call Angie too." She dials her cell number and leaves a short message. "There, that is done."

"Maybe, Kate, like a big brother, I should give you a few shooting lessons. Come on. Let's go up to the house. Lunch is almost ready. Things are pretty quiet in the office for a change. It was a light morning with no real emergencies."

Richard locks up the vet office, and he and Kate head toward his house. They pass the small corral where Richard's prize Tennessee walker, Muffin, nervously trots around the post-and-rail fence.

"I wonder what ails her," he says. "She really seems jumpy." She whinnies.

He pulls open the gate, and they walk toward the water trough. "Well, there's plenty of water in there, so that's okay." The barn door is open, and a shadowy figure passes behind it. "I wonder what is going on. That door should be latched."

Richard freezes and listens. Kate is by his elbow, staring at the barn door. "Hey, who's in there?" He feels the lump of his gun under his jacket.

Suddenly, they hear a high-pitched gunshot.

Water begins to spew out of a small hole in the trough.

Kate and Richard dive behind the trough as he tries to pull the pistol from his belt. He fumbles with it, and it hits the trough's edge, plopping into the water. "Grab it, Kate," he hollers.

Suddenly terrified, Kate is too startled to grab it. She awkwardly scrambles behind the leaky trough.

Muffin is whinnying again. She snorts and paws at the ground.

Richard tries to pull his legs out of the way. Another high-pitched shot goes off.

"He's trying to kill us!" Richard says. "Ouch, my leg. He got me!"

Kate reaches in and grabs the gun out of the trough, and somehow slowly, nervously, she cocks it. Her hands are slippery and shaky. The gun is wet. She sees a red stain on her brother's pant leg.

The guy is walking toward them, a gun in his hand, pointed at her. A silly, evil grin spreads over his face. His black, greasy hair flops over his eyebrows.

Kate stares, hatred and fear in her eyes.

There is a torn, jagged slit on his sleeve above his elbow and some mud splattered across the knees of his jeans as he walks toward them.

Instinctively Kate raises the pistol, her teeth clenched. She stares him down. She nervously points the barrel at him, with both hands grasping the gun stock. She squints at him in half-closed eyes. She rises to her knees behind the trough and steadies herself. A look of determination stares him down.

"Well, look who it is. Pretty Mrs. Remington." He sneers. "I know you won't pull the trigger. It's probably not even loaded. Ha! You're just trying to scare me. First, your husband and now his pretty wife. I'm settling the score because he fired me."

A mouth full of decayed-looking teeth appears between his tight grinning lips. The evil smile returns. He looks straight at her as he walks slowly toward them, his gun still raised and cocked.

Kate raises the gun with a steely stare at him. Her teeth are clenched together. Her jaw is set. Every muscle in her body is tense. She knows what she must do. She squeezes the stiff trigger.

Bam!

A high-pitched blast echoes around the corral. The kick from the gun's blast knocks her backward. She falls back against the fence railing. The gun is jolted from her hand as she plops down. It falls in her lap.

The beady-eyed stranger has flipped backward and lands in the corral's soft dirt. He tries to roll over on his side. He gives a deep groan and a gasp. Fresh blood stains his shirt in the chest. He coughs and tries to rise but falls back down in the dirt. His eyes roll up in their sockets as his eyes squint, then become tightly closed. There is a low gurgling cough.

Richard rises behind the trough and looks at the stranger, then at Kate, and rubs his sore leg. He tries to stand and pulls himself up to the trough. Kate bends over and retrieves the wet gun. Disbelief and shock are in her eyes.

Richard screams, "You got him, Kate! What a shot! Good old dead-eye Kate!"

There is no movement, not even a twitch. The man's eyes are closed. There is a slight gasp from his lips. The sneer is gone. His hands still grasp his gun. His finger lies limply on the trigger.

Kate stares at her hands and her pistol. She stands frozen.

No one moves a muscle. They stare at the unmoving body. Minutes pass. It feels like an eternity.

The slamming of the kitchen door breaks the silence. Joyce runs out of the house, the dog behind her.

"What is all the commotion? Was that a gunshot I heard? What is going on?" She approaches the corral, stops dead in her tracks, and sees the crumpled body in the dirt. "Oh, no! What happened?"

She gasps. She sees the gun still in Kate's hand and the stunned look on their faces. Kate breathes heavily.

Richard begins to smile proudly and scratches his head. He tries to stand, but the pain in his leg from the gunshot wound makes it hard to keep his balance. Reality suddenly sinks in.

"Call the police and an ambulance quick. I think we got one wounded soul and one dead body here," Richard calls to her. Joyce turns and runs breathlessly back to the house.

Kate still stares at the crumpled body. She nervously stands and gains her balance, then walks over and kicks the gun loose from Buddy's clenched hand.

Richard rubs his leg. His left pant leg is bloody. He takes a red handkerchief from his pocket and ties it around his leg. He twists it into a knot. The bleeding slows down. "I think his last bullet grazed my leg. I don't think it is very serious, but it throbs like crazy."

Kate is quiet and stunned. She stares down at Stewart and shudders. "We could have been killed. He was aiming his gun right at me. This is that crazy Buddy Stewart. I recognize him from the picture big Jim Watson dropped off at the house. I think he's dead. He's not breathing. Now what do I do? He kept coming at me with that crazed grin and his gun pointed at us." She gasps. "What was I supposed to do?"

Kate takes a deep breath. "I've never shot anyone before. I've never even had a gun like that in my hands before. I just saw that mean grin and evil stare coming toward me with a loaded gun, and I saw that blood on your leg, I guess I figured it was him or me. It all happened so fast."

There is still no movement from Stewart. Kate's eyes are fixed on him.

Richard leans over and takes his pistol from Kate. "Kate, there was only one shell in that gun."

She shakes her head.

Joyce returns and runs toward the corral with the barking border collie at her heels. "The cops and an ambulance are coming. They should be here real soon. Are you two okay? What in the world happened?"

She looks and sees the blood on Richard's leg, then glances over and eyes the bloody body of Buddy Stewart. "Is, is he alive? How did he get here? Oh, my! You two could have been killed. I feel faint."

Joyce plops down on the edge of the trough. Her face is pale, and her hands are trembling. She pushes her hair away from her eyes with her sleeve. "I wish the police would hurry up and get here."

Richard whispers slowly, "Kate took aim and fired. I think she hit him squarely in the chest, maybe the heart. He's not moving. Everything happened so fast." Richard looks down at the unmoving body and tries to recall the split-second event.

Kate moves closer and feels for a pulse in Buddy's neck. She looks over at Richard and shakes her head. "The police should be here any minute. What is taking them so long? It feels like forever."

Fifteen minutes pass. Then in the distance is the wail of sirens. Muffin begins to prance around the corral. Her head is held high as she softly whinnies. She kicks up a little dust with her hooves.

Richard glances toward the road. "Here come the ambulance and the police."

The cars came up the gravel lane and stop at the side of the small red barn. Lights are still flashing and sirens still screaming. The car doors fly open, and two troopers jump out and rush through the gate.

Kate stands quietly and points at Stewart. "I shot him. He's dead!"

The troopers look at each other, scratch their heads, then look at Kate. Trooper Madison surveys the situation as the other trooper turns and heads back to his car. The EMTs look first at Kate, at Richard, then back at the bloody body. The EMTs kneel and feel for a pulse. No pulse and no response. They pull open his shirt, see all the blood, and notice a bullet hole over his heart.

"Wow! Look at that! Let's get him in the ambulance. It's no wonder he's not moving. There's not much we can do for him. He's a goner." They place him on the wobbly stretcher and cover him with a sheet.

Trooper Madison steps up and retrieves the pistol from Richard. The other trooper is in his car and begins to talk quietly on his phone. "I guess I'll need a statement from all of you. This has been quite an eventful day."

Kate's hands are trembling, and her knees begin to buckle. She watches as they haul the body away. She plops down next to Joyce, hugging the edge of the trough. Beads of perspiration show across her forehead as the cool winter breeze blows around the corner of the barn. A shiver causes her to zip her jacket close and wrap her arms tightly across her chest. *What a nightmare!* "Tell me exactly what happened," as Trooper Madison speaks to Richard.

The other trooper returns and places the gun in a plastic bag.

Richard says, "He was in the barn, and he let my horse out. We saw that she was real jumpy and running around and around in the corral. That's how I knew something was wrong. Big Jim Watson called here a while ago and told us what had happened at the plant and warned us that the culprit escaped over the fence and that he might be headed to Kate's house and for Kate not to go home.

"Then this guy, Buddy Stewart—I guess that's who he is—came out with a loaded gun and started shooting at us. He got me in the leg, but I think it's not too bad. My gun fell in the trough when I tried to pull it out of my belt. Kate grabbed it with both hands and cocked it. We dove behind this horse trough. Kate has never had a gun in her hands before, but she took aim and pulled the trigger."

Kate nods in agreement.

"She saved our lives." Richard takes a deep breath. "Kate landed smack up against the railing of the fence after she fired it. She was quick to duck and react. He fired two shots, but dead-eye Kate here got off one shot and hit him squarely in the chest. Joyce, my wife, called this fiasco in. We have barely moved from this spot. I guess we are still in shock." Kate nods. "There was only one shell in the gun. I don't know what we would have done if she missed him. He is really an evil-looking guy."

Madison smiles and scratches his chin. "You're not going to believe all the damage this guy did early this morning. He set several buildings on fire at the plant in Elkton. I think the fires are still going on. He wrecked the back gate and then made his getaway by crawling over the back fence. You just saved us a lot of time and energy. Mrs. Remington, do you have anything to add?"

"I guess when I aimed and fired the gun, I didn't intend to miss him." She pushed her hair behind her ear and looked at the trooper. "Everything happened so fast. I don't remember ever shooting anyone before, much less killing someone."

She glanced over at Richard. "It's a funny feeling. It was either him or me."

Around the bend of the country road comes the white van with "WELK News" printed in purple letters. It pulls up alongside the parked vehicles. The perky, little reporter jumps out and looks around, her camera around her neck. Her ponytail bounces back and forth under her cap. She pushes her sunglasses over her forehead and looks over the scene.

"This sure has been a busy day," she says. "I see the ambulance is just leaving. Was someone badly hurt? Someone from the office told me there was a shooting out here. I jumped in the news van as quick as I could. Who was it? What went on here? Can I get some kind of statement?"

"The vet here is going to need some medical attention," Madison says. "I suggest you follow them to the emergency room. He might need a tetanus shot. You can probably catch up on the news there. I'll have to go over it again anyway and write it all up. You can listen in and get all the particulars then. I don't see where there will be any charges filed, but it will have to be reviewed. Someone will have to notify the next of kin. It looks like a clean-cut case of self-defense." He puts his pen and tablet away. "Let me help you to the car so we can get you to the ER and have your leg looked at."

The trooper steps over and helps Richard, who hobbles into the back seat of the black-and-yellow police car. The ambulance is now gone, and the other trooper in his car is still busy on his phone.

Kate's cell phone rings as she looks around for her purse. "Where did I drop it? The phone continues to ring. "Here it is, behind the water trough. In all the excitement I must have thrown it out of the way. It's full of corral sand and dirt."

She puts the phone to her ear. "Kate here," she answers. "What? Are you kidding? It's Matt." She turns toward Joyce. "Are you all right?" She listens intently and hangs up. "You're not going to believe this. Matt stopped at home and found the back door busted open and the kitchen phone pulled out of the wall. A kitchen chair was also upset. I guess Stewart found my house and yanked the phone from the wall. Maybe he listened to the message from Jake's boss, Jim Watson, and found out where he could find me. Matt said Stewart must have gotten there after I left that message. Anyway, Matt turned on his cell phone and got my other message a little late. Stewart must have gotten somebody to drop him off nearby and then ran over here. He is really a scary person and a very sick kind of character."

Kate clicks off with a trembling hand. "I'll follow with my car and meet you in town at the ER." Her voice is a little more in control now. The reporter takes some pictures and then hurries to her van. Joyce walks with Kate to her car, and they follow the cars out the lane. Kate's hands are still a little shaky as she steers the car down the road and into town.

"You may just make the front page of the newspaper, picture and all. Kate, you are a real hero. He would have killed us all. He's a real crazy man. I'm glad it was you that took aim and pulled the trigger and not me. I would have been too scared and probably would have missed him for sure. Anyway, I hope Richard's leg is going to be all right. It didn't look too bad. This has been some day around here. I'm not used to all this excitement."

"I don't think the shot was real deep, but it sure was a bloody mess. Maybe things will quiet down now that old Buddy Stewart is gone. I suddenly feel safer. I'm glad Matt didn't get home right when Stewart was in the kitchen. He might have shot him too. I guess the Lord's guardian angels are looking after us after all."

Chapter 8

News spreads around the county about the shooting, and the phone constantly rings at Richard and Joyce's house. Well-wishers congratulate Kate and want to know all the particulars.

Kate politely removes the phone from the cradle and sits down next to her brother. "They can read about it in tomorrow's paper, pictures and all. I am so tired from all the excitement. That little reporter jotted down every word. She has had a busy day too." She heaves a sigh of relief.

Joyce is in the kitchen, preparing a fried chicken supper, and the aroma fills the rooms. Richard rests quietly in his lounge chair with his leg elevated and an ice pack perched precariously across his leg. Matt's stomach gurgles. He has already missed one meal, and fried chicken is one of his favorites. They spent three hours in the ER, and everyone is glad to be at home with Richard and Joyce. The seven stitches are hidden beneath the tight dressing.

"I think that awful tetanus shot hurt worse than the whole gunshot wound." Richard rubs his right arm up and down. A set of crutches lean against the sofa. "I guess I'll have to close up the office for a few days and stay off this leg like the doc said. Maybe I'll even get breakfast in bed." He chuckles.

Joyce comes around the corner from the kitchen. "I think you'll be able to make it to the table in the morning." She winks at Kate. "Now let me help you up so you can eat your supper. I think you're going to milk this pain for all its worth." He manages to get up and hobbles over to the table with Matt by his side.

"See that, Matt. There is no mercy shown in this house." He tries to keep the mood light. Everyone smiles as he or she settles down for the tasty meal. Grace is said, and the fried chicken is passed around. Baked potatoes, peas, and applesauce soon fill their plates. No one is talking; all the mouths are full.

Kate stares at her plate, unable to swallow her food. She vividly remembers the evil tone in Stewart's voice and that sinister grin as he pointed the gun at her. She recalls the split-second decision she had to pull the trigger. She lifts her head and looks around the table. She tries to smile. Her fork begins to tremble.

Richard can read her thoughts. "It's okay, Kate. You couldn't have done anything different. Like you said, it was either him or you. I'm just glad it was you who pulled the trigger."

Matt speaks up, trying to change the subject. Kate takes a sip of her iced tea and blinks back a tear.

"Oh, yeah, I called the locksmith and the telephone company," Matt says. "They will be out in the morning to repair the damages at home. I'll stay home from class until they are gone."

Richard looks over at Matt and gives him a wink and an approval nod.

"Thanks, Matt," Kate says. "I feel like this has all been a terrible nightmare. I guess the aftershocks are just settling in. Maybe I'll take you up on that idea of a vacation sooner that I thought." She tries to smile. "I can't go anywhere until the investigation is over, though I don't think it should take very long."

"You could always pay a visit to your friends in Wyoming. It should be nice and peaceful out there. I'm sure Mary what's-her-name and Dolly, the diner gal, would be glad to see you. Maybe Matt could go with you." He pauses. "Matt, when are your classes done for the semester?" Richard glances at Matt.

"Not until June, Uncle Richard. It would be a nice trip. I'd love to see that part of the country."

Kate is quiet and begins to toy with her food. "I don't think I'm ready for that kind of trip yet." She takes a deep breath and looks around the table. "I think I need a good night's sleep. No dessert for me, Joyce. I am full, and thanks so much for the tasty meal."

Supper is over, and Matt and Kate begin to stand. "I must be going," Kate says. "It's been a long day."

Richard shifts in his chair as Joyce hands him his crutches.

"Come on, Matt. Help me to clear the table, and then we must be going."

"It's okay, Kate. You two go on home," Joyce chimes in. "I'll finish up here. Take your mother home, Matt. She looks weary."

Chapter 9

A few weeks pass. The kitchen door and the locks are now repaired. The phone company has come and gone, and the hole in the wall is covered with plaster and fresh paint. Matt has returned to his classes, and Kate is trying to settle into a routine again. Her restless sleep keeps her awake most of the night, so an occasional nap helps her to get through the day.

Dreams of Stewart's face, his evil sneer, and the look down the barrel of his gun still dance in vivid color across her forehead in the still of the night. Kate tries to dismiss her dreams and realizes she has to go on, day by day. She stares out the kitchen window as dried leaves skitter across the lawn.

She cannot let these past fears dictate to her how she will live her life. In her mind she thinks, *I must go on. I cannot be so fearful. I will overcome these nightmares. Oh, God help me!*

The phone suddenly rings and jolts her back to reality.

"Mrs. Remington, can we reschedule you to see your attorney at two p.m.? Attorney Samuel Smith is out of the office but will return then. Can you come in at that time?"

"Yes, that will be fine." Kate looks at the calendar and hangs up. "Oh my goodness, I almost forgot about that appointment for today." Kate hurries to the bathroom, showers, and dresses quickly. She made the appointment days ago on the advice of her brother to have a lawyer present when the state police review her statements about the shooting.

Her attorney, Sam Smith, has been a friend of Jake's for a long time. They used to play ball together. Kate remembers the last time she saw Sam was at Jake's memorial service. He was visibly upset too. He always seems so down to earth, just like Jake, a real friend of the family. He might make judge someday. She knows this official visit is just a formality and shouldn't take long since the whole incident was determined to be self-defense. Richard will be there too to tell again just what he saw when she pulled the trigger. *I'll be so glad when this whole thing is behind me. Maybe then I will get a decent night's sleep.*

Kate enters the garage and gets in her car. She yawns and mindlessly backs out and heads into town.

Parking the car in the reserved spaces, she sees Richard just arriving too. *Well I guess I'm at the right place after all.* He waits for her as she walks up to the courthouse door. "I can't wait for this nightmare to be over. Maybe then I will get some much-needed rest." The wind blows her hair around as she tries to pat it down. She shivers as he nods and puts a caring arm around her shoulders.

"Just relax. This shouldn't take long. You look like a bundle of nerves." Entering the courthouse, they walk down a long-paneled hall with old pictures in dusty frames of previous judges, and then they turn right into the small reception area off the main court room.

Attorney Smith comes toward them and greets them with a warm handshake. His ready smile and casual manner immediately put Kate at ease. They enter his corner office, with a desk piled high with papers.

"Have a seat," he says. "The police captain and trooper Madison will be here soon. How about a cup of coffee or tea? Kate, I know you are a tea drinker."

Richard speaks up. "I'll have a cup of coffee. Thanks."

"Nothing for me. Thanks anyway." Kate sits down in the straight-backed chair, looks around, and sighs. The office is dusty, and the wastebasket is piled full of shredded papers. There is only one sun-streaked window peeking out from behind a set of wrinkled and faded gold-colored curtains. An old faded-blue tassel holds back the drapes hiding the deep wooden and cluttered windowsills. There are a few extra wooden office chairs and a small old-fashioned oak work table beside his desk. The walls are lined with bookcases, and a computer sits amid the cluttered desk. *Typical for a busy man.*

Sam begins to pour the coffee in odd-colored coffee-stained mugs as two men come to the doorway.

"This is Police Chief Edwards and Trooper Madison. I believe you have already met Trooper Madison. He talked with you both in the ER and out at the vet clinic." They shake hands all around as they pull chairs closer to Sam's desk.

The chief extends his hand and merely nods. He recognizes Kate. "I have your statements written here for you to review. Take a look at these and see if they meet with your approval." Kate and Richard read the documents slowly and approvingly; they hand them back to Sam. They nod and shrug. Trooper Madison clears his throat and looks at Kate.

"We checked into Buddy Stewart's background and notified his father in West Virginia. He had a couple of brothers and one sister. His father did not seem too surprised at what happened, and his brother wants his body to be buried down there. They all seemed to be accepting of his untimely death. I don't think you will be hearing from any of them. Hopefully, this will be the end of this nightmare for you."

Kate nods and nervously twists around in her chair. Her eyes are riveted on Trooper Madison as he sits, reading over the papers.

Chief Edwards's deep voice echoes against the small office walls as he continues to review the shooting incident step-by-step. "As you may or may not know, we found a piece of Stewart's jacket on the fence behind the plant where he climbed over. It matches the tear from the one he was wearing at the time of the shooting. We have no problem believing he was the same one who set the plant fires and killed your husband. We found his beat-up truck with your husband's blood on the front bumper too. Kate, you continue to amaze me. I remember when the FBI searched high and low for you and when your husband was notified by your doctor friend out there that you were living in Wyoming. It was quite a story!

"Jake and I became good friends over the course of that year. I miss those lunches we used to have together. I was so sorry to hear of his sudden death. He will be greatly missed." He pauses, then smiles as he scratches his head. "You certainly are a survivor and continue to surprise me. I'm not sure many women could have reacted as fast as you did with your brother's gun." Kate smiles and nods. "The judge is going to have fun reading this report."

Questions are asked over and over again, always answered with the same responses. Soon the chief and Trooper Madison seem satisfied with the proceedings since their answers and reactions are still the same. Sam smiles across the desk as Kate takes a deep breath. Richard puts his arm around his sister as Sam glances over at the pair. There is a quiet pause.

"Everything seems to be in order and agreement. I don't think there will be anything else but to file these papers. I have looked into Buddy Stewart's assets, and he had practically nothing anyone could get from a lawsuit. The plant was considering a lawsuit, but they have decided to let their insurance handle everything. They will be looking into the investigation too. There will be no reason to prosecute anyone, but we will need a formal hearing to file this information. That may take a month, unless someone comes forward to object. These findings will be posted in the newspaper too."

They hand the papers to Sam and rise to leave. Sam stands as does Trooper Madison, while Kate and Richard struggle to get up. They shake hands all around, and the policemen leave the room.

"I'm glad that is over," Kate says as she sinks back down in her chair. "They seemed real understanding."

"Kate, I'll keep in touch and let you know when that date is set for the final hearing," Sam says. "The way the law works, it may take a couple of months. We have to post the hearing and make sure all parties, including Stewart's family, are notified of the final outcome. It will just take time."

"Come on, Kate. How about an early lunch?"

"I think your sister will need a nice, long vacation soon. Take good care of her. I'll talk to you later." They rise and head out the door, leaving Sam standing behind his desk.

"You know, Kate, a vacation is not a bad idea. Maybe Matt can drive you somewhere, maybe just for a couple of days. He should be finished with his classes soon."

"Matt seems to be my guardian now." Kate chuckles. "Yeah, maybe he would like to take a trip somewhere. I'll think about it."

Chapter 10

Uneventful days and weeks pass, and Kate begins to settle back into a routine, feeling a little safer. The county newspaper has finally filled its front page with the usual daily happenings of all the car accidents and the comings and goings of the locals. A lot of the excitement around the shooting has died down. Still there is a hush in the little milk store when Kate arrives, and eyes follow her as she shops for bread and milk.

Low murmurings can be heard as she leaves. "She's the one that pulled the trigger. Yep, shot him dead!"

The official inquiry and judgement have been declared as purely self-defense and can now be put behind her. Stewart's family is resigned to his awful fate, and they seem to want to move on too. After a few months, the plant slowly rebuilds its workshop and storage areas, while new guidelines are put in place with better safety measures.

The seasons are changing, and spring is in the air. The rain helps to sprout new spring flowers and brings a bright-green glow to the frostbitten lawns. Kate now looks forward to the new life and a newborn due in August to Angie and Dan. She keeps busy helping to plan the remodeling changes for Angie and Dan in their new but old farmhouse.

Matt is finishing his courses at college and is preparing to play summer ball with his friends. He has a part-time job at the local community college as their baseball coach and computer mentor. There is a new sanity in the Remington household.

Kate continues her occasional email contact with Mary Crawford in Wyoming, wondering whether a vacation visit would be good for her at this time. Unsure of her needs and feelings, she stares at the computer screen, but her heart silently prays, *Lord, what do I do now? You have seen me through so many trials, even though this stubborn amnesia hangs on, and*

I still feel some bitterness toward my circumstances, and yet in that letter I found from Jake, he wants me to be forgiving, happy, and willing to follow my heart. I wonder what Pastor Perry would say about all of this. Lord, what is your plan for my life? I don't have all the answers and am not even sure of the questions. Please fill in the blanks of my life. I'll go where you want me to go, and I'll do what you want me to do.

She blinks back at the computer screen. *I wonder how Mary is and what she is doing now. She never says anything about Brad; she only fills me in on casual ranch news. I can just picture the ranch as the snow is melting, the streams are filling up with bone-chilling water, and the days are growing longer with those gorgeous sunsets. Maybe Matt and I can take a road trip sometime soon. He would love that part of the country. He could get to know Peter, Brad's oldest son, and they could talk on and on about baseball. That might be quite a pair. A road trip would give Matt and me some quality time together. I suppose Brad's younger son, Jeff, is busy with medical school and probably doesn't get home very often. I'll approach Matt about it and see when he could take off. I hope Mary is okay. It's been months, and I haven't heard from her lately. I guess I've been a little too busy to keep up my end of our email correspondence too.*

Kate takes a deep breath and begins to think about a possible road trip to Wyoming. She hears a click as the kitchen door opens. Matt walks in, wearing a red baseball cap, black running shorts, and a sweaty dark-blue T-shirt. Dirt and grime cover his face and arms. A bloody scraped left knee shines between muddy knee braces. His jacket is slung over his shoulder.

"Ball season is here, and I think I just tore a ligament in my knee. The coach said to have it looked at before I can play again." He hobbles over to the kitchen table and sits down, removing the knee braces. "I've got somebody to help me with the coaching over at the community college. So I guess I can miss a few days over there."

"Go get a shower and get cleaned up. I guess we will have to take a trip to town to have you checked out. I'll give our doctor a phone call and see when he can see you. I need to talk to you anyway."

"Well, talk away. I'll try listening, but I need to sit here a few minutes. This knee really hurts." He grimaces. "I think I did some serious damage, and besides, I was out at third base. Can I have a glass of iced tea while I'm resting?"

She smiles and shakes her head. Kate goes to the refrigerator and pours Matt a tall glass of lemon-flavored iced tea. She hands it to him as his sweaty aroma fills the kitchen.

"You need to get into the shower pronto and get those filthy clothes off. You are making the whole kitchen stink. You remind me of Jake when he used to come inside after working on the lawn last summer. He was full of sweat too—such a stink!" She stands with her hands on her hips and looks down at Matt. "If the doc says, 'No playing for a couple of weeks,' what are you going to do?"

"Aw, I hope it's not that bad, Mom. Let's see what the doc says first." He sits and rubs his left knee. Kate dials the phone number and gets Doc Shaffer's nurse on the line. Matt can hear her making the appointment arrangements.

"Yes, we can come in. In about an hour? Yes, we'll be there. Thanks, Tammy." She hangs up. "The way you were limping, it doesn't look too good." Kate steps back and smiles. "I've got an idea. How would you like to take a nice, restful road trip to Wyoming? It is beautiful this time of the year. What do you say? We could take turns driving."

"I know you could probably use a nice vacation after what you and all of us have been through, but going out to an old broken-down dude ranch is not my idea of a vacation."

"Who told you it was an old broken-down dude ranch? I think you will be pleasantly surprised. It's beautiful wide-open country, very peaceful and restful."

"Well, you and Dad never said much about it before, and I just thought you were glad to be leaving that place. It sounded a little desolate." Kate stares down at Matt. "We need to do some serious talking, Matthew. Let's get you ready to go to town and see the doc. Hurry up with that shower. He will probably order an X-ray. I hope there is no permanent damage. This family doesn't need any more bad news this year."

Dr. Shaffer's office is clean, neat, and cool. A ceiling fan slowly turns, making only a tiny breeze around the waiting room. Two elderly patients look up and then quietly return to their reading. An aluminum walker is by the lady's side.

Kate and Matt sign in with Tammy and take a seat as Kate picks up one of the recent movie magazines. She leafs through it and looks over at

Matt, who grimaces while lifting his foot up and placing it on a vacant chair. A strand of wet, dirty-blond hair falls over his eyes.

Finally, the room is empty except for Matt and Kate. The two elderly patients have been called in, and Matt shifts around uneasily in his chair.

"Matt Remington," Tammy calls out, "the doctor will see you now. Do you want to come in too, Mrs. Remington?"

"Sure, if that is okay with Matt."

"Come on in, Mom, so you can hear the bad news too." Kate helps Matt stand as he hobbles into the exam room. Tammy takes his blood pressure, weight, and temperature; and she gazes down at his left knee.

"It looks like you slid into home plate."

"Actually, I got tripped up at third base. On top of that I was out too, and it was only a practice game." Tammy just smiles. "The doc will be with you in a minute. Make yourself comfortable." She leaves the room.

"Now Mom, how can I make myself comfortable? It hurts like the devil. I hope the doc hurries up. Do you think he will order a set of crutches? It is beginning to swell, and it hurts to put my weight on my leg." He continues to contort his face.

Kate just smiles. *Poor boy!* "I'm sure he'll be here soon, son. When it comes to something hurting, you are just like your dad. He didn't have much patience either. Remember when he had to have stiches after he cut his hand on the butcher knife last Thanksgiving? He was ready to do his own stitching and not wait for the doc. It was the tetanus shot he really complained about. Just be patient, son."

There is a soft knock on the exam room door, and Doc Shaffer enters. He looks at Matt and the bloody knee. "Well, what do we have here? I bet it was a baseball accident. Were you safe or out?" He smiles and winks at Kate.

Matt makes a face. "Out at third."

"Let's get an X-ray. I'll have the technician next door get a wheelchair and push you over to the next suite. You look like you are in a lot of pain. I'll tell Tammy to give you an ice pack while I write you a prescription. No driving with this pain medication."

Ted, the X-ray technician, arrives and pushes Matt over to the machine. Kate waits in the waiting room.

A half hour passes, and then Doc Shaffer comes out and sits beside

Kate. "It looks like a bad bruise and a slightly torn ligament. It's quite swollen. He'll be off his feet for a while. I'll order some crutches. It'll be quite sore too. Here's a pain medicine prescription for him. Keep ice on for twenty-four hours. He'll need a few weeks to recuperate."

"Would it be okay if he took a road trip with me for a couple of weeks? Since it was his left knee, he might be able to help with the driving. The pain shouldn't be too bad in four or five days."

"Keep him off that left leg, use the crutches, and keep ice and that brace on it for the first twenty-four hours. He should be feeling better soon. A road trip to where?"

"I've got some friends in Wyoming that I have been wanting to see, so I thought if he felt up to it, maybe we could take a ride out west. He's got a substitute to help him out with his baseball coaching, and his exams are over in a few days. It would keep him from moping around the house."

"I guess the ride wouldn't hurt him. Just try to keep most of his weight off it. He'll feel better in a couple of weeks. It's not too bad of a tear. He's young. He will heal quickly." Kate looks up and sees Matt hobble into the waiting room, complete with wooden crutches, an ice pack under his arm, and some instructions held between his teeth.

"Here, let me help you with all of this." Kate takes the ice pack and the papers as Matt gingerly manages his new crutches and heads for the door. "We can stop at the pharmacy on the way home. Doc Shaffer says we can take a road trip in a week or so, when you are feeling better. I'll email Mary Crawford and let her know our plans. It will be a nice break for both of us."

"Yeah, be careful how you use that word *break*, Mom."

Kate winks at Doc Shaffer and helps Matt out the door.

Chapter 11

It's late July, and Kate and Matt are buzzing down the highway. Kate is in full control of the speed. The speedometer is reading sixty-nine miles per hour. The weather is warm and humid, but the sky is clear, and there is a fresh, clean smell in the air after an evening of light rain.

Matt sits up front with an Ace bandage covering his injured left knee just below his tan Bermuda shorts. The radio is tuned low to a country-western station. They already passed through West Virginia and are now in Ohio. Their early-morning departure put them ahead of most of the town's business traffic. Kate's new shiny, red Buick hums along the interstate. It has been four weeks since Matt's "third-base slide," and his crutches are tucked neatly in the trunk.

Kate turns to glance at Matt. He is busy reading the local fast-food signs while trying to gauge the best time to stop for lunch. A road map is by his side. Kate tries to ignore the food signs and wants only something to drink.

Matt's stomach growls as he points at the next exit sign. "Let's stop there. They have sandwiches and milkshakes."

"Well, okay. I can use a milkshake. I suppose you want a full-course dinner." She looks over and smiles at Matt. "That should hold you until we stop for the night."

Kate pulls into the little fried chicken and burger joint and brings the car to a halt. She orders a vanilla milkshake, and Matt gets a full order of french fries, a burger, and a soda. They eat at the picnic table under the shade of an old oak tree.

"Matt, I need to explain to you about some of the people we might see at the ranch. You've heard me talk about Mary Crawford, remember?" He nods. "She's in her eighties now and probably not getting around too well.

Her son, Brad, is the one who runs the ranch, and he has two sons, Peter and Jeff. Peter used to play professional ball until a fast ball shattered his elbow. He now helps his dad run the ranch. It's not a small ranch either, hardly a dude ranch."

She pauses and looks up. "It is about one thousand acres, a real working ranch, complete with beef cows and working cow ponies." Matt stops chewing and puts his burger down. He eyes his mother. Kate continues, "His other son, Jeff, is in medical school. You may not get to meet him."

She has his full attention now. "It's true. I used to cook for the young cowboys, but it was purely a labor of love. I loved it there. There was something new happening every day. Colts were born, and calves were branded. There was the smell of fresh air blowing across the fields every day. There were beautiful sunsets at night."

Kate shifts her eyes and gazes now over the waving fields of wheat and corn of the far-reaching Midwest. She pauses and takes a deep breath. "You might get to meet Dolly and her dad too. They run a real nice eating place, Dolly's Diner. That's where I learned those new recipes that I cooked for you and your dad."

Matt continues to eat. He listens intently. "So, it's not some godforsaken place." He swallows, eyebrows raised. "Really, over a thousand acres. It sounds interesting. What else should I know?"

Kate pauses and looks down at her milkshake. "I think you will find Brad Crawford to be a very interesting guy. He's a lot like your father, very down to earth and hardworking, kind of good looking too."

"Mom, what are you trying to tell me? Just how well do you know this good-looking guy?"

Kate cocks her head and looks off in the distance, wondering what to say next. Matt is getting really curious.

"Well, it's like this." She stops as if trying to remember something. "Your father liked him too—that is, after he got to know him. Maybe that's all I should say until you meet him and his family. Mary, Brad's mother—she's a real dear too. I hope she is well."

"You know, now that I think about it, you and Dad never told Angie or me much about your time out there. I have often wondered how you managed to survive with complete strangers. I always thought you would just push that time right out of your mind. I know they called you Rose because you didn't know your real name or anything about your past. That must have been real scary, Mom."

"It was at times. It was a life-changing journey, Son. Sometimes, Matt, I still feel like Rose. It's a chapter of my life that I can't let go of. I got that name from the trucker I hitched a ride with. His name was, as I recall, Duke Andrews from North Carolina. He saw me stranded along some dark highway, where I had wandered, quite bewildered. I didn't know where I was or how I got there. I must have looked a fright. I was scared to death and covered with mud and was quite confused. I was running from something or someone. I didn't know which. My head was aching, and I couldn't even remember my name. He was a kind old soul and very concerned about me. He let me sleep a lot in the cab of his tractor trailer. He thought my husband had beat me up and left me for dead."

Kate stops and feels the old scar behind her ear. "My head felt like a hammer pounding away between my ears, and I had dried blood all down my red blouse. I was a total mess. He stopped at a truck stop for something for us to eat, and I sneaked into their ladies' locker room. I took a quick shower in their facility and got somewhat cleaned up. It was there that I saw a pink waitress uniform hanging up on a hook."

Kate takes a deep breath and looks over at Matt, wondering whether to continue. "So I literally stole it. It fit just fine. I never looked back. I was desperate. That started my journey as Rose. It had the name Rose embroidered on it over the pocket. From then on, I was just plain old Rose. That's all the clothes I had for a while: the muddy jeans I had on when I crawled out of the sinking wet van and that waitress uniform. I even washed and dried my wet shoes under the heater in his cab."

She stops and looks over at Matt. He has stopped chewing. His eyes gaze intently at her. The hamburger is still in his hand. She has his full attention. She smiles, wondering whether to go on. He pushes the hair away from his eyes.

"Mom, I've never heard this part of the story. No wonder Dad always said you were a survivor."

Kate takes another breath and continues. "After Jake was contacted about me, by my friend Doc Adams, and then proceeded to drive me home, I found I had certain responsibilities toward you, Angie, and your dad. That decision made me decide to give my old life a try. I was in quite a turmoil at first. I felt like I was leaving a very safe and comfortable place at the ranch. Your father was very patient with me. I had to learn how to be a wife and mother again. I didn't even remember how to get to the grocery store. I had to weave my life into yours all over again.

"Those first couple of years at home, as you can recall, were not easy. I felt so very strange. I even found myself daydreaming of Wyoming and of my friends out there. I caught myself not even answering to the name of Kate. I had no memory of my previous life. Do you remember how awkward things were?"

Kate pauses. Matt nods. "The pictures in that family album," she says, "helped to cement my previous life in my mind. If I didn't have those to reflect back on, I'm not sure where I would be. After we talked with that specialist about head traumas and concussions, your dad became real concerned and much more understanding. It was almost like living with strangers. We sat up many nights and just talked and talked as I tried to remember even just little things. I still don't remember my own childhood or growing up. So to find a new life out west was really refreshing and challenging. Everything was new and exciting to me."

Kate laughs. There is a different lilt in her voice, like a happy anticipation. "Somehow different experiences from my past would jump out of my memory and surprise me. Some of my nursing experiences would pop out, and I figured that I must have had some medical knowledge in my past. I didn't even know I knew how to play golf until Brad took me golfing, and I actually beat him a couple of times."

"You actually played golf with this guy?" Kate is finishing her milkshake and nods.

Matt gulps down his soda and swallows the last of his fries. They get up, throw their trash away, and head for the car. Matt gets in on the driver's side and turns on the ignition. He still has a little limp in his walk, but he gets comfortable behind the wheel. He pulls out onto the highway as he glances over at Kate.

"What else should I know about this guy? Is he married? You haven't mentioned a wife?"

"No, his wife, Rachel, died a few years before of cancer, and he was managing the ranch and his two boys by himself. His mother, Mary, moved in to help out for a while. Then she fell and broke a hip, and that's when I became employed by him to help take care of her. I slept in a little bedroom under the stairs and then started to cook for the ranch hands he had working for him, a real nice group of young guys." Kate smiles as she remembers. "You may get to meet some of them too."

"So, this guy is single with two kids, and you're sleeping in the same house he is. Mom, I'm beginning to wonder what kind of setup this was, and you're cooking and cleaning for this guy?"

She looks over at Matt. "He paid me real well. I was even covered by his health insurance." Kate laughs. "After Mary got on her feet, I moved into an old apartment over Doc Adams's office. Mary loaned me some furniture, and I would go out to the ranch every morning. I even got a driver's license and drove her old Chevy out every day.

"This part of the story I knew about. Does Angie know about all of this?"

"Actually no one knew about this part of my life except your father and of course the Crawfords."

Matt continues to drive, deep in thought. Miles of black-tarred highway stretch out before him.

Kate breaks the silence. "I guess we should start looking for some place to sleep tonight. Any ideas?" Soon they pass road signs that say, "Welcome to Indiana." "If you still feel like driving and you're not tired, maybe we can find a place in Illinois. These roads seem like they go on forever. The weather has been decent, nice and sunny, so we can go a little farther. When you get tired, I can take over driving for a while." Matt nods and shrugs.

The pair motor on down the highway, taking in all the scenery and small towns. Matt is now quiet, and Kate begins to snooze off and on. Road signs and exit signs appear while the sun goes down, and dusk begins to settle in. The full moon glows among distant clouds.

Matt pulls off the road and sees a sign for food, gas, and lodging.

"Let's stop at this Cracker Barrel and get something to eat. My stomach is growling, and there is a nice motel right over there. We can sign in and get some gas, then grab a bite to eat. I'm really hungry. Our snacks are almost gone."

Chapter 12

After a restful night and a big bacon-and-egg breakfast, they continue down the road again. Kate drives, and Matt rubs his knee. "I guess I drove too long yesterday, because my knee this morning is a little stiff." He begins to stretch out his long legs against the floorboards. He pushes his hair away from his eyes. "Tell me about this ranch again."

Kate glances over at him and smiles. "I think I'll just let you be pleasantly surprised. It's a whole different life than what you are used to. Look over there." She points at the mountains and the cloudless skies as she refocuses back on the highway.

The roads begin to stretch out endlessly with hardly any other vehicles in sight. The barbed wire fences march up and down the hills, and grazing Black Angus cattle can be seen in the distance. Silvery white wind turbines can be seen standing tall and erect across the vast fields and mountains, far in the distance. They slowly turn their long outstretched arms in the gentle wind.

Kate looks over at Matt. "Traveling this far from home, I will have to keep in contact with Angie though. I want to make sure she is okay, you know, being pregnant and all. You did ask Jim Burns down our street to look after the house while we were gone, didn't you?"

"Yeah, he said, 'No problem. Just take your time and enjoy the trip.' Angie is going to collect our mail, so I think I have things covered, Mom. She has our cell phone numbers too. But getting back to this Crawford guy, how well do you know him?"

Matt looks intently at his mother. She looks away and stares down the highway, her hands firm on the wheel. Her sunglasses give a reflection back in the sunlight. There is a smile on her lips.

"You've been home for four years now, and a lot of things out here might have changed."

"I guess you are right about that too. But one thing I know won't change is the friendship I had with his mother, Mary. I'm really anxious to see her too. She knows a little of what we have been through this year. I didn't fill her in with all the gory details."

Kate tries to change the subject. She clears her throat. "I hope she isn't working too hard. She doesn't talk about herself very much in her emails, but I know she must be slowing down. She is in her eighties. They have had a hard time keeping help in the kitchen to do the cooking for all the cowhands."

She pulls into a rest stop. They get out and stretch their legs and arms. They grab a few snacks and something to drink. It's Matt's turn to drive.

Kate settles down in her passenger seat, closes her eyes, and wonders whether Mary told Brad about her and Matt coming out on this road trip to the ranch. It's been over six months since Jake was killed, she thinks, as a tear forms in the corner of her eye. She sniffles. She quickly wipes it away and readjusts her sunglasses.

Jake was such a rock! So much has happened since then. I wonder what Brad will think when he sees us. I wonder if he is seeing anyone special. Maybe this trip is not such a good idea after all. Mary has been so secretive about him.

They sped through Iowa and Nebraska, and now see exit signs for Wyoming towns. After stops for food, gas, and lodging, they approach signs that advertise western boots and saddles. Billboards ahead brag about their best eats "this side of the Rockies." Pickup trucks crowd around mom-and-pop eateries. The two push on wearily, knowing they need to stop somewhere to get out and stretch their legs again.

Their dusty red sedan hums along the black-topped roadway while soothing country music plays classic tunes. Kate and Matt sing along with some of the old favorites. Route 80, a ribbon of a highway, continues up and down faraway hills. It splits the countryside in two and seems to go on forever. Matt now drives while Kate yawns and tried to read the road map in the glaring light.

Suddenly, over the hill a road sign appears. Matt reads it aloud. "Arlington, ten miles ahead. Hey, Mom. Look, another sign! Dolly's Diner just ahead. Isn't that the diner you were talking about a couple of days ago?"

"It sure is, Matt. I can't believe we are so close. We have to stop. I am tired and weary, and I know you are hungry. You have got to meet Dolly and her dad. I wonder if Sally, her daughter, is working with her. Sally may be married by now."

Kate is suddenly awake and sounds excited. "Oh, by the way, there's a Country Inn around here somewhere, run by Sue Carter. We can stop and get a room there. It should be just around the bend. It's funny how I can remember things like that."

Matt looks over and shakes his head in disbelief. "Just how long are we planning on staying out in this Wild West territory?"

"I don't know. How long can you stay away from your ball team? You don't have any serious or permanent job commitments yet, or do you?" Matt shakes his head. "You may want to stay out here awhile." Kate laughs. "You may not want to go back to Maryland."

Matt looks over at her and continues to shake his head. "You can't be serious! What have I gotten myself in for?" His voice rises. "All my friends are back there and my ball team. Unless …"

"Unless what?"

"Unless, of course, I meet the cowgirl of my dreams out here." Matt laughs too.

"You never know who you might meet out here. I know you're not going with anyone special, or are you? You have always been so secretive about your so-called love life."

"No, no one real special, but I've got my eye on Laurie. She's the soloist in the church choir. She has the prettiest blue eyes and such a terrific voice. A lot of the guys are eyeing her too."

"It sounds like you have some real competition." Kate continues to laugh. Matt is finally opening up about his personal side. He has always been such a deep thinker and so quiet about his feelings.

"Look, Mom. There's that sign again, just a mile ahead to that diner. I'm getting hungry. That's my stomach growling. How about you?"

"Sure. Pull in when you get to it. Dolly is really going to be surprised. There may be a lot of ranch hands in for lunch. This is one of her busiest times. I wonder what her special is for today."

Matt sees the neon sign on its roof up ahead, Dolly's Diner. He pulls in and parks under one of the shade trees. Old redwood picnic tables sit empty. "Look at all those dented, muddy pickup trucks," he says. "This is some place! This must be the only eating place in town."

He shuts off the motor, and they awkwardly step out of the car. They both begin to stretch and bend from side to side, loosening up their joints. Kate leads the way to the door. The door opens suddenly, and a string of rough-looking, denim-clad cowpokes stream out the door, bumping into Kate. She steps back.

"Sorry, ma'am. Sorry, ma'am. We were just leaving. Have a good day." One tall cowboy tips his weathered, sweat-marked Stetson and smiles. Their worn and muddy boots clop down the wooden steps as they nonchalantly swagger toward their pickup trucks.

Kate and Matt nod and smile. They enter, looking at the twelve red vinyl and chrome stools sitting in front of the red Formica counter. There is a color TV overhead, giving out the latest weather forecast. Empty dirty plates and used knives and forks are still on the counter. Half-filled cups of coffee are left near empty pie plates. A clash of dishes and metal pans can be heard coming from the back kitchen area. The sweet aroma of fresh-brewed coffee fills the air.

Kate and Matt slide into one of the windowed booths. A few older customers talk quietly in the next booth, sipping coffee.

Kate winks at Matt. "Watch this. Matt." She yells, "Hey, can we get some service over here?"

Suddenly there is quiet. Kate stands and smiles. A gasp can be heard as all eyes turn toward the two newcomers. A bent-over man turns around from washing the pots and the pans at the sink, and a tall blondish woman stands nearby with her hands on her hips. She stares, not believing her eyes, and shouts.

"Pop, it's Rose—I mean, Kate. Look, there is some kid with her."

Kate smiles broadly and waves her hands. Moisture clouds her hazel eyes. Matt looks on and slides sheepishly down in his seat.

Dolly rushes around the counter, arms outstretched, while Pop, throwing his apron off, follows. Hugs and kisses pass from one to the other. All eyes are on the commotion. "What a surprise! I'm so glad to see you," Dolly exclaims. "Why didn't you call and tell me you were coming? You look great! It's been four years since I've seen you."

"How have you been?" Pop chimes in. His wet, soapy hands wipe a tear from his eye. He clears his throat and chokes up a little, then turns and looks down at Matt. He releases Kate. "And who is this nice-looking fellow?"

"This is Matthew, my college graduate son and protector." She winks and smiles proudly. Pop reaches over and to shake his hand. Matt is grinning.

"He looks like his father. And oh, yes, Mary told us about the accident with Jake. So sorry, Kate. Such a tragedy! It sounds like you all have had quite a winter. We were all wondering how things were going for you and your family." He pauses, looks up at Kate, and changes the subject. "So Kate, how long can you stay?"

"Maybe a week or ten days. We are not sure." She looks down at Matt, who is quiet. "It's been quite a year so far, a lot of ups and downs. I feel like I've been on an emotional roller coaster. But I do have some good news though. My daughter, Angie, and her husband, Dan, are expecting their first child in August. They are in the process of fixing up Dan's grandmother's old stone farmhouse. Hopefully that job will be done when the baby arrives. Matt thought I needed a vacation, so here we are. Surprise!" Matt nods.

"Well, it's about time. Pop and I have really missed you. Sally is off today, but she has been working with me too. Oh yes, there may be a marriage in the future for her with her old flame, Butch, someday soon. Good help is so hard to find, and I am so glad to have her around again. By the way, I know someone else who has really missed you too. Things aren't the same out at the ranch."

Dolly smiles. Matt looks up at Dolly's face, then back to Kate's. He cocks his head. Dolly changes the subject. Her hands are back on her hips. "How about some lunch for you two? It's on me. The diner special today is meatloaf, gravy, mashed potatoes, peas, and applesauce. And oh, yes, apple pie for dessert."

Matt smiles. His stomach does a slow growl. "Now Matt, if this meatloaf tastes familiar, it's because I've stuck with your mother's recipe. It's one of our customers' favorites. I'll be back with the drinks, iced tea and a soda?"

Matt and Kate nod in agreement. The other customers tip their hats as they begin to file out past the counter. Matt and Kate settle down for a late lunch.

Lunch is served, hot and steamy, oozing with rich, brown gravy. Dolly and Pop crowd into the booth, each with his or her cup of coffee, to catch up on all the Remington news. Matt sops up the extra gravy with a warm roll and listens as Kate and Dolly reminisce. Pop listens intently and nods in agreement.

Finally, Matt speaks up. "Did you hear the story about dead-eye Kate shooting the guy that ran over Dad?" He laughs. "That's what the whole town has started to call her. She even made the front page of the paper." Matt's eyes twinkle as he grins.

"What?" Pop speaks up. "Kate, you shot a man? Mary didn't tell us the whole story. She did say they caught the guy. What have you been up to, Kate?"

"Maybe I should let Matthew tell you this story." She looks over at Matt. Matt swallows hard and begins.

"Well, Mom was out at Uncle Richard's vet clinic when this Stewart guy showed up. He had already crashed into the gates at the plant where Dad worked and set some of the buildings on fire. It was quite a scene. I heard there was greasy black smoke and debris all over the place. So then this guy shows up at the clinic and lets my uncle's horse out of the barn. They had been warned that this guy, Buddy Stewart, might be heading their way, so my uncle gets his pistol out of the clinic and tucks it into the back of his pants. Then."

Matt pauses. He has Dolly and Pop's rapt attention. They lean forward not to miss a single word. Their mouths are wide open.

"So here he comes, walking out into the corral with a gun in his hand, pointing it at Mom and Uncle Richard. Stewart actually fired the gun and shot my uncle in the leg. Mom and her brother dove behind the water trough, but Uncle Richard's gun fell into the water while he was pulling it out from his belt. Mom picks it up, aims, and hits the guy right in the chest, right in the heart, and he falls down dead."

Dolly and Pop let out a gasp. Their coffee cups are still in midair. Matt looks admiringly at Kate. "Yep, front-page news. That's my mom."

Kate's face turns a little red as she looks down at her plate. "Actually, it was a lucky shot. I probably couldn't hit the broad side of a barn door now if I had to."

"Wow!" Dolly's voice is excited. "That is some story, Matt. Kate, that is amazing. You weren't kidding when you said you have had some ups and downs. Kate, adventures seem to follow you wherever you go. Hopefully, this journey will be a little less action packed. I can see why a little vacation is what you might need." There is a lull around the table.

Kate speaks up. "Now, to change the subject, does Sue Carter still have the Country Inn? We need a place to stay. We can head out to the ranch after we drop our bags off."

"Yes, she does. She runs a real nice motel out there. I guess you know that she and Tom, Brad's foreman, got married. They seem real happy. Tom still works for Brad though, and you can still hear him whistling around the barns. He'll be glad to see you all too. Brad's son, Peter, has stayed on and works the ranch with his dad too. Jeffery, the younger one, is in medical school and doesn't get home a lot." She looks at Matt. "You'll like it out there. Lots of wide open spaces."

"Well, Mom, maybe we should roll out of here and check in. I am stuffed. I won't need to eat for a week." He pats his stomach. Pop pipes up as Dolly prepares to stand.

"If Brad puts you to work at the ranch, you'll be ready for your next meal real soon." He winks at Kate as he begins to slide out of the booth. He and Dolly stand and hug Kate all over again. He shakes hands heartily with Matt again.

Matt and Kate step away from the booth and head for the door. The tile floor creaks beneath their feet. There is a little *ding ding* as the door opens. Dolly and Pop wave as the door closes.

"I wonder how Brad will react when he sees Kate," Pop says. "I wonder if the flame is still there. Brad was quite smitten with her when she was here. It sounds like Kate did the right thing by renewing her marriage with Jake. Matt sure seems like a nice boy. He and Peter should get along fine."

Dolly stares out the window and shakes her blonde head, hands on her hips. "Time will tell. It should be interesting, especially since Charlotte Hamilton, the real estate lady, has her designs on Brad. She has been spending a lot of time out at the ranch. They were seen going to the movies last week. You know, we hear a lot of gossip about those two. I wonder if Mary told Brad when Kate and Matt would be coming. She can be quite secretive at times. Mary and Kate were quite close when Kate worked out there. They formed a real bond. You know what they say. 'The plot thickens.'"

Chapter 13

Matt and Kate reach Carter's Country Inn and see Sue behind the counter, busy at her computer with paperwork all around her. She looks up, surprised, and recognizes Kate. "Well. hello there. It's been a long time since you were in this part of the country. Welcome back. It's good to see you. Who's the young man with you?"

"Sue, this is my son, Matt." Matt nods. "We would like to rent a couple of rooms during our stay. I'm not sure how long we will be staying, maybe just a week. I'm on my way out to the ranch now. This is kind of a mini vacation for us. Matt has never seen this part of the country before."

"Well, Matt, I sure hope you enjoy your stay. That ranch is beautiful this time of the year. Things are a little slow around here right now, so you can have your pick of the rooms. Let's see, how about rooms seven and eight? They have an adjoining door with separate baths. I'll even give you my discount rates."

Sue laughs. "Tom. You remember him from the ranch, right?" Kate smiles and nods. "Well, he and I got married two years ago, but he is still working with Brad, so he comes home here every night. We built a separate little apartment that's hooked onto the left side of this motel. It's real nice having a man around here again. He can fix most anything!" She laughs. "Most of the young ranch hands live nearby, so he doesn't have to stay with them at night very often. They seem like a nice bunch of guys. Of course, they do love to eat. I've heard a lot of stories about how you spoiled them with your great cooking." Kate blushes again.

"Brad has had a hard time keeping decent kitchen help. Mary, his mom, can't keep up with all the work anymore. She's not getting any younger, and her hip now has a little arthritis in it. She'll be glad to see you. Watch out, Matt, or he'll put you to work too." Sue laughs again.

"Tom told me that your husband died in a weird accident a while ago. That must have been awful. I'm very sorry to hear that. I hope you can enjoy your time out here."

"Thank you. I appreciate that. If it will be okay, Matt and I will put our things in our rooms and come back later tonight." Sue nods.

Kate signs a credit card, and Matt receives their keys. Mother and son hurry off to the car and then to their separate rooms. The rooms are quite spacious and done in a western motif, with horse and cow-roping pictures lining the walls. Indian designs on the bedspreads give the rooms a real western flavor too. Giving the place a quick once-over, they quickly dump their suitcases and head back to the car.

Kate's stomach churns, and her hands become sweaty. She seems a little distracted. Matt notices her nervousness. "Are you okay, Mom? You look a little flushed. Too much gravy on that meatloaf?"

She gives him a quick glance. "No. I'm just a little warm. Must be hot flashes." Matt smiles, turns the car around, and says nothing.

The ride to the ranch is quiet and uneventful. Along the narrow country road, strong cool breezes cause the hardy branches of tall oak trees to dip and sway as they pass under the cloudless blue skies of the West. Neither talks. Matt seems deep in thought. Kate shifts and twists, uncomfortable in her seat. There is just a little background country music seeping out of the radio speakers.

Up ahead, Kate can see the long ranch lane lined with the stark white fence. She readjusts in her seat again and turns the off radio. "Turn in here, Matt, and be careful of the dry ruts."

Matt slows the car. A cloud of dust trails behind them with the crackling of gravel under the tires. He holds tightly to the steering wheel and stares straight ahead, taking in the whole view. Kate's jaw is tight. and her muscles are tense. Off in the distance a two-story ranch house appears along with a row of barns and sheds.

The corral has a few brood mares and frisky colts in it. The sun reflects off the gleaming green roofs of the outbuildings. Black Angus cattle graze on new grasses on one side of the lane, while stocky cow ponies kick up their heels in the opposite field. Their manes flow in the wind.

"Wow," Matt whispers. "This is a real ranch. It is so big."

Kate nods and glances over at him. "This place goes on forever. It stretches far beyond that tall mountain over there." She points to the far pasture. "There's a nice little mountain stream about a mile down there in the back pasture. The water is always real cold." Kate remembers the episode between Brad and her when she got tangled up in the rope with the young heifer and nearly fell in the stream. She wipes her sweaty hands across her jeans and adjusts her sunglasses.

The car eases up to a gravel parking area, and whistling is heard from one of the barns. "I bet that is Tom, Sue's husband, whistling. That is the first sound I heard when I came down this lane for the very first time too. Maybe things haven't changed too much." She takes a deep breath. "There doesn't seem to be much activity right now. I wonder where everyone is."

Matt turns off the car motor. They get out and stretch their arms and legs.

"This is Friday afternoon," she says, "and I bet Mary is inside, tidying things up a bit. Let's go up to the porch door."

They approach the large white gabled porch. The wooden steps creak under their feet. The welcoming white rattan chairs with soft-blue cushions soak up the hot afternoon sun. The porch swing still sways in the breeze as Kate reaches for the unlocked screen door. Kate knocks on the inside oak door and waits. She knocks again and listens, her ear to the door.

There is a slow shuffling sound approaching the door. It opens a crack, and two wrinkled eyes peer out. Kate straightens up and looks in. The door is suddenly pulled wide open.

"Oh, my word! Look who it is! It's Rose—I mean, Kate!" Mary screams. Her eyes glisten. "I don't believe it! Come in. Come in, Kate, where it is cool. I can't believe it's you. I wasn't sure when you might be arriving. Your last email didn't give me an actual date. How are you? You look so well."

She grabs Kate and gives her a strong emotional hug. Her cane falls to the floor. Tears trickle down their cheeks. Kate chokes up and swallows hard. Matt steps back and looks on.

Kate steadies Mary as Mary turns to Matt and releases Kate. "And who, just who is this young man with you? It must be your son, Matt. He sure looks like his father."

Kate can only nod. Mary steps slowly back as Kate retrieves her cane. "Come in. Come in and sit a spell."

"Yes, this is Matthew." Kate finally finds her voice. "He has been my driving companion and my right-hand man." Kate looks at Matt and smiles, then pats him on the shoulder. Matt just looks on, eyeing the emotion between the two women.

Mary steps back unsteadily as she beckons them to come in. Matt looks around and eyes the dark wooden floor and high wagon wheel light fixtures, complete with little globes on each spoke. Ten large oak chairs surround a long rough-hewn oak table, with salt and pepper shakers paired in the middle. Crumbs can be seen sprinkled randomly across the table. Clumps of dirt and straw lay beneath the table, and footprints lead right to the kitchen door. Mary slowly makes her way to the living room, cane in hand, and plops down in the overstuffed recliner. She raises her right foot up on the matching stool and grimaces. Kate eyes the slowness of her steps and the deep breaths she takes. Her face is flushed, and her loose clothes signal a loss of weight.

Kate looks around. She sees a pile of newspapers by her chair and a bunch of unfinished knitting stuffed in a wicker basket. There is an empty coffee cup sitting on the end table. Kate pushes a wooden stool over and sits down on the flattened plaid cushion. Matt still surveys the whole house.

"It looked like nobody was home when we drove up, although we did hear Tom out there whistling in the barns."

"Well, Kate, Tom is my protector when no one is around. We have had some problems with somebody sneaking around here at night. Our watchdog died last year, so we have no warning of strangers. Someone sneaked in the barn, broke a lot of the hay bales loose, and let a lot of the heifers out. Brad and some of the boys are out there right now, rounding them up. I'm just glad they didn't set anything on fire. Brad thinks it is some of the boys from across the county line looking for some devilment. Some of the other ranchers have had the same problem too. It's always something." Mary pauses and takes a deep breath. "So, tell me about your trip out here. How was the weather?"

"The weather was fine, a little rain here and there. Matt did a lot of the driving. He is still nursing a torn ligament in his left leg, but he is a good driver. Maybe we should put you two side by side so you can share the cane."

Mary laughs. There is a twinkle in her eye.

"It is so good to see you both. Matt, if you would like, take a walk out there and see Tom. He can show you around the place. Your mom and I need to reminisce. There are some sodas in the fridge. Help yourself to anything else you might see. You look like a growing boy."

"Thanks, Mrs. Crawford. I would like that. I'll see you two later."

Matt makes his way back to the kitchen and grabs a cold soda. He can hear Tom whistling as he heads out the door. He stops on the porch and surveys the vast pastures and snow-tipped mountains. He sips the frosty soda. Miles of fence divide the grassy fields as he shades his eyes from the sun.

He turns and sees a tall tanned cowboy with a dusty hat approaching him. His wrinkled cowboy boots clink across the gravel. He waves.

"Hi, I'm Matt Remington."

He limps over and extends his hand.

"You must be Tom. I could hear you whistling a tune when Mom and I drove up." They shake hands.

"I was wondering who was here with a Maryland license plate on that car. You must be Kate's son." Tom's voice has a slight Midwestern drawl. "You sure look like your dad. I think you might even be a little taller. I heard what happened to him. So sorry, son. Such a tragedy. I couldn't believe it. Mary said they caught the guy."

Tom shakes his head. "I guess your mom is inside with Mary. They have a lot of catching up to do. Come on out into the barns. I'll show you around. Brad, Peter, and some of the boys are out rounding up some strays that somebody let out of the box stalls last night. They should be back soon. Some are on horseback, but Brad is driving his pickup. I've just finished cleaning out some of the troughs. There is always some cleaning up to do around here. Have you ever been around a ranch before?"

"No, not really. My uncle runs a vet clinic and has a small barn out back of the office, but I've never been to a working ranch like this. This place is beautiful and so peaceful. Look at those blue skies! They stretch on forever. My mom was trying to describe it to me but said I would have to wait until I got here to appreciate the real thing. She was right."

"It looks like you have a sore knee and a little limp. What happened?"

"I was playing baseball, and I slid into third base and tore a ligament in my left knee. To top it all off, I was out too."

Tom smiles, lifts his hat, and scratches his head. "You and Peter should get along fine. He played big-league ball for a while until his elbow got messed up."

"The doc seems to think some rest will help it heal, so I guess I'm on the disabled list for a while. He did say I could drive if I was careful. I'm trying to be careful, but the knee stiffens up after sitting for long periods." Matt rubs his knee. "It feels good to be out of the car and walking around."

"It sounds like your family has had quite a year, with your dad's death and all."

"Yeah, Mom has been through a lot too, and everyone has told her that she needs a vacation, so here we are. We are staying out at your Country Inn."

"Oh good. I'll probably see you out there sometime. Is your mother going to take over some cooking duties while she is here? We haven't eaten so well since she left." Tom grins. "I'm just kidding. Come on, I'll show you around."

Chapter 14

Mary and Kate huddle close together while laughing, talking, and catching up on all the news. Then Mary stops and looks squarely into Kate's eyes.

"What is it, Mary?" Kate asks. "Are you okay?"

"I haven't told you everything yet." Mary pauses and takes a deep breath. "There's a real estate woman from town who has been chasing after Brad. Oh, she's nice enough and all that, but she thinks Brad should sell this place, retire from all the hard work, and marry her. She says he should travel and see the world—you know, Paris and London and all that. I don't think she realizes that for a rancher, this *is* his world. He's still in his forties, Kate, and she wants a husband really bad."

Mary takes a long raspy breath. Kate listens intently. "She has no children, though, and Peter doesn't seem real fond of her either. Brad is not ready to retire. He has a son in college." Mary's voice rises. "He loves this ranch. What would he do? Where would I go? Look at me, barely getting around!"

Mary's arms wave around. Kate jerks back, almost falling off the stool, unable to speak. Finally, she stutters awkwardly, readjusting her position on the footstool.

"Really?" Kate says. "What does Brad say? Is he really serious about this woman?"

"I don't know. He doesn't say much. You know him. He keeps his feelings very private." Mary settles back in her recliner and lowers her voice. "Oh, they go out here and there—you know, to the movies and sometimes to the cattlemen dinners. I think he likes the extra company and somebody other than me to talk to. I try not to say too much, but I got to thinking. What would Peter do if not ranch work? Besides, Brad is helping Jeff pay for medical school. Jeff's scholarships don't pay for everything. Doc Adams is really hoping Jeff can take over his practice when he graduates, so he has to finish college and then do an internship and probably a residency for general practice. When he comes home, Jeff is off with Doc, making house calls. We hardly get to see much of him. He is such a good kid and a hard worker. I love him dearly." Mary shakes her head back and forth, taking deep breaths.

"Mary, I didn't know all this. Maybe Matt and I should leave. I don't want to cause any problems or hard feelings."

"Don't worry about that. If Charlotte shows up, I'll just say you're an old friend of the family who popped in to surprise me. What's wrong with that?"

"I'm a little nervous about this situation. After all, I haven't seen or spoken with Brad since Jake was here and carted me home four years ago. Speaking of home, I really had a lot of catching up to do. It was not easy. I found I had certain responsibilities to my newfound family and decided I had to try my best to make up for lost time. Jake was real patient with me. That concussion from that hard garage floor really did a number on me. I still don't remember my childhood or our early marriage. But anyway."

Kate stops and changes the subject. "Angie is now married and expecting her first child in August. I called her before we got here, and so far the pregnancy is going well, but I do want to be there and help her out the first couple of weeks with the new baby. So I won't be staying here very long. I've told Matt that we are here merely to have a mini vacation and to see you. Neither Matt nor Angie knows about all the events of my past here at this ranch."

Mary nods and sits back in her chair. Her hands are folded in her lap. "I see." There is silence and then a sly smile. "Hmmm. Well, I will tell you one thing. This place has not been the same since you left with Jake and restarted your old life. Brad moped around for weeks—actually months. I want to be there when he sees you again."

She winks at Kate. Kate's face turns red as she nervously shifts on her stool again. She looks away, remembering Brad's marriage proposal over four years ago.

"By the way," Mary said, seeming to interrupt her own thoughts, "Mrs. Garcia still comes and cleans for us. She will be glad to see you too, but the meals from the new cook, Emma, are a little lacking. Emma still has trouble making a good pot of coffee, and her gravy always has lumps in it." Mary chuckles. "There are no extra mouths to feed tonight because Brad usually pays them on Fridays, so the young guys go into town and back to their own families. Peter, Tom, and Brad usually manage things over the weekend. Things stay pretty busy around here. It's hard for me to keep up. I get short of breath if I do too much or get real excited, but I've learned to pace myself." Kate can see the tiredness in her face.

"Well, while I'm here, how about I fix some supper for you, me, Peter, Matt, and Brad?" Kate stands, hands on her hips. "What's in the freezer?"

Mary smiles broadly as a sly smile crosses her face. "I think there is a roast of beef in there. Make yourself at home. Fix whatever you find out there. I'm sure it will be good." Mary nods her head. "It feels like old times. Brad will be surprised that he is not eating fried chicken again. He sometimes goes down to that chicken place on weekends and gets food for us when the cook is off. You know where everything is kept, so have fun. This evening should be very interesting." Mary chuckles again.

Kate can see the twinkle in her eyes. "You sit still, and I will see what I can pull together. How about I fix you another cup of coffee?"

"That would be great. My old bones need to rest awhile anyway. My hip has been slowing me down. Doc says I'm just getting older and that arthritis has set in. It can be real painful at times. Ha! He is no spring chicken either. If anyone needs to slow down, it is him. By the way, you should stop in and surprise him. He would love to see you. I told him you might be coming out this summer. I didn't give him a definite date though. I will admit, Kate, that I did not tell Brad when I thought you might be coming either. I thought we could surprise him too."

Kate stands here, looking down at Mary and shaking her head. She steps away and heads for the kitchen. She finds the coffee and plugs in the coffeepot. Everything is right where she arranged it before she left. Opening the freezer door, she finds a nice roast of beef. She next rummages around in the larder and finds some potatoes, canned beans, and applesauce. Kate opens the flour canister and finds just barely enough flour for some homemade biscuits.

Ah, the guys will like these. Someone will have to go to the grocery store real soon if I use up all of this stuff.

She begins to hum as she prepares the meat and potatoes. She wipes down the table and sets the plates out for five. The coffee begins to percolate, and the aroma fills the kitchen. A little snore can be heard coming from Mary's direction.

Kate pours the coffee and quietly places it on the end table. Smelling the coffee, Mary awakens and straightens up in her chair. "Boy, this is service. This smells great. I see you have not lost your knack for making coffee." The steam rises from the mug as Mary, her hands shaking, takes a sip. "Ah, this is real good." She places the mug down on the table and closes her eyes. She begins to doze off.

It's six o'clock, and Kate looks out the window and sees Matt and Tom sitting on a bale of hay, talking and laughing. *Well, it looks like Matt has found a friend.* Kate opens the porch door and steps out onto the porch. She takes a seat on the swing, still swaying in the breeze. She begins to rock gently back and forth. Her feet are barely touching the floor.

Oh, the memories of this side porch.

The late afternoon sun warms her back. She can hear the whinnies of the colts and mares in the corral. She peers down the lane, where a car approaches, a cloud of dust following it. It is a late-model car, bright blue, with only one passenger. *I wonder who this is.*

A lady stops in the gravel parking area and gets out. She waves to Tom and approaches the porch. She sees Kate. "Hi, I've come to see Brad. Is he home?"

"No, but he should be real soon. Supper is almost ready. He's out gathering up some strays with the boys."

"My name is Charlotte, and you must be the new cook. I smell something delicious in there."

"Well, um, I'm Kate Remington and yes, I did cook up some supper. Mary is inside. Do you want to see her? She's taking a little nap, but I'll wake her if you need to see her."

"No. I'm here to see Brad. What did you say your name was?"

"Kate. Kate Remington. That's my son over there with Tom on that bale of hay."

"Why does that name ring a bell with me?"

Kate shrugs and shakes her head. She remains silent and thinks, *So this is the famous Miss Charlotte! Quite professional and pretty too; nice hairdo, smart navy-blue business outfit. Really a take-charge person.*

"If you would like, I could tell Brad you stopped by. Did he know you were coming?"

"No, I don't need an invitation to stop by. Maybe I'll stay for supper. It certainly smells good. Besides, Brad and I are practically engaged. We've been going together now for over a year."

"Oh, I see." Kate smiles innocently. "Would you like to have a seat out here and wait for him?" She begins to feel a little anxious. "He should be here real soon. Would you like a cup of coffee?" She wants to disappear.

"Sure. It really smells good. Make it black. I don't take cream and sugar," she replies sharply. Charlotte turns her back to Kate and looks toward the corral. "This is really a quaint and lovely place, don't you think? I have a little trouble with all the animal and barn odors though. I could never live this far from town. I need my stores and shops close by. Say, how long have you worked for Brad and his mother? I don't recall him saying anything to me about hiring anyone new."

"Oh, I just arrived today. I'm an old friend of the family." Kate gives a little smile.

She's a little bossy too. I wonder how Brad got hooked up with her.

Kate excuses herself, gets up, and heads into the kitchen. The screen door slams behind her. She looks back over her shoulder and sees Charlotte settling down in one of the porch chairs.

She checks on the roast. The potatoes are beginning to boil. She pours another mug of coffee and stops. There is suddenly some commotion outside.

A truck door slams shut, and there are horse whinnies and a lot of laughing coming from male voices. A dark, dusty pickup has arrived, and four sweaty guys are leading horses into the corral.

That must be Brad and his cowboys. Now what do I do? Should I go out there or stay in here? Hmmm, he doesn't know Matt. Well, here goes.

She picks up the coffee mug and timidly steps out onto the porch.

"It's about time you got home, honey," Charlotte hollers. She waves and tries to get Brad's attention. "Oh, Brad, honey, I'm over here. I'm so glad you're back. I've missed you." She quickly steps off the porch.

Brad is talking to Tom while looking Matt over. Tom points toward the house. Brad puts his arm around Matt's shoulder and motions for Peter to come over. Kate can see Brad nod and extend his hand to Matt. Peter comes over, shakes Matt's hand, and slaps him on the back.

Charlotte hurries to Brad's side, waving as she goes. Her blue high heels twist her ankles in the loose gravel. Kate remains motionless on the porch with a steamy mug of black coffee in her hand. Matt turns and waves to his mother. Brad ignores Charlotte's closeness and turns toward the porch. His eyes light up, and a broad grin spreads across his face.

Charlotte reaches up for a little kiss on his cheek, but Brad ducks away. His eyes are on the porch. He sees Kate, her auburn hair blowing in the breeze, standing tall and trim in the late afternoon sun. Their eyes lock on each other, and Kate gives a little wave. A shiver runs down her spine as she takes a step back.

Brad begins a fast walk to the porch, grinning widely. Charlotte is left standing beside Tom and Matt, looking dejected, a pout on her face with her arms folded across her chest. She quickly realizes there is a special connection between these two and wonders just who this Kate Remington really is. She suddenly looks lonely and deserted, though surrounded by all those young cowhands. They all turn and look toward the porch, ignoring her.

"Hey, Brad, what's up? Wait for me," Charlotte yells after him. She takes a few steps but can't match his stride. She nearly stumbles in the loose gravel. She stops to fix her loose shoe.

Brad doesn't slow down but continues up to the porch, skipping the steps, and stops right in front of Kate. They are just inches apart. Kate sets the coffee mug down and grins too. His bright-blue eyes beam right her own, and he stares lovingly at her blushing face.

A tear trickles down Kate's cheek. She smiles and blinks. His strong, tan arms reach out and wrap around her waist, and he lifts her off her feet. He swings her around as his cowboy hat flips to the floor. Her head is tucked in against his chest. She can feel his strong heart pounding against her cheek. She can smell the day's sweat in his shirt. His day-old beard pricks her chin. She pushes against his strong embrace. He laughs heartily and throws his head back.

"Brad, put me down. People are watching you!"

He sets her down slowly, holding her tightly, with his unblinking eyes locked onto hers. Kate is breathless. She straightens her pink blouse as her cheeks blush a bright red.

All the cowhands watch the sudden embrace and wonder who this woman is. They see their boss swing her around and hear that hearty laugh. Matt and Peter stare at their parents with surprised looks. Tom stands there a minute and smiles. He pats Matt on the shoulder and nods. He wanders over to his truck and gets in, still grinning, and gives a little high-pitched whistle.

He hears Kate's voice. "Brad Crawford, put me down."

"Kate, Kate. What a great surprise! Welcome home. I mean, welcome back. You look great, really great." Brad says with a grin, "When did you get here? Mom said you might make the trip out here. She just never said when."

Charlotte hurries up on the porch behind them, sees the embrace, and hears part of the conversation. "Oh, Brad. Just who is this long-lost friend of the family anyway?" She sounds indignant and eyes Kate suspiciously.

Kate wipes the tear from her eye. Brad is still grinning and ignores Charlotte. His eyes stay latched onto Kate's. "Just a long-lost friend, Charlotte. Just a long-lost friend." He releases Kate and turns his head. "Something smells good in the kitchen. I think we are eating something special tonight."

"It's a roast of beef, cooking slowly." Kate clears her throat. "Are you hungry? I know that's a stupid question. You never miss a meal. Your mother said you were tired of fried chicken, so I found the roast in the freezer and thought I'd help her out with supper. I guess I'm your new temporary cook."

Kate laughs and looks at Charlotte. "You're welcome to stay too, Charlotte. I'll put out another plate for you." Charlotte stares first at Kate, then back at Brad. He takes a little step back from Kate.

"Yes. I think I'd better stay. Thanks." There is a sharp tone in her voice. Charlotte looks suspiciously at Brad and then at Kate. Kate feels her icy glare. Kate tries to regain her composure. She steps back from Brad as he drops his arms.

"Brad, I see you have already met my son, Matt. He and Peter seem to be getting acquainted over there by the barn. Why are all the other guys still lingering around the stables? I thought they should be on their way home."

"Oh, I almost forgot. Today is their payday. I'll be right back." He gives a quick wink to Kate.

Brad hurries into the house, past Mary, who is waking from her nap, and goes into his office. In a minute he returns with several envelopes. "Let me give their checks out. I'll be right back, then we all can sit down and eat. I'll send Matt and Peter in to get washed up." He rushes pass Charlotte and heads down to the barns, while Kate returns to the kitchen area. Kate begins to add another plate, complete with silverware. She turns toward the stove.

"Supper is just about ready. I need to mash the potatoes." Kate is tense since Charlotte now follows her around the kitchen. Kate scoops up the beans into a large bowl and removes the biscuits from the oven.

"Just how long have you known Brad Crawford? And where are you from?" Charlotte eyes Kate. Her eyes move up and down over Kate's slender body.

Kate stiffens and begins to mash the potatoes. She clears her throat as beads of perspiration appear on her forehead. Kate tries to ignore Charlotte's presence and her suspicious stare.

Mary stirs in her chair and hears the jealous question. Mary comes to her rescue and calls out, "She's an old family friend, Charlotte, from Maryland, and she's a good cook too."

Mary manages to rise and hobble with her cane to the table. She senses the tension.

Matt and Peter saunter in like old friends, laughing and smiling. Brad is right behind them. The door closes with a bang. Kate places the potatoes and beans with the applesauce on the table. The uncut roast is slid over near the head of the table near the steamy, hot gravy. Fresh baked biscuits are covered with a napkin in a little basket.

"Wash up over there, boys, and then grab a seat. It looks like roast beef tonight. Here, Mom, sit here by Kate." Brad turns to Charlotte. "Charlotte, sit anywhere you like. I'll sit on the end. This looks like a good supper tonight."

Charlotte plops down in her chair next to Brad and faces Mary and Kate across the table. She fixes her stare on Kate. Matt and Peter take the two empty places next to Charlotte. Kate shifts in her seat and seems a little uptight.

"So, tell me, Kate," Brad says, "how was your trip out here?" He begins to carve the meat. "I see you brought a nice-looking fella with you." He winks at Matt. "Tell me what you all have been doing back in Maryland."

Matt speaks up, reaching for the biscuits and gravy. "Did you hear about how Mom shot that guy that ran Dad down?"

Everyone stops chewing, and all eyes are now on Kate. Even Charlotte stops chewing, her fork in midair. Brad stops carving.

"Now Matt, you don't need to go over that story again." Kate sounds apologetic. "I'm sure they have all heard about it."

"Heard about what?" Peter interjects.

Charlotte seems interested now and surprised. "You mean, you actually shot someone? Did you kill him too?"

Matt looks over at his mom. She looks a little embarrassed. Her face reddens. Everyone is staring at Kate. Brad grins from ear to ear and shakes his head. Even Mary stops chewing.

"Sorry, Mom. I don't think Pete heard about the dead-eye Kate story." He laughs. "Maybe I should save that story for later. I guess Mom didn't make the front pages out here in Wyoming. Maybe people get shot out here all the time." There is laughter all around the table. The tension is lessened. Mary chuckles.

"Yep," Matt adds, "she shot him dead."

"I guess you didn't go into all the details about the shooting, Kate. I mean, in your emails." Mary is curious now and says, "I thought the police caught him, and one of them had the big shoot-out." Eyebrows are raised around the table as curiosity is raised. "Maybe there is a part of the old west still in Maryland. Kate, you never cease to amaze me."

"Matt, you can go into the details later, but for now, just eat your supper." Kate wants the story dropped for now. She feels a cold glare from Charlotte. She looks over at Matt with a stern look. Brad winks at Matt. Peter leans forward, hanging on every word.

"Wow! I think we have a real celebrity here," Peter says, quite impressed. "We can talk later, Matt. This sounds like a real interesting story."

Charlotte continues to gaze at Kate while pushing her food around on her plate. Brad catches the glances as he enjoys his last mouthful of roast beef. He tries not to smile at the icy situation. He sees Charlotte glare at Kate, and Kate stares down at her food. There is an awkward quietness. The boys sense something is up. Matt and Peter nudge each other. Mary tries to break the silence.

"This is really a tasty piece of meat, and the gravy has no lumps in it. I'll have one more of those biscuits. Thanks, Kate, for putting supper together."

Charlotte moves closer to Brad and places her hand on his arm. "Brad, honey, I think I am quite full. I can't finish my meal. Maybe we could take a ride into town tonight and see a movie. I'm sure Kate can clean up these dishes by herself." She smiles slyly.

Kate looks up and raises her eyebrows. "Sure, Brad, go ahead. Have a good time. Matt and I will be leaving soon anyway. We are staying out at the Country Inn. Mary and I can do more visiting tomorrow. We are tired, and a good night's sleep will do us both some good."

Charlotte seems satisfied and a little smug. Her hand is still on Brad's arm. Kate sees Brad move his arm and then fold his arms across his chest away from Charlotte's touch and push his chair back. He looks around the table and eyes the two boys whispering to each other.

"Say, Matt, why don't you spend the night here with Pete. You two can get up early with me and help me fix that broken-down fence out back. How does that sound?"

Pete's eyes light up as he smiles in agreement. "Come on, Matt. We can make a real ranch hand out of you. What do you say?"

"All my clothes are back at the inn."

"I can outfit you with some jeans and boots. How about it? We are about the same size."

"Well, Mom, what do you think?"

"I can drop off some of your clothes tomorrow when I come back to see Mary. I suppose it will be all right. Go easy on him, Peter. He's not used to ranch work. The callouses on his hands are from playing ball, not from throwing bales of hay around."

Matt smiles as Peter pats him on the back. Mary smiles, rolls her eyes, and pushes her chair away from the table.

Brad begins to stand. "I don't think I'm ready for a movie tonight,

Charlotte. I think I'll read the newspaper and go to bed early." He glances over at Kate. "Unless someone needs help with the dishes."

Charlotte suddenly throws her napkin down, pushes her chair back, and stands. Her eyes cast daggers at Kate as she lashes out at Brad.

"So, you are willing to help this long-lost friend with the dishes, are you? That's a first, Brad Crawford. I'm sorry I didn't cook your roast beef supper tonight." There is sassiness in her voice. "So! No movie or stroll up Main Street for us tonight! I guess I know where I stand."

She flings her head back with one hand on her hip. Her face is crimson, her voice high pitched and intimidating. Her icy stare is penetrating.

"Look, Charlotte, maybe another time. Now calm down. I just don't feel like getting all cleaned up and getting back late tonight. I've put in a full day's work today." Brad casts a look at Kate as she begins to stack some dirty dishes and silverware at her place.

Kate rises, pushes her chair back, and keeps her eyes lowered. She carries the dirty dishes to the sink. Brad looks for some help and suddenly feels trapped. The situation is tense. He realizes he misspoke. Everyone knows Brad Crawford doesn't do dishes. After a long silence, Peter finally speaks up. He nudges Matt again, looks across the table at his father, and grins at his predicament.

"Dad, you really do look tired. Maybe you should go to bed early and get some rest too. You're not getting any younger." He sees a surprised look cross his dad's face. "I think Matt and I can fix the fence in the morning. We can take Tom along too."

Kate continues to clear the table, saying nothing as a fork drops from the plates. Brad bends over and picks it up. Mary pushes up away from the table with her cane and turns to go to the living room.

She hollers back over her shoulder, "I'm going to bed early too. It's getting dark, and I need my beauty sleep. Good night, all. I've got some reading to do, and then I'm heading for the shower. I'll see you all in the morning." A smile creases her lips as the *tap tap* of her cane fades away toward he room.

Charlotte stares at Brad. There is tension in the air, and Charlotte isn't happy.

"Well, it's early, but it looks like everyone is heading to bed soon." She taps her high heels against the floor. "I see ranch work and washing dishes take precedence over me around here."

She looks first at Brad, then at Kate. "I see no reason for me to hang around." A little sarcasm is in her voice. "I'll see you tomorrow, Brad Crawford. Good night, Mrs. Remington or Kate or whoever you are. Enjoy your dishes. I'll see myself out."

Matt and Peter hear the sarcasm and step back as Charlotte heads for the door, heels clacking against the hardwood and purse tucked under her arm. The door slams shut, and she is gone.

"Whew!" Brad shakes his head. "She has quite a temper." He turns to Kate. "I guess after all that, I'm obligated to help with the dishes." The two boys burst out laughing. "It's been a long time since I helped in the kitchen." He moves close to Kate's ear and says, "We have some catching up to do."

Kate looks up at him with a large greasy spoon in her hand. "Brad Crawford, you have put me in a very awkward situation. She told me that she and you are practically engaged. I'm not here to get in the middle of your love life."

"She'll cool down. She knows nothing about my so-called love life. She thinks she has me roped and saddled. I've got a surprise for her. She wants me to travel all over Europe with her and see the sights. I'm not sure this cowboy wants to see all those sights. I'm perfectly happy viewing the sights from my back porch."

He pauses. Matt and Pete are all ears. "Now about these dishes—we can put some of these in the dishwasher and wash up these pans by hand. We can be done in no time. Then we can talk." He turns to the boys. "You two boys go out and check on those heifers we found today and make sure there is enough feed out there for them."

"Sure, Dad. Come on, Matt. I think he wants us to get lost." Pete grins. Matt looks back at Brad and then raises his eyebrows at his mother, wondering just what is going on, as Pete pulls him away. The two young men head out the door, the door bangs shut, and Matt tugs at Pete's sleeve.

"Hey. What was that all about?" Matt says. "I'm not sure I know why your dad suddenly wants us out of the house."

"Matt, you can be real dense. You don't know what went on between my dad and your mom while she was out here? Poor Charlotte doesn't know either but suspects something. Boy, was she mad!"

"What do you mean? What did go on while Mom was out here?"

"Your mother had no idea who she was or where she came from when she took care of my grandmother. Because of her terrible amnesia, she had no recollection of you, your dad, your sister, or your home in Maryland. We all called her Rose. That's all I knew her as. Then Doc Adams started helping her to inquire about missing persons by way of the Internet. Your mother and Doc knew she must have some kind of history from somewhere. That's how your dad was contacted, but while she was here, my dad and she had a thing going. Dad was even ready to ask her to marry him. He moped around for months after your dad found her and took her home to Maryland."

"I am beginning to understand some things now, Pete. You see, I was never told all about that side of her adventure out here. Pop and Mom were always a little secretive about her time spent in Wyoming. Pop always said she was such a survivor and marveled at how she managed to get this far. But she came back with him and started her life all over again. She seemed so different. I remember Dad saying he felt like he was married to a completely different wife. Now I know what she means when she says she feels like two separate people at times. No wonder it was hard for her to settle in with us. She didn't even know us. Dad was always explaining things to her. I guess that gash and bump on her head really rattled her brain."

Matt takes a deep breath and pushes hair away from his eyes. "She was really hesitant about taking this trip out here, but several people encouraged her to do it. They said she needed a vacation after all the family had been through. First, the sudden death of my dad. Then we were warned about that crazy guy who ran him over. He tried to burn the whole plant down to get back at my dad for firing him. Then he came looking for Mom, and she shot him, right in the heart too, at my uncle's vet clinic." Matt's voice rises. "He had already shot my uncle in the leg. She had never handled a pistol before. She was a nervous wreck." Peter listens intently. "Then I slide into third base and tear a ligament in my knee, which put me on the disabled list for a while. And now here we are."

"It sounds like you all really needed a vacation, so welcome to

Wyoming!" Pete laughs. "I think ole Charlotte knows there was something special between those two, at least more than just an old family friend, who just happened to show up here. Did you see how my dad swung your mom around on the porch? He couldn't take his eyes off her. Charlotte saw that too." Pete smiles. "I had to laugh when Charlotte got mad and stomped out of the kitchen when she found out Dad was going to help with the dishes. She was fuming, just as mad as an old wet hen."

Peter lets out a loud cackle as they walk into the barn. "I bet she'll be back tomorrow to catch up on who Kate Remington really is. This is real comical, and I love it. I have never seen my dad pushed in a corner like that before, especially by two women. Your mom played it real cool and didn't say a word. I noticed a smirk on Grandmom's face too. She excused herself real fast too and headed for her room. I bet she is still chuckling."

Matt is deep in thought and trying to process the events of the evening. He pushes his hair away from his eyes and ponders his thoughts. "Do you think those feelings are still there? Do you really think my mom still has feelings for your dad? What about Charlotte? She sounded like she has some definite plans for your dad. She was really giving my mom some evil stares at supper. Now I know why Mom has been real cool about this trip out here, although I have noticed some unusual nervousness when we approached the ranch today. She said mainly that she wanted to visit Mary, your grandmother. She has said nothing about your dad."

"Maybe she wasn't sure how things might have changed. I don't think there has been any communication between them, only a few emails from my grandmother to your mom."

"You know, Pete, I have to give my mom a lot of credit. She had to learn all over again about Angie and me. She was practically a newlywed to my father. I heard them sitting up all hours of the night. talking and laughing. Angie and I often laughed because she got lost one day just going into town. She would cook up some of the most delicious meals after Dad brought her home, and I never realized where some of those recipes came from. I guess some of them came from Dolly out there at the diner. I think some of the pieces are finally falling into place for me."

Matt continues to follow Peter around to the many box stalls and corrals. Peter grabs a bucket and shovels some grain into it for the young heifers. "There, that should hold them until morning. These are the ones that need branding. Maybe you can hang around and give us a hand the first of the week. The other boys will be back Monday morning. The boys like to rope them and tie them down while Pop brands them. He puts a Circle C Ranch brand on them. He never changed the brand after my mother and he got married. Her name was Rachel and only in her thirties when she passed away from cancer. That brand is the same brand my grandfather used when he ran the ranch."

There's a drop in his vocal tone, and he becomes more serious. "It took a long while for Dad to get over her death. He kept his emotions penned up for a long time. He seems at peace with it now. I guess Jeff and I went through a long mourning period too. Then Grandmom moved in to help out, especially with the meals and all. We have a Mrs. Garcia who comes and cleans. Her son, Joe, is one of the hired hands too. Then your mom arrived, and everything changed. She had a way of putting everything in order, even my dad."

He laughs. "He had a new spring in his step, and you could tell he was becoming very happy and content again, especially when he was around her. She was such a blessing. He even started to go to church again, and Grandmom's hip got better too. I was playing big-league ball in Arizona and making a name for myself until I got hurt. I got my elbow shattered by a line drive. I still can't straighten it out completely. Jeff, who wasn't sure of what he wanted, even settled down and took off in a new direction. He's doing great in medical school. You'll meet him if he gets to come home anytime soon." Peter's expression changes. "Are you okay Matt?"

"I guess so. I never knew about my mother's other life out here. She tried to tell me a little about it on our way out here, but I never thought she could love anyone other than my dad. Do you think Brad and she were in love?"

"I'm pretty sure my dad was. He only knew her as Rose and knew nothing of her past. For all he knew, she could have been wanted for murder." Pete laughs again. "I'm just kidding, Matt. She seemed content to live out here too until she found she had certain obligations to you and your dad and your sister. They were both in a bit of turmoil. But I can understand now how she was so conflicted, and I can see how she had to make a big decision and, I guess, the right choice. Someone had to be a winner, and someone had to be a loser. My dad was the loser. He moped around for months. Now, dear ole Charlotte is in the picture. I wonder what will happen next."

Both boys smile and head up to the house again. Pete whispers to Matt. "I wonder if the dishes are done." They laugh again. "I have a TV in my room. Why don't we head upstairs and watch a good movie tonight. We can let those two get reacquainted."

Chapter 15

Matt and Peter step quietly into the kitchen and see Brad and Kate finishing up the last of the pots and pans. "Hey, guys. We're headed upstairs to watch some TV. See you in the morning."

They wave to Kate and Brad as they tiptoe by Mary's room. Mary's light is still shining brightly under her bedroom door as they hurry up the stairs to Pete's room.

The house is quiet, and the sun has long ago set in the west. In the distance, the moon is beginning to peek through a few clouds. Darkness closes in around the ranch as a cool summer breeze makes a rustling sound through the trees.

Brad wipes his soapy hands on the side of his jeans, while Kate grabs a dish towel and dries her hands too. The two look at each other and smile. Kate looks down.

Brad knows the time has finally come. They are alone. The house is quiet.

He puts a strong arm around her waist and gently lifts her chin with his other calloused hand. He lowers his head and delivers a long and loving kiss. Her lips respond as he moves his hands to encircle her face. It is such a gentle, but loving kiss.

Tears again dot Kate's cheek. Her arms encircle his waist. Kate trembles, and her cheeks are crimson. She drops her arms and tries to pull away. She looks up, smiling.

Kate speaks first. "What about Charlotte?"

He caresses her neck as he still holds her close. "Don't worry about her. She has her own agenda. I wanted to do this since I laid eyes on you this afternoon."

Kate's heart pounds while she tries hard to control her emotions.

"Let's go out on the porch and talk," he says. Kate gives a nod. His arm is around her waist as they quietly open the porch door and settle down on the porch swing. His arms pull her close as he places one around her shoulders. Kate is quiet.

They begin to swing back and forth. The swing gives out a little rusty squeak. She feels so comfortable here with his strong arms around her. She begins to relax. The red in her cheeks begin to fade. She can see the moon clearly now and hear the soft whinnies of the mares. The night breeze tosses her hair across her face.

He looks into her hazel eyes and pushes a strand of hair from her forehead. "This is where I enjoyed my first kiss with you. You acted a little embarrassed." He laughs. "Do you remember that? I guess I was a little forward." Kate nods again. "We even had to explain the whole thing to my mom. Do you remember that episode at breakfast when I landed on the floor, covered with egg?"

Kate begins to laugh and nods. She shivers a little in the night air. His arms pull her closer.

"Yes, I do. I think that is when I first started loving you, but I was afraid to show it. You, so big and strong, were so helpless and innocent looking, sprawled out on the kitchen floor, with scrambled eggs dangling from your jeans pocket."

Kate laughs, remembering the incident. "I didn't want you to get your feelings hurt because I didn't know what the future held for me. There were so many ifs, ands, and buts. So much has happened since I was here. I have two great kids, a married daughter with a baby on the way, and the terrible death of my husband. I even shot and killed a man in self-defense. He was the one who ran Jake down at the plant. He had already shot Richard, my brother, in the leg. It was either him or me. I can still see his ugly stare from those evil eyes boring a hole right through me. We both had a loaded pistol, pointed at each other, and when I pulled the trigger, I guess I won."

She smiles. "It went right through his heart. I was shaking like a leaf. That's the story Matt started to tell at the table. There was a big writeup in the paper, and people would come up to me and pat me on the shoulder and say they were proud of me. I even tried to hide in the grocery store because all sorts of people would nod and recognize me. I guess I was quite a celebrity."

"That's why I love you. Did you hear that? I'm still in love with you. You never back down, always charging ahead. You are such an amazing, surprising woman and even more beautiful than I remember. I don't think Charlotte knew just who she was tangling with, poor Charlotte."

Jake laughs aloud. "Kate, even your husband, Jake, knew just how special you really are. He loved you dearly too. I was so very jealous of him, but I couldn't get mad at him. I moped around here for months after you left. I would have done the same thing. He was right in taking you home. After that serious talk in the barn, he and I understood each other completely. Jake was a great guy. I wanted you to be happy, even if I was miserable. It must have taken a lot of strength on your part, with your amnesia, to walk in and start all over with a new life with complete strangers. I can tell Matt is a lot like his father, a really great boy. He even looks like him. You have done a great job, Kate." He stops. "But I still want to call you Rose, because that's where our story started." Brad looks down at her left hand and sees the gold wedding band.

Kate sees the glance. "Give me some time and space." She takes a deep breath and looks out over the distant pastures. "I've got some explaining to do, especially to Matt and Angie. You have rekindled some old emotions I thought were buried and forgotten." Looking out at the distant pastures, she continues. "This place is such a solace for me. I love everything about it. I feel like I have actually left some of the past bitterness and hatred behind. I'm beginning to think Matt is loving it here too. He and Peter seem to be getting along just fine."

Brad turns her face toward him and lifts her chin. "He's not the only one who is loving it." He pulls her close as their lips meet once again. The kiss is long and tender. Her head drops to his shoulder as the swing rocks back and forth in the darkness. The rusty squeak is gone. His arms cradle her shoulders. A distant owl hoots in the hay mow and breaks the silence. Kate is startled and straightens up. He soothingly rubs her back.

"I really must be going," she says. "I've got to get back to the motel. Brad I really should go." She tries to pull away. She looks into his eyes. "I'll be back for breakfast. Plug the coffeepot in for me in the morning. Don't forget to add the coffee." She smiles as she rises and steps off the porch.

He grabs her hand as he walks her to the car. He leans over and gives her a little peck on the cheek. Her purse and empty snack bags still lie on the seat. Matt's knee brace lies rumpled up on the floor. She leans over and picks it up. "Here, give this to Matt for his knee. He may want this in the morning." She settles in the front seat.

"Be careful. I'll see you in the morning."

The car starts, and she gives a little wave. Driving back to the Country Inn, Kate's emotions are ready to burst.

What have I let myself get into? Do I know what I am doing? Maybe things will seem clearer in the morning. Oh, Lord, help me!

Chapter 16

Entering the motel room, she drops her purse on the bed, and the white envelope falls out. It's Jake's note she found in the pocket of her suit in her closet after Jake's funeral. She unfolds it and reads it again. The last two sentences stare back at her.

"You have so much love to give. Always follow your heart."

Kate stares at herself in the motel mirror. She sniffles.

Is Jake giving me permission to love again? What does this mean? She folds it over and holds it close to her chest. *Where do I go from here?*

Kate begins to unpack a few things as she prepares for bed. Thinking about the day's events, she decides to get a good night's sleep and then begins to gather her thoughts.

Everything will be clearer in the morning. I'll have a good, long talk with Mary tomorrow. She can help me sort some things out.

Kate endures a fitful night's sleep, and morning seems to come early. The sun shines between the curtains, and a *caw caw* can be heard outside her room. She peeks out the window only to see a big black crow perched on a tree branch, staring at her window. It is seven o'clock. She grabs her things and heads for the shower. *Breakfast might be a little late this morning.*

In no time, Kate is speeding down the road, heading back to the ranch, her hair still damp and the car window down, wondering what to cook up for breakfast. She can feel the July humidity on her cheeks.

As she approaches the ranch, she slows at the gate and catches her breath. The cattle are grazing with calves on one side of the meadow, and the colts on the other side are following their mothers around while kicking up their heels. Driving down the gravel lane, she hears the crunch of small stones beneath the wheels. A small trail of dust follows the dusty car.

Standing on the porch, waving at her, are Matt and Peter. Matt is dressed in boots, jeans, a plaid shirt, and a straw cowboy hat. He looks right at home. Coming to a stop, she sees Brad come out of the barn and approach the car.

"Well, aren't we the late one this fine morning? Breakfast is over, and I am heading out with the boys to mend that fence. I made us all pancakes this morning. There are some leftovers in there, so help yourself. They were pretty good too, if I do say so myself." He grins as he tries to pat himself on his back. He helps her out of the car and plants a soft kiss on her lips as he lifts her gently in the air.

"Brad Crawford, you are so unpredictable. Put me down." He smiles that toothy grin again. Oohs and aahs can be heard from the porch. Matt and Pete are taking it all in. Kate's face reddens.

"Fix yourself a little something if you don't want the pancakes," Brad says. "Mom has not eaten yet, so help yourself to whatever you find. We'll be back for lunch. There are some frozen pizzas in the freezer. I'll need to go to the grocery store later today." He winks. "It feels like old times."

She looks up at him. "Behave yourself. What will those boys think?" He puts his arm around her, pulls her close, and walks her to the porch.

"Just so you know, I had a nice talk with them at breakfast, and even Matt seems to understand now. He didn't say too much, so I think he's just thinking things over. He's really a nice kid, Kate, really smart too. I may just make a cowboy out of him yet. He filled me in on a lot of what has happened in the last seven months. It sounds like you could use some kind of rest and relaxation. He and Pete have really bonded too. They are both baseball nuts." They step up on the porch as Kate looks up at Matt.

"I don't think you are ready to go horseback riding yet," she says to Matt. "Your knee is still not completely healed."

"Aw, Mom, I can manage. It's been a long time since I've been on a horse. Peter is going to give me an old slow horse to ride. I'll be okay."

Brad interjects, "I'll tell you what, Matt. You can ride with me in the pickup. There's no sense in causing any more problems with your knee. Maybe Doc Adams can check you over too."

Kate nods in agreement. "I should run in and see Doc Adams anyway while I'm here. I just may have him check you out. He may order another X-ray. I found your knee brace on the car floor last night. Please keep it on for a few more days." Matt nods. "Matthew, I just want you to be careful.

We don't need any more injuries." Matt glances over at Peter and rolls his eyes, then looks back at his mom.

"Yes, Mother. I know, I know. I'll be careful." He looks back at Brad. "I guess I'm ready. I'm anxious to see the rest of this ranch." Brad, Peter, and Matt pile into the truck, loaded down with fence posts and wire. She waves as they head out into the back pasture.

Kate continues into the kitchen and sees Mary sitting alone at the table. "Good morning, Mary. How did you sleep last night?"

Mary has dark circles under her eyes and seems short of breath. "I hate to say this, but I hardly slept a wink. I ran out of some of my medicine, and I feel so tired. Maybe we can call Doc and have him drop by. He would love to see you again." Kate casts a worried look at her. Her lips appear a little blue, and the wrinkles on her face are deeply creased. Her hair looks uncombed.

"How long have you been feeling this way?"

"Oh, it comes and goes. Some days I'm good, and some days I can hardly get out of bed. Doc has been making house calls and bringing my medicines out to me. I hate to bother Brad with all my aches and pains. I guess I'm just getting old." She sits back in her chair and takes a deep breath. "A cup of coffee would taste good."

"I think I'll call him and see if he will make a house call today, since this is Saturday. He can stay for something to eat too." Kate manages to find his phone number and leaves a message on his cell phone. She pours a cup of coffee for Mary and casts a worried look across the table. She then begins to have for herself some slightly warm pancakes, orange juice, and a cup of tea. "Would you like some toast or cereal with that coffee, Mary?"

"Oh, I'm not hungry. I'm just so tired because I didn't sleep well last night." She glances out the window. "I see the guys are all gone." Mary manages a little smile. "How did you like our dear Charlotte, now that you have met her?"

Kate takes a sip of tea and says nothing. Mary pauses and takes a deep breath. "We need to talk." There is a real seriousness in her voice. Kate looks across at her and nods. "I think Charlotte is history, and she knows something is up." Mary laughs. "That was quite a scene last night at supper. Those two boys got quite a kick out of seeing Brad squirm. He's still in love with you, Kate. It's not often he offers to do the dishes."

"I know. I felt like I was in the middle, and I could feel Charlotte's daggers too. I don't want to be the bad guy here. I've also got to fill Matt in on some things too, though I'm not sure what all Pete and he have discussed."

It's Kate's turn to take a deep breath now as she looks over at Mary. "Brad and I had quite a discussion out on the porch swing last night, actually more than just a discussion. Mary, I'm falling for him all over again. Jake was killed last January, and I guess I need some time to get my feelings sorted out." Kate sips her tea again. "I found a letter that Jake wrote to me over a year ago that was hidden in my suit pocket. I haven't shown it to anyone, but I would like you to read it. I've carried it with me since I found it."

Kate reaches for her purse and hands the wrinkled letter to Mary. Mary can see the tear-stained, blurred words written in ballpoint pen ink as she begins to smooth out the crumpled edges of the worn letter.

She adjusts her glasses and looks up at Kate. "Are you sure you want me to read this? Some things should be kept personal."

"Just tell me what you think. It's okay. My life seems to be an open book anyway."

Mary lowers her eyes and slowly reads the letter. Kate finishes her pancakes. There is silence as Mary refolds the letter, smooths it out, and hands it back to Kate

"Jake was such a great guy. He loved you dearly. He wants you to be happy. It sounds like he is giving you permission to love again. It's not often a woman can find true love again, twice in her life."

"What should I tell Brad?" She raises her eyebrows. "What about Charlotte? She has some definite plans for him. What should I tell Angie and Matt? I need to get back home soon. I promised Angie I would be there for her when the baby comes. I just can't leave my old life and restart a new one out here. Angie, Matt, and I have really bonded through all of our trials. I wonder if they would understand if I married Brad and moved out here. There is so much to consider, and what about my house in Maryland?"

"Maybe you should let them read this letter."

Kate is quiet as she sips the rest of her tea. "I have had so much turmoil and hatred boiling up inside of me ever since those awful guys kidnapped me. How can I forgive that kind of person? Then Buddy Stewart ran Jake down and killed him, and I am supposed to forgive people like that? I was actually relieved after I shot him, but I still feel like there's a black cloud hanging over me at times."

Mary looks at Kate and points to the letter. "What did Jake say in there?"

"He wants me to be 'happy, contented, and forgiving.' There's that word again, *forgiving*. Even Pastor Perry back home preached on forgiveness."

"What does the Bible say, Kate?"

"It says to forgive 'seventy times seven.'"

"You are right. That is from Matthew 18."

Kate fumbles with a napkin and wipes her mouth.

"Now you have got to let those feelings of hatred go. Let the Lord work in your heart. I believe the work has already started, Kate. You have been through so much, and I can understand how you feel justified by hanging onto those feelings of despair and hatred. It is only human nature to want to get back at someone who has wronged you. As Christians we have to rise above that. Remember the Lord's Prayer where it says to 'forgive us our debts as we forgive our debtors.' Then Jesus goes on to explain it further. 'For if you forgive men when they sin against you, your heavenly father will also forgive you. But if you do not forgive men their sins your Father will not forgive you.'"

"Mary, I guess I never thought deeply enough about the effect of carrying such a burden of unforgiveness. I can remember standing in my kitchen with Jake and pounding my fist against the counter and saying how I have come to hate the guys who actually caused this amnesia. I felt justified because I lost a vital part of my life with my children and husband. Now I'm out here with you and Brad, and I feel like I want to restart my life, but that black cloud of hatred wants to follow me wherever I go. I know I should have a forgiving spirit."

Mary looks into Kate's eyes and leans over to her. "Let's pray about this."

The women bow their heads and grasp each other's hands as Mary begins. "Oh Lord, hear our prayer. You promised where two or more are gathered, you will be in their midst. I pray now for Kate to be able to relinquish her feelings of hatred and despair and to receive your forgiveness in her heart and mind. Remove the dark cloud of despair and give her a new freedom of strength and love as only you can provide by your Holy Spirit. Help her to put aside the past wrongs and love again. Help her to be the woman she was born to be, grateful, loving, caring, and forgiving. Lord, we know you have a special plan for all our lives. Help us all to do your will and stay close to you. Protect us, Lord, guide us, and give us your wisdom to do the right thing. We ask all these things in Jesus's name, amen."

"That was beautiful, really beautiful, and right to the point." Kate swallows hard as tears roll down her cheeks. She wipes them away with her breakfast napkin. She looks up at Mary. Mary's eyes are tearful as a gradual smile parts her lips.

"I have been praying for you since the first time I met you. When you wrote to me about Jake's death, I prayed that you and your family would somehow be able to rise above the crisis and come out stronger because of the trials you were facing. Kate, you have come through a mountain of trials, and I feel that the prayers of God's people have brought you strength and healing to where you are today. You, my dear, have been in my prayers every day—yes, each and every day."

"Thank you, Mary." She smiles. "I feel like I have been on a long journey and that I can finally look up and feel that the heavy burden of guilt and hatred is finally being lifted. I feel like the black cloud over me is being taken away. I actually feel a certain peace." Kate smiles as a new radiance appears on her face. "Now what do I do?"

"I think you need to reread Jake's letter. He says to 'follow your heart.' I believe he wrote that letter so you would find it when you needed it. He was following the Lord's plan too. He had your best interest in mind and wanted you to be taken care of. Jake was a very special person too. As a Christian, the Lord has a plan for us, though we may not know or understand it at times. We have to trust in him and have faith that our lives will be lived for his glory, not ours."

She takes a deep breath. "I also believe that your trip here at this time was no accident either. Maybe the Lord wants to give you some real rest and a time to relax. Emma, our young cook, will be here on Monday morning to prepare meals for the guys, so maybe, just maybe, you can enjoy your visit here with no workload."

"You're right about one thing. I do need to relax, and I do feel relieved and unburdened about a lot of things. That prayer was just what I needed. Mary, you are the mother I don't even remember and a friend I really and truly can share my deepest longings with. Thank you for your loving friendship and your special spiritual understanding. You are so special."

Mary reaches out and pats her hand.

"I really don't mind helping out here with the meals and with the errands. I need to stay busy. Maybe you could give Emma a little vacation for a week while I am here. I enjoy the cooking. It will be good for me to stay busy. I know Matt is enjoying his time here too."

"Kate, don't let my son push you into anything until you are ready. I see the way he looks at you. He definitely has some plans in his head for you. Pray earnestly about your next step. The Lord will hear your prayers."

"Yes. Brad has really rekindled some old emotions in me, and I can't say that I'm not excited about the possibilities too. Mary, I'm falling for him all over again. I get tingly whenever he comes close to me. I feel like a love-struck teenager. I am a grown woman, and I need to sort some of these feelings out. Should I be feeling this way?"

Mary nods and smiles. Kate leans closer. "Mary, I have certain responsibilities to my family. Could I adjust to a new way of life? It's an entirely different lifestyle out here. Could I leave a new grandchild and two kids whom I have come to know and love too? Mary, Jake left me with some pretty good investments and a surprising insurance policy, and I'm trying to navigate through a lot of investment jargon. I've even had to hire a financial adviser. It is unknown territory for me. Matt is helping me understand some of this computer business."

Mary nods. "Talk these things over with your children. You may be surprised at their reactions. Yes, I believe Matt is liking his stay here too. He and Pete seem to be hitting it off real good."

"Yeah, it's all talk about baseball and sore arms and knees."

Mary laughs. "They sound like they have more aches and pains than me."

The phone rings, and Kate rises to answer it. "Hello. Doc?" She pauses. "Yes, this is your old friend Kate. Remember me?" She pauses. "Yes, I'm out at the ranch, and I think Mary needs to see you. She says she needs some more of her medicine." Kate casts a worried look at Mary. "Her breathing is still labored at times."

She hangs the phone up. "He says he will be out about noon and can grab a bite to eat here too. It will be good to see him again. He must be eager to retire soon. He's not getting any younger either."

"Doc, yeah, he's the same old Doc Adams. What would I do without him? He has kept this old body going for up to eighty years now. It would be real nice if Jeff could step in and relieve him a little. Most of his housebound patients already know Jeff. It would be a nice transition. Doc thinks the world of Jeff, just like a son he never had."

Mary begins to stand and reaches for her cane. "I think I'll get a shower and then catch up on my reading." She wobbles out of the kitchen and heads for her room.

Kate watches from a distance. A worried look and a grim expression appear on Kate's face. *She's such a trooper!* Kate begins to tidy up the kitchen and looks around for a broom. She sweeps the floor clean of its barn dirt and little straw strands. Kate tiptoes toward Mary's room to check on her and listens. She can hear the shower going and a little hum as Mary enjoys the warm water.

Kate goes back to the kitchen and stares out the door, her arms folded across her chest. Her mind relives all the what-ifs. Time passes as she stands quietly and takes in the bucolic scene.

The sun is shining. The birds are singing. There isn't a cloud in the sky. There is a hint of humidity in the air. The porch swing sits still. The pastures rise and fall over each little knoll as they stretch out toward the rugged mountains.

Could I be happy and content living out here? What would the kids think?

She hears Tom whistling out in the barn. *Well, he sounds like a happy and contented soul.* Her mind is brought back to reality when she hears a shuffling and a *tap tap* in the living room. It's Mary heading for her easy chair, her damp hair curls on top of her head. "I think I'll just rest here awhile. I could use another cup of coffee if there is any left."

"Oh, sure, I'll fix you one. It might need warming up."

"Kate, you looked deep in thought, staring outside. I guess you have a lot on your mind."

Kate carries a mug of coffee over to her and settles herself down on Mary's footstool.

"It's just that my life has taken so many twists and turns. Sometimes I feel like two different people. I'm thinking about so many things and trying to keep a clear head, but my emotions are running wild, and my heart is beating a mile a minute."

"Deep down you are just one person, just with different circumstances and responsibilities surrounding you. You have been very fortunate to have loving and stable people around you. Kate, you have been given a second chance at love and a family. I know of no other person who deserves it more. I feel that many of the things that you are worried about will work out and surprise you. Remember what Jake wrote, to 'follow your heart.'"

Mary sips her coffee and closes her eyes. She smacks her lips and nestles comfortably in her chair. She begins to doze off.

Kate takes the mug of warm coffee from Mary's hand and places it on the end table. Kate rises and looks around the room. Things are a little dusty with a few clumps of dirt from the barn scattered here and there. The braided oval rug still lies over the wide-plank floorboards. The fireplace still holds some old family pictures on the mantel. The tan-and-brown overstuffed chairs still hold their rumpled seat cushions.

Kate steps forward into Brad's office. His desk is still piled high with papers, and a computer sits off to the side. The large bay window allows the glare of the sun to shine through. The curtains are pulled back, bringing real warmth to the room. The threadbare rug is gone, and a fairly new rug with gold-and-brown Indian prints has taken its place. Mary's room is next, and the door has been left open. Her bed is unmade, and a wet towel has dropped to the floor.

Kate steps inside and proceeds to make her bed, then picks up the wet towel. She can hear a gentle snore from Mary as Kate quietly closes her door and tiptoes past her. The clock in the kitchen ticks loudly, trying to outdo Tom's whistling in the sheds.

Kate moves to the freezer and removes three large sausage and cheese pizzas. *I wonder if Doc likes pizza. I know the boys do. Maybe I should fix something else for him. He should be here soon. There's not much food left around here to fix. Maybe I can find a can of soup. Someone needs to go to the grocery store, and soon.*

Kate looks out the window and sees a car drive up. *That must be Doc.* She moves out to the porch and waves as he climbs out of his car. *Same old Doc. Same old car.* They move toward each other and give each other a welcoming hug. She steadies him as they walk toward the porch.

"You certainly look good," he says. "It's so good to see you again. I heard by way of Mary what happened to Jake. I'm so sorry, such a terrible tragedy. Jake was such a nice guy, even though I only met him when he came to cart you home. I still remember that day in my office. You almost hauled off and hit him. You had no idea who he was. I still chuckle over that. By the way, how are those two kids of yours? I know they must be grown up by now."

"They are fine. We had a lot of catching up to do, but first, I'm a little worried about Mary. She is in there snoozing in her chair. She gets really short of breath with exertion, and her color doesn't look good."

"Yes, she has been battling congestive heart failure, and she won't go to the hospital for some tests. I think she wanted to be here when you arrived. She can be stubborn when she wants to be. I guess we all get that way when we get old, just don't get old." He laughs. "I'll let her get her nap. We can catch up out here." Kate sits down on the creaky swing, and Doc plops down in one of the soft wicker chairs.

"Aren't you about ready to retire too?" she said. "I hear Jeff has been helping you out when he gets home. Is he going to be able to take over your practice?"

"I sure hope so, though I've cut back on my office hours. My old patients still want me to make house visits. Not many doctors leave their offices nowadays. Technology has taken over so much now. You can even send an EKG over the phone into a computer, which will spit out a diagnosis for you. Jeff knows all about that stuff. I still keep up on some of the electronic stuff, but I must admit, times are changing fast."

"I know. My daughter, Angie, is a nurse, and she talks about all the new advances in medicine, but she is expecting her first child in August, so she will be taking some time off. I hope to be there when she delivers. Matt, my son, is out with Brad and Peter fixing a broken fence. He just finished college and graduated early. He is all into computers and baseball. That reminds me. He pulled a ligament in his left knee and has been wearing a soft brace on it. I'm wondering if you would have a look at it."

"I didn't know I would be seeing two patients today." They both laugh together. Hearing a rattling in the distance, a sound coming up from the back pasture, they see a dusty red pickup heading for the barn. It rumbles to a stop with tools, wire, and fence posts rolling around in the truck's bed.

"Here comes the hungry boys and Brad." Kate announces.

Brad jumps out of the truck and waves. Matt and Pete laugh about something as they pile out too.

"Hey, Doc," Brad says. "How have you been? Is Mom okay?"

"Yes. She is in there taking a nap. Kate and I have been out here reminiscing. I've got some pills for your mother when she wakes up."

"Hey, Mom!" Matt says. "Are those pizzas ready? We have worked up an appetite, and we are starving."

"Let me put them in the oven. I wasn't sure when you guys would show up. Doc, how about you? Do you feel like having a slice too? There's not much in the house to eat. Someone," she says as she looks over at Brad, "needs to go to the store. I could fix you a cup of soup if you would like."

"Actually, Kate, pizza would be a nice change. Pizza is fine."

Brad rushes past the boys and plants a little kiss on Kate's cheek. She looks surprised as her face reddens. Doc looks a little surprised too. "Well, Brad, are you picking up where you left off four years ago?"

Brad grins. "I'm trying, Doc. I'm trying."

Matt and Peter burst out laughing. Furious, Kate turns quickly and goes in the house. The screen door slammed behind her.

"It's okay, Doc," Brad says. "The boys know where I stand. We have had a couple of good talks about Kate and me. They are coming around to accept the obvious. I think I need to go in there and apologize to her. I am constantly embarrassing her. Wait out here."

Matt and Pete watch through the screen door as Brad approaches Kate. They see him put his big, tan arms around her shoulders; he turns her around and lifts her up. She has a wooden spatula in her hand, and she begins to wave it in front of his face. Even Doc is peeking through the screen and watching the scene unfold at the stove.

Kate can see their nosey faces watching their every move. Brad says something, and Kate continues to wave the spatula toward his face. Brad laughs heartily.

She raises her voice. "Brad Crawford, put me down and behave yourself. Everybody is watching us! You are so impulsive! I never know what you will do or say."

He smiles broadly as he releases her and waves for them to come in. "Come on in, guys. I want my favorite people to hear this," he hollers as he beckons them in. He throws his sweat-rimmed Stetson in a chair as he suddenly turns and walks hastily into his office.

Kate is left standing there, perplexed, one hand on her hip, the other hand holding the spatula, wondering what he will do next. She shakes her head. His noisy cowboy boots click across the solid wooden plank floors as he enters his office. Desk drawers can be heard opening and slamming shut.

"Finally, ah-ha! Here it is!" Brad exclaims.

Mary wakes up to the commotion and sees the trio entering the kitchen. Doc, Matt, and Peter move closer to the table. Doc plops down in a hard chair. Mary struggles to get out of her recliner and finally ambles over with her cane, looking first at Doc, then at Brad and Kate, wondering what is happening. The smell of pizza begins to fill the kitchen.

Brad walks slowly toward Kate, one hand behind his back. "Let's make this official Kate." He drops down to the kitchen floor on bended knee and looks squarely into Kate's eyes. "Kate Remington, I love you. Will you marry me?" He pulls a velvet ring box from behind his back and opens it carefully.

All eyes are on Brad. His rough, calloused hands cradle the box gently. A beautiful one-carat diamond ring glows in Brad's hand. Surrounding the center gem are numerous other little diamonds twinkling on the gold band.

There is silence. No one is breathing. Matt is wide eyed, staring first at his mother, then at Brad. Peter's mouth is wide open. They stare at the ring. Doc and Mary grin and shake their heads.

All eyes are on Kate now. She looks first at the ring, then at Brad, then at Matt. She grabs hold of the sink's edge to steady herself. Her knees are trembling. The spatula drops.

Brad's eyes are on Kate alone; he steadies himself on one knee. There is shock, then surprise on Kate's red face. She pushes a wisp of hair away from her eyes. A gasp is heard as she hangs onto the sink.

"It's beautiful." she whispers. She looks up at Matt again.

He smiles and nods. Peter has his arm around him, whispering something in his ear. Doc looks over at Mary and winks as Mary slides onto a hard, wooden chair.

"Brad Crawford!" Kate says. "You never fail to surprise me. I have only been here two days, and you come out with this." She looks at all their faces. She wipes a little tear from her eye.

Matt smiles too. He nods.

She stutters. "Yes, I guess so. Yes, I mean, I guess so, if it is all right with Matt and Angie. I have to talk this over with them."

Kate smiles as she nervously holds out her left hand. Brad rises and slides the new ring next to her old wedding band. There are shouts of "Hooray, hooray!" from the onlookers, and they all clap their hands. Loud congratulations are heard from Doc and Mary. Matt rushes over to his mother and eyes the ring; he gives her a little hug. Kate is teary eyed. They are oblivious to the sound of a car door slamming.

"It's okay, Mom, really. I've had a long talk with Pete and Brad." Pete puts up a thumbs-up sign.

Brad embraces Kate and swings her around. He plants a quick kiss on her neck and then on her lips. Her arms encircle his neck. He gives a cowboy yell and laughs heartily. Loud oohs and aahs are heard as the commotion suddenly comes to a halt.

The screen door slams shut. The clapping stops. All eyes turn to the loud noise.

Charlotte stands there with her purse and some papers in one hand; her right hand is planted on her hip. She stares at Brad and Kate. She fumes, her face crimson. She sees their embrace and the quick kiss. Her eyes are but slits, and her lips barely cover her teeth. Her right foot taps. She takes a step forward, and her high heels click across the hard floor. Her eyes dart back and forth as she surveys the gathering. Every hair on her head is in place, and her black tailored suit signifies she means business.

"What is the meaning of all this noise? Just what is going on here?"

There is a sudden silence as Charlotte's piercing gaze is directed at Brad. He sets Kate down and takes a deep breath. He looks around the kitchen at the startled faces. He stares at Charlotte.

Matt and Pete slink back to watch the exchange. Mary and Doc grimace as they hide their faces in their hands. Doc leans over and whispers quietly to Mary. "Time for a showdown, and Brad is on his own." Doc smiles and nudges Mary. "This should be interesting."

Mary shifts in her seat and nods. She glances up at Brad.

Brad knows there is no help coming. He stands there, looking around the room, and digs his hands into his faded jeans pockets. He blows a wisp of hair off his forehead.

Kate takes a step backward, rubbing her left hand, covering the new ring. She sees Charlotte's questioning and beet-red angry face. The little bell dings on the oven. The pizzas are done, but no one moves.

"Charlotte," Brad says, "I need to explain something. Now just calm down." He clears his throat as his voice cracks and wavers a little. He squares his shoulders and pushes his hair from his forehead. Her fierce stare makes Brad shift his weight as he takes a protective step in front of Kate. A new sign of courage and determination is beginning to show in his square-set jaw. His deep-blue eyes are unblinking. His face is flushed, and beads of sweat dot his forehead.

He looks squarely at Charlotte and slowly begins. "You and I are not getting married, and I am not selling this place, and I am not traveling all over Europe. There. I said it!" He heaves a deep breath. "I'm sorry if I led you on for the past couple of years." He steps forward. "I plan to marry Kate." Kate peeps around from behind him and feels icy daggers penetrating her from Charlotte's eyes.

"Brad Crawford," her voice screeches, "I have in my hand papers for you to sign. They will make you a very rich man. I have worked hard on this sale. The offer for this place is over four million dollars, and you and I will be able to do and go anywhere in the world and leave this little nobody behind!"

She waves the papers in his face. There is a burnt odor coming out of the oven. Kate steps up to open the oven door. The kitchen begins to fill with wisps of smoke. Kate reaches over to turn off the oven and grabs a hot pad.

Brad steps out of the way as she pulls the pans out and sets them on the counter. The pizzas are singed around the edges and dried out in the middle.

Charlotte slams the papers down on the table and looks around at the silent faces. "I hope you know what you are doing and what a fool you are! Go ahead and eat your burnt pizza. Call me when you change your mind."

She turns toward Kate and catches the sparkle on her left hand. She sees a huge diamond glowing amid little diamonds set on a gold band, right next to a gold wedding band. "I hope you know what you are getting yourself into, little Miss Kate."

She turns briskly and heads for the door. It slams behind her, and they all take a collective deep breath. Brad stands stoically still.

Stray pieces of gravel can be heard hitting the side of the porch steps as Charlotte speeds out the lane. No one has moved. Matt and Pete stand off to the side, arms folded across their chests.

Pete whispers to Matt, "Whew! There goes hurricane Charlotte!"

Doc dryly comments, "The pizza is not the only thing hot in this kitchen. I think more smoke was coming off Charlotte than off the pizza." A bit of nervous laughter begins as Doc rises and looks over at the pizza. "Now what do we do for lunch?"

Mary speaks up. "I'll settle for a bowl of soup and some crackers."

Peter looks over at the pizza. "Well, Matt, I guess we have some crispy pizza to eat."

"Mary, I'll have some soup with you and maybe a piece of this overdone pizza." Doc looks at the dried crispy crust.

Brad regains his composure and takes a deep breath. He grins. "Kate, I'll take you out for an engagement celebration lunch to our favorite 'high-class' chicken place, and then we can go grocery shopping. How is that for a big date?" Brad grins that broad infectious smile. He puts a comforting arm around Kate's shoulders. There are smiles all around.

Kate nods and looks down at the glowing ring. "I guess I can't say no to such a big date as that, especially with all these witnesses." She lets out a nervous laugh. "Let me open a can of soup first for your mom and Doc, and then I'll be ready. I found some cheddar cheese in the fridge too. You can add that to your big lunch of soup and crackers." Kate smiles. "I guess the boys will be satisfied with some of this overdone, crispy pizza. There is some extra tomato sauce in there too for you two to doctor up your slices. Maybe we can bring home something decent for supper. Oh, yes. Leave the exhaust fan on and the door open for a while. It will help to rid this place of some of the odor and smoke."

"Speaking of smoke, I thought Charlotte's hair would go up in flames. She was really on fire." Doc chuckles as he pretends to wave his hands in the air to clear the smoke away.

"Doc, I think you rather enjoyed that little episode," Brad says teasingly. "What else should I have said to her?" He looks around. "One thing is for sure. I don't think I have heard the end of this yet." He looks at Kate and smiles. "When Charlotte gets upset, the whole county hears about it."

Chapter 17

Sunday morning arrives, and a breakfast of eggs and bacon appears on the table with warm biscuits and orange juice. Kate arrived early from the motel and prepared the tasty breakfast. With food in the house, she feels quite at home. A change of clothes lies neatly across one of the kitchen chairs. The grocery store outing was what was needed to pack the shelves and the refrigerator.

She is dressed in a long skirt and a white, airy summer blouse. Her hair is brushed back and still damp from the morning shower and humidity. A long white apron from the pantry hook covers her front as she makes herself busy with the breakfast.

Brad arrives first as the smell of fresh coffee and bacon lures him to the kitchen. He sneaks up behind Kate and gives her a surprise hug and a soft kiss on her neck.

She at first appears a little startled but relaxes and begins to enjoy the tight squeeze. He sees her check her watch. "Church is at eleven o'clock, and I don't think Mom is feeling up to it. She has missed quite a few Sundays. The boys may like to go though. How about it?"

"I remember the last time I went with you. Those pesky, nosy Simpson sisters tried to corral me and started asking me a bunch of questions. I suppose they are still there." She looks over her shoulder.

"Oh, you mean Harriet and Hannah. Yeah. They are still the town gossips. What would we do without them?" He chuckles.

"Are you sure it is okay to leave your mother here alone? She doesn't look all that well, but she won't complain."

Brad rubs his chin. "I'll check on her. I think I heard her in her bathroom." He heads over to her room and sees Mary standing at her door. "Hi, Mom. Do you feel up to church this morning? You look rested."

"No. But I do feel better. Those pills that Doc gave me helped me get a better night's sleep. I feel like I can breathe easier now. I think I'll stay home this time and rest up, but you all can go. Say hi to the Simpson sisters for me." She laughs. "I'll give our little cook, Emma, a call and give her a week off. It smells like Kate has taken charge of the cooking now that you went to the store and stocked the pantry." She shuffles her way to the large plank table as other footsteps are heard coming down the steps.

Matt and Pete rub their eyes and approach the kitchen.

"Something sure smells good. Boy am I hungry!" Matt heads for the bacon while Pete rubs his stomach.

"You are always hungry, Matt," Kate says. "You have never missed a meal since you were born. You two sit down here and eat breakfast. We have to leave soon if we are to catch the eleven o'clock service."

Sunday morning moves along at a leisurely pace. Chores are put off until later as the four of them ride to town in Kate's car. The morning air is sticky, and the temperature is ninety degrees as the sun begins to rise high in the sky. People in jeans and plaid shirts are seen entering the little Bible church as Kate turns into the gravel parking area.

"Hi" and "Howdy" are the greetings of the day as the men duff their hats and take their seats. Matt and Peter file in beside Kate and Brad. Taking the only available seats, they find sitting in front of them two "blue-haired" giggly women, the Simpsons.

Brad nudges Kate's arm. She smiles and whispers something to him. He picks up her hand and squeezes it. The other arm goes around her shoulder.

Matt looks over the congregation as Pete eyes some friends. There is a pretty blonde, who acknowledges Pete as he slyly waves to her. Matt sees the connection and jabs Peter in the ribs. Matt whispers to Pete, "So this is the reason you come to church." They both smile as they settle in their pew.

The ceiling fans over their heads whirl away as warm air can be felt against their cheeks. The plain church windows are open wide, and a little bee buzzes in and out. The service starts with "How Great Thou Art" as the whole congregation stands. The preaching begins, the offering plate is passed, and the hour passes. A final hymn is sung, and their voices carry into the church yard. Soon the amens are heard as the service ends; once again greetings are heard as they shake hands all around.

Brad and Kate hurry to make a quick exit but see that the Simpson sisters have held up the boys. Peter introduces Matt and tries to sidestep their questions. He looks around and finds that Brad and Kate have ducked out the side door. They are left on their own.

Hannah grabs Matt's hand and shakes it heartily. "You are new here, aren't you? Where are you from? I saw you were with Brad Crawford. Is that a new girlfriend he was with? Where is Charlotte Hamilton? She often meets him here."

Matt looks back at Pete for some help. He gulps.

"I am new here, and I'm a friend of Peter's. I'm Matt, I'm from Maryland, and I really must go. Nice to meet you, ladies." He nods. With that he and Peter step aside and head for the side door too. They leave the two women staring after them, looking a little frustrated.

"What did he say his name was?" Hannah and Harriet look at each other. "Matt from Maryland, I think. That woman with Brad Crawford looks very familiar. Where have we seen her before?"

Harriet continues to ponder this question as they slowly move toward the door with other parishioners. They shake hands with the pastor quickly and hurry to catch up with Crawfords; they see all of them get in the red, dusty car and head out of town.

"Well, how do you like that? We didn't even get to say hello to Brad and his new girlfriend. I wonder who she is."

Driving home with the air-conditioning putting out some cool air, Brad finally breaks the silence. "Well, the Simpson sisters are still in grand form. I saw where they cornered you two, and I wonder if they recognized Kate."

Kate shakes her head. "Maybe I'd better stay out of town for a while." She laughs. "It was a good sermon, even though they caused a little distraction, sitting right in front of us. I'll try to remember the part of the sermon about loving your neighbor."

Peter pipes up and kiddingly asks, "Does that neighbor include Charlotte too? I didn't see her in church this morning. I wonder where she will show up next."

"Now, son, be nice. We just left church. Try not to spoil a good day, and besides I think we can forget about Charlotte." Brad now drives as he continues to have one arm securely around Kate's shoulders. He looks at Kate and grins that innocent cowboy smile.

She shakes her head and glances over her shoulder. She eyes Matt as he pokes Peter in the side. Playful muffled noises are exchanged in the back seat. Soon tires going over loose gravel are heard as Brad steers the car up the ranch lane. The car comes to a halt, and the group climbs out.

Mary is on the porch swing, going to and fro, her feet barely touching the floor. The little squeak blends in with the chirping of the birds. She smiles and gives a little wave as they ascend the steps.

"Hey, Mom. You look better. How are you feeling?"

"I'm feeling much better. I slept much better last night. How was the sermon?"

"It was just fine, all about loving your neighbor. Matt and Pete got cornered by the Simpsons. Other than that, it was a good morning." He looks over at the pair. "Okay, you two, there are some heifers that need tending to. We need to get those branded in the morning, so separate those from the others out there. The other cowhands will be back in the morning, so we will be ahead of the game if we can have them ready when they come."

Peter salutes his dad and pulls Matt with him into the house to change their clothes. Kate plops down beside Mary and leaves Brad standing by himself. He scratches his head. "What's for dinner?"

"Brad, you are worse than those two boys, always hungry." Kate slides off the swing and stands. The squeak stops.

"We bought some thick steaks at the store yesterday. I'll put on some vegetables while you hook up to the kitchen grill. We can have dinner ready in no time." Kate is giving the orders now. Mary nods as Kate heads to the kitchen.

"When it comes to food, son, I think Kate is in control."

Brad settles down on the soft cushions and twiddles his thumbs. He closes his eyes. His long legs and size-eleven boots are stretched out across the porch floor. Strands of gray hair fall across his forehead.

"Call me when you want the steaks put on," he says as he stretches. Mary watches Brad give a contented yawn as he settles down in the chair.

"Brad. We need to talk. Are you listening?" He nods and opens one eye. "I don't want you pushing Kate into something when she is not ready.

You need to back off a little and slow down. She has some emotions she has to sort out and some decisions to make."

Brad straightens up and squints. "I hear you, Mom. Anything else?" There is annoyance in his voice. "I've already talked to Matt and Pete about my feelings, and they seem to understand the situation quite nicely. Don't worry about it or worry about us—that is, Kate and me. I'm a grown man, and I think I know what I am doing."

Mary is upset by the tone in his voice. "Kate and Matt will be leaving soon. She has promised Angie, her daughter, that she will be there when she has her baby. Give her time to take care of some things at home. Don't push her into something you both may regret. She needs time for some rest. She and her family have been through a lot in the past eight months."

"Yes, Mom, I hear you. Stop worrying. We are going to talk about a plan for us real soon."

Kate emerges from the kitchen. "Okay, fire up the grill. The veggies should be ready when the steaks are done." Kate has changed into shorts and a bright-blue summer blouse. "How about some iced tea while we are waiting?"

Brad pulls himself up in his chair and pulls Kate down beside him. "I'll get the iced tea for you both and fire up the kitchen grill. You and Mom can sit out here while I get things heated up. The boys should be done in the barn soon, and I know that when they smell the steaks, they will come in as hungry as hounds." Brad leans over and gives Kate a little peck on the cheek; as he stands, he winks at his mom. Kate's face turns a bright pink.

"I'll be right back." He disappears into the kitchen, the screen door slamming behind him.

"Brad is acting like a different person since you arrived, Kate. He's not acting his age." She laughs. "Though, I really like that new spring in his step. The twinkle in his eyes has returned."

Kate nods and smiles. Brad reappears with two cold glasses of iced tea. "Here's to my two favorite ladies. So just sit back now, and I'll cook those steaks to your perfection." He hands the iced tea to Kate and Mary. Mary continues to swing back and forth and looks up.

Brad has donned the long white chef's apron and bows before them. The women laugh as he steps back into the kitchen.

A warm summer breeze brings the aroma of newly mowed hay across the porch. The sizzling of the steaks and the noise of busy cowboy boots against the hard, wooden floors can be heard between creaks of the swing. Mary and Kate sip the cool iced tea and swirl the ice cubes around in their glasses.

Kate checks her watch. "I think I'd better check on the vegetables. I'll be right back." The delicious aroma of the searing T-bones fills the kitchen and wafts into the summer air. Kate checks the fresh veggies and quickly sets the table.

Brad is busy turning the steaks and testing them for doneness. "Just a few more minutes, and these steaks will be done. I'd better call the boys."

"No need. I hear them coming up to the porch. They probably caught the smell of those steaks clear out in the barn. I'll call them all in."

The creaky noise of the swing stops as Mary, Matt, and Pete open the screen door and enter the kitchen.

"Something really smells good," Pete says. "Boy, are we hungry. Matt and I are salivating. There's nothing like grilled steak for a Sunday dinner."

Mary looks up at Matt and Pete, and points at them. "Don't forget to eat your veggies. Growing boys like you two need all the vitamins you can get. This is your grandmother speaking." She smiles broadly. "Just save a small piece of meat for me." Mary's eyes twinkle as she laughs.

The group settles down around the table and watch as Brad brings the steaks to the table. Kate has provided fresh broccoli, carrots, and cauliflower with coleslaw on the side. Grace is said, and there is an unusual quiet as everyone savors the delicious steaks and fresh vegetables.

Brad catches Kate's eye and winks. She blushes. Mary watches Matt and Pete devour their T-bone steaks, then sit back and pat their stomachs. Their veggies are still piled high on their plates. They glance at Mary and feel a better-clean-your-plate stare as they slowly dab their forks into the broccoli mix. Matt nudges Pete. They wash each mouthful down with a gulp of iced tea. Brad catches the unspoken rule from his mother and smiles.

There is a real peace and understanding around the table. Mary looks around the table. "After this meal, I feel a nap is in my future. I'll settle for some dessert a little later, maybe some ice cream. I'll let our experienced dish washer help with the cleanup."

Mary looks over at Brad and teasingly smiles. Brad catches the inflection as he takes a deep breath and grins that toothy cowboy smile.

He puts the fork down by his plate. "I'll be glad to help, Mom. Maybe we won't have the Charlotte sideshow today." The boys give a hearty laugh and look over at Kate.

Kate tries not to laugh, but a wide grin breaks through as she chuckles. "Poor Charlotte! I wonder if she has calmed down."

"Don't say 'poor Charlotte,'" Brad says. "That woman can be as sly as a fox. You don't know her the way I do. She has pulled off some amazing real estate deals. When she sets her mind on something or somebody, watch out. I don't think we have seen the last of her." He twirls his fork around with the final piece of steak on it.

Chapter 18

Monday morning arrives early, along with the hot, humid, sticky heat of summer. There is a lot of bawling and commotion from the young heifers and steers in the corral. Choking and coughing can be heard from the hooves and boots of the cowboys kicking up the dust. The young calves run around in circles before they are lassoed and pulled down to their knees.

Matt stands off to the side as Brad brings a searing, red-hot branding iron down on the hips of the heifer. A scarring Circle C Ranch brand is being permanently burned into its hide. Peter, Ben, Rick, and Joe are busy roping and tying calves' legs together for a fast branding. The smell of burnt flesh permeates the whole corral. The shirts of Joe and Rick, the experienced cowhands, are drenched in sweat. Their shirts stick to their backs, outlining their youthful muscles. Their reddened faces glisten with perspiration as they wipe the sweat from their eyes.

A cloud of corral dust is kicked up as a heifer with the lasso tangled about her feet drags Ben. Pete grabs his rope and hurries to Ben. All eyes turn to see Ben as he releases the rope. He staggers to his feet, looking disgusted, and wipes the dust and sand from his Levis. His blond hair is now a dusty brown. Matt walks over, picks up Ben's sweat-brimmed cowboy hat, and hands it to him. Ben nods a thank-you and smiles.

Pete approaches Matt with a lasso. "How about trying to rope some of these critters? There are only a few left to brand."

Matt looks at Pete with a little uncertainty in his eyes. Brad drops the branding iron into the fire and walks over to Matt. "Maybe you would like to help me hogtie these critters down while I do the branding."

"I don't mind helping, but this stuff is all new to me. I've never roped anything in my life, let alone helped someone brand young calves.

The stench of burnt flesh is sickening. How do you guys stand that? My stomach is churning."

"It's all what you get used to, son." Brad wipes the sweat off his forehead. He pokes the red handkerchief back in his pocket. "Come on. I'll make a cowboy out of you yet. You can tell all your friends back east what you have been doing." Pete, Rick, and Joe stand off to the side, taking a little breather, hands on their hips cowboy style. Ben is over by the horse trough, dusting off his pants.

"Hey guys, let's watch this. This should be interesting." Pete's voice is low.

Brad takes Matt over to the huddled calves, waving the lasso lazily.

"Just swing your rope easy up in the air a little and a little ahead of the loping calf and let it fly. She should run right into it. Watch!" Brad swings the rope out in a wide circle. The rope rises in the air and then drops easily around the startled calf's neck. She stops suddenly and comes to a quick halt. She jerks her head. There is a little snort.

"Got her!" Brad pulls the rope snug. The guys wrestle her down and tie her feet. "Now you try."

Matt looks at Brad. He doesn't move. He scratches his head. "I've never done anything like this before. Don't laugh when I fall flat on my face." He pauses. "Oh, all right. Hand me the rope."

Brad steps over and twirls the lasso around. He pats Matt on the shoulder and hands him the stiff rope. Matt picks it up and fingers it gingerly. The lasso is full of stiff calf hair. He looks around the corral. All eyes are on him.

The calves are huddled in the corner. The dust has settled. Matt begins to twirl the rope around his feet. The calves burst out of the corner and head for the water trough. Matt quickly follows them, twirling the rope over his head.

A small Black Angus calf darts out from the others. Matt shifts his weight around and lets the rope fly. The rope lands over the calf's head and quickly flows down around its belly. Matt yanks the rope tight as the calf takes off. The rope burns through his hands.

The Angus heifer kicks up her heels as the rope tightens around her hips and jerks Matt off his feet. He struggles to regain his footing as the heifer pulls him awkwardly around the corral. Dust blinds him. He heads for the trough as the calf nimbly jumps over it. Matt hangs on and struggles to keep his footing. Too late.

He stumbles and falls in the trough, the rope left flying in the air as it slips off the heifer's hips. Brad rushes over to the soaked Matt. The scared heifer breathes hard and runs to the corner. The other calves are scattered throughout the corral. Matt stands, dripping wet and a little bewildered. He looks around and sees the surprised faces of the other cowboys.

"Are you all right, son? That was quite a show." Brad helps Matt out of the trough. Matt moves his arms up and down and pushes the hair from his forehead.

"I guess I'm all in one piece. I didn't see that water trough coming. My side is a little sore. I guess I hit the side of the trough when I fell in. I don't think anything is broken." Water sloshes in his boots, and his Levis stick to his legs. "I think I need another lesson, but for right now, I'm content to just watch." The other guys crowd around him and check him over. Smiles come to their faces once they see Matt is all right.

"Hey. It's okay. We all have been through it," Ben speaks up. "We all have stories to tell. Ain't that right, Pete?"

"Yeah. Don't remind me. I actually got myself tangled up in the rope one day, fell to the ground, and that stupid calf stood over me, straddling my whole body." With that everyone lets out a loud howl, and Matt doubles over, laughing. Matt feels like he is one of them now and right at home. The howls and laughter can be heard throughout the barnyard as Tom comes to the post and rail fence and leans over.

"It sounds like you guys are having too much fun. What happened to you, Matt?"

Matt empties his water-filled boots. All eyes turn to Brad.

"He got a little tripped up and fell in the trough," Brad says. "He actually got cooled off. You know these guys from back east always find a way to go swimming." More laughs and shaking of heads come next as Brad offers an explanation. He gives Tom a little nod. Tom smiles. He knows exactly what really happened.

"I think we should break for some lunch. Matt, you need some dry clothes. We can finish up this business later." The guys dust off their pants as Brad puts the branding fire out. They herd the remaining calves into a side box stall and fasten the gate.

Chapter 19

Days later, all is not well in the Arlington Real Estate office. Charlotte paces around her paper-filled desk, formulating a plan and seeking revenge for "a woman scorned." "I'll not have my plans upset by any little nobody! Just who is this Miss Kate anyway? I'll fix her! Now let me think." She looks up and sees her secretary enter from her side office.

"I thought I heard you talking to someone. Was someone here? You look upset."

"No, Caroline, there is no one here. I guess I was talking out loud to myself. I'm fine!" She drops down in her swivel desk chair. Her hands are clenched as she breaks a pencil in half. There is a look of determination on her face. "Do you know anything about this Kate Remington who is friends with Brad Crawford? She seems to have come from nowhere. He has never mentioned her to me in all the years that I have known him. She seemed quite at home at the ranch when I stopped in with that sales contract. Now Brad says the sale of his ranch is off. I'd like to know what is going on. I thought we were making marriage plans, and from the money of this property, we would be set for life."

"I know one son, Jeff, is studying to be a doctor. He follows Doc Adams around when he comes home from college. He was in my graduating class and is a really nice guy. The other son used to play professional ball and got his pitching arm hurt real bad, so he is working with his dad on the ranch. But, no, I've never met or heard of this Kate that you mentioned. Who is she?"

"Caroline, I'm not sure who she is, but when you want to know some gossip, you go either to the beauty parlor or to those Simpson sisters. I'll see what I can find out. So, my hair needs to be trimmed a little. I'll be back later. Take care of the office for me." Charlotte marches out, slamming the door behind her.

"Wow. Charlotte really seems upset. I wonder what she will do next!"

Charlotte hustles down Main Street, her high heels clicking loudly against the hard, cracked sidewalk. She enters Sue's Hair Salon. The door slams behind her and grabs Sue's attention. Sue's artificial eyebrows arch up, and a low "Oh no" echoes throughout the salon. All the other beauticians stop and stare and then glance over at Sue.

Charlotte marches herself over to where Sue is putting the finishing touches on a little lady's fingernails. Charlotte glances around and senses the sudden quiet. She bends over to Sue and whispers, "I need a quick trim on these loose ends. I don't have much time. Can you fit me in?" Charlotte straightens up and steps back.

"I'm almost finished here. I'll see what I can do. You may have to wait ten minutes. We have really been busy this morning. You should have called earlier for an appointment." Sue sounds frustrated.

"I know, I know, but I have some questions to ask you too. It's about that woman out there visiting Brad Crawford. Do you know anything about her?"

Sue smiles a little grin. "Oh? What woman?"

The salon is very quiet now. The scissors have stopped snipping, and all ears are tuned in. Everyone is aware of the designs Charlotte has on Brad Crawford. She has bragged about their cozy relationship for over a year now. The gossip hounds are constantly up on Charlotte's activity.

"Maybe it's a relative or an old friend. I haven't seen anyone new lately come into my shop. Now, just who could it be?" Sue enjoys this little game and the perplexed look on Charlotte's face. Perhaps for once she knows something that maybe no one else is aware of. Sue is aware of the grapevine in this town because she is friends with Doc Adams's nurse, Annie Murray. Annie is aware of Doc talking on the phone and of making a house visit to the Crawford ranch. Annie told Sue about Kate's return to the ranch but made Sue swear to secrecy. Sue knows the connection between Doc, Kate, and Brad Crawford but loves to see Charlotte squirm. Sue shakes her stiff curls, rolls her eyes, grins, and says nothing.

"I know you must know something about this situation. When are the Simpson sisters due in? They know everything that goes on in this town."

Sue shakes her head and ignores her as she helps the elderly lady out of the chair. A few minutes pass, and Sue returns to her chair. Charlotte has plopped down in it with her purse at her feet. "Can you just snip a few of these loose ends off. I am in a big hurry."

Sue sighs and pulls out her snipping shears. Sue stares at the top of Charlotte's head and pumps the chair up. "Let's see. Turn this way and put your head down." Sue begins to snip around Charlotte's neck and takes a little off around her ears."

Ten minutes pass. "There. That should do it. You won't need another trim for a month." Charlotte rises, checks herself in the mirror, pulls out some cash, then stashes it into Sue's pocket. Her shoes click across the floor as she heads out the door.

Sue takes a deep breath and drops down in her chair. "That woman is going to drive us all crazy. Who does she think she is? I believe Brad Crawford is too good for the likes of her. She can be so controlling. No wonder he has found someone different." The shop becomes quiet once more as patrons begin to file out. It is lunchtime.

Charlotte continues up Main Street and stops at Cramer's Variety Store. She browses the aisles when she hears a familiar cackle. She glances over and sees Harriet and Hannah Simpson poking through the sale racks. She slowly sidesteps over and comes up behind them. "Well, this must be my lucky day. Such a nice surprise! How are you two girls doing this fine day?"

"Oh, we are just fine. Just looking for a few sales. How's the real estate business going, Charlotte?"

"Well now, Hannah, it was going just fine until a few days ago. Say, I was out to the Crawford ranch the other day, and I thought Brad was ready to sell his ranch to this easterner, but I met a lady out there, a Kate Remington. You wouldn't happen to know who she is or where she came from, would you? Mary said she was an old friend."

"Oh, Charlotte, that must be the woman who was in church with Brad on Sunday. I wish I could remember where I have seen her before. There was a young man with Peter too. He said he was from Maryland."

"Hmm, from Maryland. Why did she come all the way out here?"

Harriet speaks up. "You know, I think she was the one that worked out at Dolly's Diner for a while about four years ago. Maybe that is where we have seen her. Nobody knew much about her past. She is really a mystery woman."

Hannah rubs her chin. "I think she must be the same woman that helped Mary Crawford recover from her broken hip too. Then she sort of disappeared."

"Well, something surely went on, because Brad Crawford just gave that woman a hefty diamond ring. I saw it on her finger, right next to a gold wedding band. I don't think she is merely a friend of the family." Charlotte sounds indignant now. "I saw them hugging and in quite a tight embrace when I walked in on them." Her voice rises as her face turns a slight red.

The Simpsons gasp as their hands cover their wide-open mouths. Other customers stop and look over at the trio when they hear her loud, squeaky voice.

"Wow! A diamond ring! This must be serious, and she already had a gold wedding band on? That doesn't make sense. I wonder what is going on." Interest suddenly perks up the minds of the Simpsons. "I'm going out to the diner. Come on, Hannah. Let's go. I bet I can find out some news out there."

The Simpsons turn and hurry out of the store. Charlotte is left standing alone and smiling a contented grin. The bloodhounds are on a hot trail.

Chapter 20

Hannah and Harriet enter Dolly's Diner amid the busy eating crowd of old-timers, ranch hands, and a few truckers. The smell of fresh-baked ham and potatoes fills their noses. There is a constant clicking of silverware hitting the plates along with the sounds of slurps and burps as the cowboys eat and talk over the day's adventures. The women hurry to an empty booth and slide across the red vinyl seats.

Dolly is busy serving up the heaping plates of food, while her dad, Dave, pours second cups of steaming coffee to the truckers. Dave sees the sisters enter and nods as he steps out from the counter duties and approaches their table.

"What can I do for you two ladies today? Soup and a sandwich? You are a little early for bingo."

Hannah looks up and giggles. "I'm on a diet, so I'll have your special apple crisp and a cup of that great-smelling coffee. Oh, yes. Add a scoop of vanilla ice cream to that too."

"How about you, Harriet? Or are you on a diet too?"

"Well, coffee and apple crisp does sound real good. I'll have the same." She winks at Dave. "Thanks, Dave. Oh, by the way, do you ever hear from that lady that helped Dolly out with the cooking here in the diner a few years ago? You know, that nice-looking, slim gal with the pretty auburn hair."

"Oh, you mean Rose?" Dave suspects something and wants to lead them on. These two never stop in here unless they are looking for some news and gossip. He steps back as if he has to think things over. He rubs his chin. "Well, now that you mention it, I heard she was involved in some sort of murder from back east. I think she shot someone."

Hannah's and Harriet's hands fly to their mouths.

"Oh my! Was she really that dangerous? I thought she looked a little sinister. You just never can tell about people. I wonder if the town sheriff can dig up any news about her. I think that guy in church was with them, and he said he was from Maryland. Maybe we could start a search from there."

Their startled looks stare back at Dave. Dave tries to hide his mischievous smile. He loves their looks of surprise. He can hardly hold in his laughter.

"I think we saw that very person in church last Sunday with Brad Crawford. Do you think he knows about her past? They seemed real chummy. I wonder what she is doing back here and who she murdered. I know dear Charlotte is quite upset about the situation. You know they were practically engaged, almost married, and now this murderous woman shows up." Dave looks away and stares innocently up at the ceiling.

Hannah interrupts, "Maybe we should tell Charlotte about this development. I wonder if there is some kind of newspaper report from Maryland we could find and show it to her." She stops and looks over at her sister. "Oh yes! Thanks, Dave. Maybe we could have that coffee and apple crisp another time."

Hannah and Harriet quickly excuse themselves and hurry out the door. Dave gives a little chuckle and shakes his head. The doorbell overhead gives a little *ding ding*, and they are gone.

Dolly comes out from behind the counter and looks at Dave's sheepish grin. "Okay, Dad, what was that all about? I saw you talking to the gossip hounds, and what did you tell them?"

"I think I should give Kate a call and tell her what I did."

"Just what kind of rumor did you start at poor Kate's expense?"

"Now that I think about it, I may have gone a little too far. I told those two gossip hounds that Kate shot someone. Now they are going to look up some news from Maryland and see what they can find out."

"You told those two that? Pop, I'm surprised at you. You get on the phone right now and give Kate a heads-up. Those two can cause nothing but trouble." Dolly is adamant. "I bet they are headed right now to see what old newspapers they can access through the Internet. Charlotte will have a field day with that kind of news."

"I didn't mean anything by it. I just wanted to scare them a little."

"The way they distort things I wouldn't be surprised if they didn't go and try to have Kate arrested. They are always looking for something to dig up on someone."

Dave walks over to the phone and dials the Crawford ranch number. After a few rings, Kate picks up.

"Hi, Kate. This is Dave. I think I may have put my mouth in gear before my brain. I just spoke with the Simpson sisters, and they were asking a lot of questions about you. You know how they are, always trying to spread gossip around. Well, I—"

"What is it, Dave? What did you say?"

"Well, I told them you shot someone, and now they think you are a murderous woman."

"Dave, that story is going to be all over town. Those two will spread that all over the place. I may have to leave town." Kate tries to laugh it off. "I wonder what people will think of Brad, especially taking up with a murderer. Well, thanks a lot, Dave. Now what do I do?" Kate isn't happy.

"I'm sorry, Kate. I just didn't think about the repercussions those two could cause."

Kate hangs up the phone and wonders what she should tell Brad and Mary.

She stands silently in the kitchen and whispers a little prayer. "Okay, Lord, what do I do now?" She wants an answer to fall out of the blue. The phone rings again. She is hesitant to answer it. "Oh, well, here goes. Hello?" She waits. "Hello?" Kate is a little anxious.

I wonder if it is the sheriff's department.

"Hello, Mom. Is that you? I tried calling your cell phone, and it just rang and rang. Are you all right?" It is Angie. She sounds a little upset and seems to be breathing hard.

"Yes, Angie. What is it? Are you all right? You sound a little out of breath."

"I think I am in early labor. The doctor just put me on bed rest this morning and told me to drink lots of water. It is really hot here. When are you coming home?"

"Well, Angie, when I spoke to you the other day, everything was fine. I'll see what I can do. Matt is really enjoying himself this week, and I have some news for you too." Kate stops and hesitates. She looks down at her ring finger.

"Mom, I'm a little worried. I have about three more weeks to go. The ICU has been really busy, and maybe I am a little stressed. There is never enough help. The supervisor has to pull someone from the med-surg. floor to replace me. Dan is working a lot of overtime. He doesn't know about this bed rest yet."

"Calm down and do what the doctor says. Everything will work out. They will need someone in your place when you have the baby, so now is a good time for them to think about that."

"I'll be home as soon as I can get Matt packed up and make sure someone is here to help with the cooking. Mary is not well, and the ranch is really busy too. Your brother is turning into a real rancher." They talk for a few minutes, and Angie sounds more composed and relieved. They say goodbye, and Kate hangs up. She heads out to the barns, trying to think things through.

I guess a week out here is enough, and we really should be traveling home. I need to talk to Brad about our future plans. I hope he is out here with the boys.

Kate enters the long barn with box stalls on both sides. She can hear a lot of chatter and laughter coming from the far corral. Tall tan-and-black Stetsons can be seen over the wooden rails. There Brad, Matt, and Pete are standing around with the rest of the guys, telling tall stories of what they went through as green ranch hands. They all look up as they hear Kate approaching.

Brad gets up and dismisses the group, saying, "Back to work, you guys. Your break is over. Finish up with the rest of the cleaning of those box stalls and then stop in for your pay. You all have had a busy week, and you can leave a little early today."

The guys scatter, leaving only Brad staring at Kate. He walks toward her, planting a kiss on her lips. "You look a little worried. Is Mom all right?"

"Your mother is fine. She is taking a nap in her favorite chair. I just got a call from Angie, and she thinks she might be in early labor. She sounds a little stressed. I think Matt and I need to pack up and head for home." She takes a deep breath and settles down on a bale of hay. "I didn't tell her about us. We need to talk."

"I see." Brad slides over next to Kate. "I knew you would have to be leaving soon but not this soon. Is there something else?" Kate nervously slides her feet back and forth against the dry straw.

"Dolly's dad called me. The Simpson sisters are at it again. He jokingly told them about the shooting. Charlotte already knows part of the story from what Matt bragged about when she stayed for supper last week. They are making me out to be a dangerous murderer. I tried to laugh it off, but I am afraid of what it may do to your reputation too. I'm afraid the truth will be a little exaggerated. You know, the Simpsons and Charlotte are not a good combination. She will try to retaliate because you refused the offer to sell this place. Plus she may feel very hurt because you rejected her. Who knows what they may spread around? A woman scorned can be a very dangerous person."

Brad sits back and takes Kate's hand. "I think I can handle whatever she dishes out. Don't worry about her."

"I have visions of the sheriff coming out to arrest me and believing the stories. It seems wherever I go, I stir up trouble."

"It will give the good town of Arlington something to talk about for a while. Don't worry about it. You just do what you have to do. As for our plans, we need to set a date. What do you think?"

"I guess you are right. I can't even think of a proper time, but someone once said, 'Absence makes the heart grow fonder.'" She smiles and looks up at him. "I have some things that need to be settled back home, so I'll just have to let you know. What should I do about the house? Matt needs a place to stay. He's not ready to get married and move out. As for me, I'll be content on living out here."

He shakes his head. "I've waited for four years. I suppose I can wait a little longer, just not too long." He rubs her back and smiles that old cowboy grin. "It will all work out. I promise you."

"I know after the baby comes, Angie and Dan will be fine. They both have good heads on their shoulders and good jobs, but I will really miss them when I move out here. As for Matt, I am not sure what we can work out. We will have to have a long conversation on the way home. There are a lot of things that I have to consider." Kate pauses and looks up at Brad. "Now, for a wedding date."

"Oh yes, a wedding date. How about tomorrow?" He smiles. "I can't wait to get you out here for good. Matt can come too." He laughs. "I can always use a good cowboy."

"Try to be serious. I'm thinking about January. Things are a little less busy then, and I should have something settled with the house. What do you think?"

"January? Are you kidding?"

"That's only about six months. I just can't up and leave everything without tying up loose ends. Can you, Jeff, and Peter make a trip to Maryland in January for a wedding? I'm not sure Mary will be up for a long trip." Brad scratches his head.

"Well, that is the slower season. I suppose Tom can watch over things until we get back. Jeff might be on some sort of break by then. I just figured we would get married in town by the justice of the peace. I don't want anything fancy or drawn out. You know, I am just a plain sort of guy." He reaches over, gives her a strong hug, and smiles. "I guess when we all get back home here, we can celebrate with some of our ranch friends and Doc, of course."

"I'll look up a good January date for after the holidays. Things settle down after that, and I can email you the date. How's that? Unless you want to make it an after-Christmas wedding, and you can still come in and celebrate the holidays with everybody. That might be fun too."

"Whatever you want and can arrange. I know I can't leave right now and drive back east. There is too much going on with this ranch business. I have to get some of the livestock ready for the fall sales. I need the money for Jeff's tuition and to keep this ranch in the black. So far everything looks good, and I have my usual buyers calling me for a sale date. The corn and soy beans look good too. I guess Christmas or January is fine."

Kate gives a definite nod and stands up. "I guess I'd better tell Matt that we will be leaving in the morning. I hope Emma is free to help out in the kitchen. Your mother doesn't look good at times. She really gets short of breath while just walking to the breakfast table. Doc wants to put her in the hospital for some tests, but you know her. She will go when she is ready."

"Yeah. She worries me at times too. I'll give Emma a call and see if she can come out, starting Monday morning." Brad stands now and looks down at Kate. He plants a soft kiss on her lips and puts his strong arms around her. They walk back to the house.

Chapter 21

It is early Saturday morning. The sun is rising, the birds are just beginning to chirp, and there is a heavy feeling in Kate's stomach. Matt's bags are packed and waiting on the side porch. Kate's things are already packed and are in the trunk of the car.

Brad stands alone on the porch, leaning over the railing, waiting for Kate to make her last-minute cleanups in the kitchen.

Breakfast was hurried and quiet. Pete and Matt ate only bagels and juice. They look at each other and smile. Mary sits quietly at the table, yawning and finishing off her last cup of coffee. There is a lone tear in her eye as she clears her throat. The time has come to say goodbye.

Kate glances down at her hands. She eyes the shiny diamond and slowly makes her way to Mary. She wipes her sticky hands on the moist hand towel and takes a deep breath. "I guess this is it."

Mary slowly rises as the two embrace for a lingering hug. Kate rubs her back and smiles. "Please keep those emails coming. I want to know everything that is going on out here. I'll be back, I promise you. Please take care of yourself." She turns and heads for the door as the humid air hits her face.

Brad turns and reaches out for her. His strong, tan arms embrace her tightly as he leans his head down for a slow, lingering kiss.

"I guess this is it, Kate." He stares into her eyes and pushes hair from her eyes as she smiles up at him. "I'll be waiting to hear all about your trip home and that new baby."

Matt and Pete see the lingering embrace and step outside. Kate turns and gives a motherly hug to Pete.

"Take care of your father for me, Pete. Don't let him get tangled up with Charlotte again." Kate laughs. "You all plan to come east for the holidays and a wedding."

Pete and Matt smile and give each other a tight cowboy hug.

"I'll see what I can do," Pete says. "Take care of yourself too. I'll see you, Matt, in December sometime."

Tears slowly drift down Kate's cheek as Matt picks up his bags and heads to the car. Kate waves a final goodbye to Mary through the screen door as she steps down the porch steps. Brad is right beside her, his arm around her waist.

Matt throws some things in the trunk and jumps in behind the wheel as Kate hurries to the passenger side. Brad turns her slowly around and looks down at her.

"I'll see you soon." The embrace is strong, and the kiss is smooth and lingering. She pulls apart and slides into the car. Matt starts the car as the door clicks shut.

Matt looks over at his mom as tears roll down his cheeks too. He clears his throat, turns the car around, and heads out the stone pebbly lane. They can see Pete and Brad wave their final goodbye.

The sky is clearing, and the humidity is rising. Matt turns up the air-conditioning and speeds out onto the blacktop road.

They are on their way home.

Chapter 22

Brad and Pete are busy with the early-morning chores, and Tom whistles in the distance. The morning is peaceful as each goes about his work quietly and contently. The young cowhands, now on horseback, have been instructed about which of the beef herd to separate for the later sales. The buyers should be coming soon to look over the stock. Some of the frisky colts will be loaded up too to be sold at the local sale barns.

Things haven't been the same since Kate and Matt left. Phone calls have been daily as Pete and Matt have been keeping in touch through cell phones. Kate and Brad tie up the lines in the evening.

Kate and Matt's trip home is long and weary. The weather has been rainy and windy. Each is engrossed in his or her thoughts. Angie calls her mother many times and remains on bed rest, but otherwise is doing okay. Matt and Kate have many serious conversations about their future. Matt feels a heavy burden of responsibility. He knows his mother will be moving out west. He is back behind the wheel again after a good night's rest and a hearty breakfast.

"So, Matthew, my next question is, do you want to stay in the house? I can turn it over to you, kind of sell to you. Angie and Dan are pretty much fixed up in their own home. Then when Brad and I come to visit, we will have a place to stay too. What do you think?"

"You know, Mom, I just never thought I would have to think about these things before. I feel like you and Brad are right for each other. I like him a lot, and I love that ranch too. It is going to feel funny not having Peter to joke around with."

"I knew you would fit right in. Now I have to fill Angie in on our plans." Matt looks over at his mother. She looks a little worried. She looks down at her new ring.

"I think she will be all right with it, once she understands the circumstances. She can meet Brad, Jeff, and Pete in December. She has Dan to lean on." Matt smiles. He changes the subject. "I wonder what good old Charlotte is cooking up."

Kate laughs too. "Don't be surprised if she sends the police after us."

Matt and Kate continue to motor on down the road.

Little do they know about the dusty sheriff's car approaching the Crawford ranch. It comes to a halt as Brad comes out of the barn and waves to Sheriff Paul Michaels. "Howdy, Sheriff. What can I do for you this fine day?"

"Brad, I need to talk to you. Charlotte, the real estate lady, and those pesky Simpson women stopped in my office the other day. They tell me you are harboring a murderer out here. They said she murdered someone back east and was hiding out here with you and Mary. They say she even changed her name. I've come to get your side of the story. They showed me a clipping from a Baltimore paper, but I don't think it had all the details."

Brad laughs aloud and scratches his head. "I knew dear Charlotte was up to something. Let me fill you in with the real facts." He takes a deep breath. "For one thing, Kate is no longer here. She left early Saturday morning for the baby."

"For the baby? Whose baby? Is it *your* baby? Brad Crawford, I have always respected you. Now I don't know what to think! What is going on out here?"

"No, it's not *my* baby. It is her baby. I mean it's her daughter's baby. Good grief, Paul, what do you think I have been doing? Her name is Rose—I mean Kate Remington. Let me get this straight." He pauses and takes a deep breath. The sheriff is hanging on his every word. "She really didn't know who she was for a while. That's why the name change. As for the murder, yes, she did shoot some guy. He ran down her husband and killed him. Everything was purely self-defense."

"How do you know it was purely self-defense? From the story I got from those women, she is a dangerous character."

"Paul, I wouldn't be marrying her if she was dangerous."

"You're serious about marrying this gal? She's not after your money, is she?"

"No. She has money of her own. Just what all did those females tell you?"

"Well, Charlotte said I should hurry out here and lock her up as a fugitive from justice. Why has this woman, Kate, suddenly left here?"

"Her married daughter is having a baby, and she felt she should go home to be with her. Plus she wants to make some arrangements about her house. We're not getting married until around Christmas or January."

"I want to believe you, Brad, because I know the reputations of the Simpsons, but I thought you and Charlotte were getting married. At least that is what she said."

"Yeah. I know what she has been saying, and she also wants me to sell this place, had a buyer and everything. I guess I deflated her balloon."

"I think you did more than that. She wants to round up a posse and put this woman behind bars. She has the whole town stirred up. Charlotte is even thinking about toting a gun. She even told my deputy that the Maryland paper didn't get it right and that it sounded like some sort of conspiracy cover-up."

Brad grins and shakes his head. "Kate is the most harmless creature I have ever met. She suffers from amnesia from a bad assault to her head. I met her when she came to take care of Mom when she broke her hip. She didn't know who she was or where she came from. Her husband, Jake—with the help of Doc Adam—traced her here and took her home to Maryland to their two kids. This guy that she shot is the one that ran down her husband and killed him. Then he came looking to shoot her. She really is quite a remarkable woman."

"Well, I'm glad I came out here and got more of the story. Now, what am I going to do with Charlotte and those two sisters?"

"What can you ever do with that bunch? Just don't turn your back on them." Brad laughs. "Come on in to the house for a cup of coffee or a soda and rest your weary bones. It's much cooler in there. Mom is probably taking a nap."

The pair head for the house and enter the kitchen. The screen door slams shut. Brad and the sheriff stop in their tracks. "Oh no, Mom!"

Mary lies on the floor near her chair. A cup of coffee has been upset and is on the floor. The wooden stool beside her is on its side. "Mom! Mom!

Call nine one one and Doc Adams quick." The sheriff runs to the kitchen phone and dials.

She is hardly breathing. Brad is by her side. Her lips are turning blue, and her face is pale. Brad raises her head up as Mary pats her chest over her heart.

"Come on, Mom. Take a deep breath. Hold on until the ambulance gets here. You are going to be all right. I wish Kate was still here. She would know what to do." He cradles Mary in his arms, a million thoughts racing through his mind.

It seems like an eternity, but the EMTs finally arrive with the ambulance. They access Mary's condition, start some nasal oxygen, and take her vital signs. They then lift her onto the stretcher and hurriedly carry her outside. The phone is ringing, and the sheriff answers it.

"Hey, Brad. It's Doc Adams."

"Tell him to meet us in the emergency room." The ambulance speeds down the lane. A cloud of dust follows them. Pete and Tom come out of the barn when they see the ambulance speed out the lane.

"Hey, Dad. What is going on? Is Grandmom okay?"

"I don't think so, son. It looks like she fell, and she was hardly breathing. I'm going to follow them into town. She doesn't look good. Take care of things while I am gone."

"Sure, Dad." He and Tom stand quietly and begin to mull things over. "I hope she is going to be all right."

"Yeah. I hope so," chimes in Tom.

The ambulance arrives at the emergency room; lights are flashing, and sirens are wailing. The EMTs hurriedly push the stretcher into the exam room. Mary is quiet, breathing very shallowly. Doc Adams comes around the corner, stethoscope in his hand, steps close to the stretcher, and begins to examine his patient.

"Mary, talk to me. Are you having any pain?"

Mary lightly taps her chest and looks away.

He turns to see Brad at his elbow. "I'm going to order some blood work, an EKG, and some other tests. I want the hospital's new cardiologist to come in on a consultation. I saw him making rounds this morning. I'll have him paged."

A nurse steps up and takes Mary's vital signs and readjusts a nasal cannula with oxygen to her nose. Her color is still a dusky gray. Doc looks back at Brad and ushers him into the hall, pointing him to the private waiting room.

"This is real serious, Brad. I'm going to admit her to the ICU. Her heart is failing, and things do not look good."

Brad glances back toward his mom. She seems to be breathing easier now, and her color has slightly improved. He walks wearily with Doc to the waiting room as nurses and technicians work busily to carry out all the doctor's orders.

"Brad, I'm sure the tests will confirm my diagnosis of a major heart attack. I could see this coming, but she was adamant about waiting until Kate got here. I wanted her in the hospital for an evaluation by our new cardiologist." He shakes his head. "I guess we all get stuck in our ways at our age. I may not be any different."

He pauses and looks at Brad. "Be prepared for the worse. This is as hard on me as it is for you. You all are my family too." Doc looks away and pats Brad on the shoulder, then quietly leaves as he closes the door.

Brad drops his tired body down on a spongy leather couch and pushes the hair from his eyes. "Now what?"

He has never thought about the immediate need of prayer before. He has always let Mom do all the praying for the whole household. There is a real heaviness in his heart. He feels a real need to do something. His needs are desperate, his thoughts jumbled. His hands catch his head as he leans forward while tears trickle down his cheeks. He offers up a quick prayer.

"Lord, I don't know where to start. Our lives are in your hands, and you know our future. Be with Mom, heal her, protect her, and guide the doctors in their treatment. She has been such a trooper." He takes a deep breath. "I must call Kate."

Kate and Matt finally reach home and haul their bags into the kitchen. It has been a long and tiresome journey. The storms have been constant, and the roads have been treacherous; they have viewed many accidents along the way. Kate and Matt have reached some very important decisions between all the fast food and rest stops. Matt has agreed to "buy" the house, at least on paper, so he will have to pay some of the lawyer's fee and take on some more responsibility. Kate can determine what she wants to take with her later, when they decide to clear out some of the accumulated odds and ends. The furniture can stay with the house, along with all the other appliances and the computer. It will be a big undertaking to sort things out, and it will be a life-changing beginning for him.

Kate is anxious to see Angie and tell her all the news. She and Matt wearily leave the house and hop back in the car to pay Angie a surprise visit. It is getting dark, and she hopes Angie hasn't settled in bed for the night. Matt is driving, and the car seems to know the way right to her back door. The lights are on, and Kate can see the flicker of the TV through the window. Dan sees the car drive up and is now holding the back door open for the weary duo.

"So, how was the trip to cowboy territory? You two look tired and exhausted. How about some iced tea?"

"Iced tea sounds good," says Matt. "It was quite a trip home. Lots of bad weather and accidents."

Hugs and smiles are shared between the trio. "Angie is in on the sofa. She will be glad to see you."

Kate hurriedly makes her way to her daughter's side. Surprise and relief show on Angie's face. She is propped up with her feet on a pillow and a tall glass of water by her side. Her rotund belly is covered by a long summer robe.

Angie extends her arms as her mom approaches. She blurts out, "Boy am I glad to see you two. What a surprise! How was your trip? Dan, did you know they were coming?"

He shakes his head and mouths a no. Angie tries adjusting her position as she hugs her mother. The two women embrace for a long moment, and Kate slides in alongside her on the couch. Matt stands by quietly and gives a little wave. He and Dan stand off to the side with tall iced tea glasses in their hands.

Angie notices the rock on her Mom's ring finger. "Mom! What is this? What have you done?"

Kate looks back at Matt and Dan. Matt speaks up.

"Angie, Mom and I have a surprise for you." Angie is suddenly quiet as she stares at the ring. "Mom is going to get married around Christmastime."

Kate nods, not knowing what to say or do next. She smiles.

"What do you mean, get married? Just what has been going on out there in Wyoming? What would Dad think?"

"Angie, calm down." Kate can see the surprise and sudden questions on Angie's face. "I need to talk to you. I was going to wait until tomorrow to fill you in, but now is as good a time as ever."

"It's okay, Angie. Honest, it is," Matt says in a reassuring tone. "You will like Brad. I know you will. He is so much like Dad."

"Just who is this Brad anyway?" Angie looks at her mother.

Kate settles in, closer to her now. "He's a rancher in Wyoming I met when I was out there for the year I went missing. Your dad met him too."

Angie cocks her head. Kate continues, "You see, he only knew me as 'Rose,' and I worked for him and his mother, Mary, a really dear soul. I took care of her when she broke her hip, and then I cooked for all the ranch hands too."

"You should see that place, Angie." Matt sounds excited. "It is a real working ranch with cows and horses and wide-open spaces. He and his sons, Jeff and Peter, are coming here in December for the wedding."

"Is this the surprise you said you had for me when we talked on the phone? Dad will only be dead one year when you marry this guy. Are you sure you know what you are doing?" There is a little catch in her voice.

"Yes, Angie, I am sure." Kate looks back at Matt, hoping for some reassurance, and then turns back to Angie. Matt nods his approval. "Your dad and I never filled you or Matt in on my life out there. I wanted to rebuild my life back here with you, Matt, and your dad, so I tried to put aside my Wyoming experiences. Brad and his mother, Mary, only knew me as Rose, because that's all I knew about myself. I can fill you in later on some of the crazy things that happened out there."

Kate pauses and takes a deep breath. "I know this is quite a surprise, and I was just as surprised as you are, but I feel there is a real bond between Brad and me. Please try to understand." Kate pleadingly looks deeply into Angie's eyes. "So"—Kate hesitates—"with our trip out there, Brad and I rekindled an old friendship and found we want to make a new life together. You need time for all of this to sink in."

Angie is quiet and continues to stare at the ring. "What about us and Matt? What about this new baby?" She looks across at Dan. He is deep in thought too. "You are going to leave us and move where? To Wyoming?"

She wipes a tear from her eye. She flops back against the couch pillows. Her eyes stare at the sparkly ring.

"Look, Angie, it is getting late." Kate sounds weary and begins to stand. "Matt and I are dead tired. We had a long and tiresome trip home. We can talk more tomorrow. You need to get some rest. I'm just glad you and the baby are fine. We just dropped in for a few minutes."

She looks over at Dan and Matt. "We need to be going. Good night, sweetheart." She gives Angie a little kiss and a hug and steps away. "We'll talk some more later." She smiles down at her.

"Really, Mom, this is some news. I never expected this. Yeah, we need to talk some more." She smiles back at her mother. "So yeah, get some rest, Mom. I'll see you tomorrow sometime." She hesitates. "So good night, Mom."

Matt walks over and gives his sister a brotherly hug. "See you later, Matt." Dan walks them to the door.

"It is quite a bombshell, but I'll talk to her. She'll come around. I think I understand. You know these pregnant women. Hormones are out of whack, and nothing makes sense to them." Dan smiles and scratches his head. "You two go home and get some rest. You both have had quite a trip."

Matt and Kate arrive home for the second time, each deep in thought— Matt worried about his new and different responsibilities, Kate concerned about Angie's response to the future wedding. Each quietly goes about his or her usual bedtime routine and then literally fall into bed. Their bags and suitcases remain unpacked on the kitchen floor.

Kate has wearily dropped her purse among the bags and suitcases. There is a muffled cell phone noise coming out of Kate's purse, but neither can hear it. The kitchen phone blinks, waiting for someone to listen to the messages. But the house is now dark and quiet.

Chapter 23

Brad waits impatiently in the ICU waiting room. There is a lot of hurried activity around Mary's bed. She has had a variety of tests done, and blood work is finished. There is a quiet knock on the door, and the charge nurse enters. "Please stay only a few minutes. Your mother is quite ill and very tired, but she seems to be resting comfortably now."

Brad approaches her bedside and sees a little pink in her cheeks. Her eyes are open. The oxygen is hissing in her nose as she raises her hand to grab his. She clears her throat. Tears again cloud his eyes.

"Hi, son." She coughs. "This old body is worn out." She pauses. "Take care of Rose. You need her."

"Mom, you mean Kate, don't you?" Tears trickle down his cheeks.

"She will always be Rose to me. Go home and get some rest." She coughs. "You look terrible." She takes a deep breath. He smiles.

"The Lord is with me," she says.

"I just wanted to check on you. I love you, Mom." Their eyes meet. He takes a deep breath and squeezes her hand. "Okay, I'll see you in the morning."

The charge nurse approaches the bed and nods. He pats Mary's hand, leans down, and kisses her forehead. He turns to leave the unit, his dirty tan Stetson in his hand. He stops and gazes back. Her breathing is not so labored, and her color is much better. The overhead monitor gives off a little *beep beep* as the heart waves flutter up and down. He pulls a dirty, red handkerchief from his back pocket and wipes his face. Slowly he turns and leaves the unit. His chin nearly touches his chest. His cowboy boots click against the floor tiles as he heads down the hall.

It is a long way home, or so it seems. The night is dark as storm clouds cover the moon. Lightning can be seen in the distance. He revs the motor and numbly points the pickup toward the ranch. The gloom hangs over his head as his mind is in a turmoil. His thoughts turn to Kate.

I wonder why she hasn't answered her phone. I hope they got home all right. They are probably in bed by now. I'll call again in the morning. This has been some experience. I hope Mom gets a good night's sleep. I'll see her again in the morning.

Brad is exhausted too. The house is dark and still as he makes his way to his bedroom and drops into bed. He tosses and turns through the early-morning hours. A soft patter of rain hits his window. His dreams turn over and over in his head. He hears a distant ringing. He rolls over and knocks the alarm clock off the nightstand.

Something is still ringing. He manages to open his eyes and glances at the clock on the floor. It's five o'clock in the morning. Everything is pitch black outside. The ringing continues. It is the bedside phone.

Who would be calling me at this hour? I wonder if something happened to Matt and Kate.

He clumsily picks up the phone and answers with a weary "Hello."

"Brad, this is Doc. Are you awake? I've got some bad news for you." Brad sits up suddenly, his pillow dropping to the floor.

"Doc, what is it? How's Mom?" He tightens his grip on the phone. A cold sweat begins to appear on his forehead.

"Brad, your mother passed away this morning. I'm so sorry." He pauses and takes a deep breath. "This hits me very hard too. I'm just so sorry, Brad." Doc sniffles. "If you want to come into the hospital. you can, or you can wait until later." Doc stops and hesitates. "I'm not sure what type of funeral arrangements she wanted."

Brad is quiet.

"Brad are you still there?"

Brad stares at the floor. Tears drip down his cheeks and onto the floor. His voice cracks. "Yeah, Doc, I'm still here." Brad blows his nose. "I wasn't expecting this. Oh, Doc. I guess I didn't want to believe she was that sick and that she would never be coming home."

He wipes his face on his sleeve and takes a deep breath. "She always said she wanted a quiet funeral and to be buried up on the hill with my dad. What do I do now?" He takes a deep breath.

"Brad, I can call the Wilson Funeral Home in town, and they can take it from there. You can make the final arrangements in the morning."

"Thanks, Doc."

"She lived a long and good life. We all need to remember the good times. I am going to miss the times we talked about the old days out there on your porch swing. She was a special lady. She's at rest now. She didn't want any extraordinary efforts done. That request was written and signed by her in her chart. She just kind of faded away. That's the way she wanted it." He pauses. "I share your heartache and grief too."

"Thanks, Doc." Brad sits on the edge of his bed, staring out the window. The sky is clearing. The rain has left only a few drops on the windowpane, and the moon is beginning to peek around the clouds. There is a soft knock on his bedroom door. Peter leans against the doorjamb.

"I heard the phone. What's up, Dad?"

"It was about your grandmother." He takes a breath. "She passed away this morning. That was Doc." Brad can hardly speak.

"Oh no, Dad." Peter looks at his dad. He can see the tired wrinkles around his eyes and the glistening of tears on his cheeks.

Peter walks over and plops down beside his dad on the bed. "I just figured she would get some rest and be home here again in a couple of days. I think she was sicker than what she let on."

He puts his arm around his dad's shoulders. Father and son stare out the window, each lost in his own thoughts. "I'll give Jeff a call later."

Chapter 24

K ate is in the kitchen, drinking a cup of hot tea and munching on an English muffin when Matt shows his face. "What's for breakfast?"

"There's not a whole lot in the refrigerator. I practically emptied it before we left, but I found some frozen muffins in the freezer. Here, have one. Stick it in the toaster. I'll have to make a trip to the store for a few things later. I want to go over and see Angie again. We need to sit and talk and catch up on a few things, if you know what I mean."

"Hey, Mom, the phone is blinking. I bet there are a thousand messages on it." Matt hits the button and listens to the messages. Most are calls from solicitors, and some are reminders of events passed. He hits the erase button. "Here's one from Brad. It says to call him right away. His voice sounds a little shaky. I wonder what's up."

"Give me the phone, and I'll give him a call. I wonder if he tried my cell number too." Kate sits back and dials the Wyoming number. It rings a couple of times, and then Brad picks up. "Hello, Brad. We are home safe and sound. It was quite a weary trip, but Matt was a good driver, and we are relieved to be back."

Brad cuts her off. "Kate, it's Mom."

"What do you mean? Is she all right?"

"Kate, she passed away early this morning. It was her heart."

"Oh no! Anything but that. I knew she was not feeling well but, oh no, not that! Oh Brad. I am so sorry. She was like a mother to me. She was just so special. Oh Brad, I am so sorry."

Kate is crying. She can hear Brad sniffling too. Matt stands off to the side in the kitchen but surmises what has happened. He cocks his head and listens intently. "Brad, what can I do?"

"You can't do a thing. Mom always wanted a very quiet funeral and to be buried up on the hill next to my dad and Rachel. Several of the old-timers are buried up there too." He pauses. "I'm on my way into town to the Wilson Funeral Home to make the final arrangements. I guess I just can't believe this."

"I can fly back out there and be with you if you want."

"No. Your place right now is with your daughter. I hope she is all right. She needs you too."

"Oh Brad." Kate weeps and tries to dry her tears on her housecoat sleeve.

Matt quietly stands by, listening. He whispers, "Mom, if you want to fly back out there, I'll stay here. I'll talk to Angie." She nods.

"Kate, just stay put," Brad says. "I should be going. Stay where you are, and I'll call you again when I get back from the funeral home. The boys will be here with me. Jeff will be coming home too for a few days. I love you." He pauses.

"I love you too." They both hang up.

"I guess I didn't want to believe that Mary could be that ill," she says. "She always had such a brave face and attitude. She had such an understanding way about her. I'm going to miss her terribly." The tears continue to fall. She flops down in her chair and looks over at Matt, puts her head in her hands, and sobs. She can barely speak. "That ranch won't be the same without her."

Matt nods. She wipes her face on a table napkin, straightens up, and takes a deep breath. "This is quite the homecoming news. I am going to miss Mary so much." She wipes her face again and blows her nose. "I know I have to fill Angie in on what has been happening too." She tries to stifle her tears. "You have some things to catch up on too." She sighs. "I guess I'd better get dressed and head over and see Angie. This has been quite a trip and quite a life-changing adventure for me and for you." She glances down at her ring. She wipes her face again.

The phone rings, but Kate is hesitant to pick it up. "Now what?" It's an odd number. She picks up anyhow.

"Mom, this is Dan. Angie is on the way to the hospital by ambulance. I'm at work here in the pharmacy. She thinks she is in full-blown labor with contractions every five minutes. I'll meet you there." Dan is excited and talking a mile a minute. He hangs up.

Kate looks over at Matt. "It's Dan. Angie is in labor and on her way to the hospital. It sounds like the baby is coming a little early." She takes a deep breath and smiles as she dries her tears. "Someone once said, 'When there is a death in the family, there is a birth soon afterwards.' There might be some truth in that. Matt, I'm not sure I can take any more good or bad news. My emotions are worn out."

"You go on to the hospital. I'll stay home and try to catch up on some of my old news. I've got to run out and see how my ball team is doing. Summer ball season is just about over. I may just drop by the hospital later."

Kate dresses and heads out the door. She slides into her dusty car and adjusts her seat. She backs out of the garage and heads down the road. She sends up a little prayer, asking for help for Angie and Brad.

Kate arrives at the county hospital and pulls into the parking garage. She hurries into the lobby and finds the elevator. Riding to the third floor, she whispers. "Oh, Lord. Take care of Angie and that baby."

The maternity floor is bustling with activity. Cries of babies can be heard coming from the nearby nursery.

Dan appears in the hall, all smiles. He's beaming as he shouts to Kate, "Angie and our baby boy are fine. She had a fast delivery. He is small, only a five pounder, but he cries real good."

He puts his arms around Kate's shoulders, looking quite relieved. "The doctor says it was good she got here when she did. Those contractions were hard and fast. She said she was having contractions all night but didn't tell me. She thought it was false labor. You know these nurses. They think they know everything."

Kate laughs. Dan beams. "His name is Jacob Daniel McCallister. How's that for a namesake? He might get little Jake for a while."

They walk into the waiting room, grab a chair, and impatiently wait for Angie to be wheeled into her permanent room. Other fathers anxiously pace the floor. Soft music is heard in the background. Soon a nurse in a scrub gown appears at the door. She smiles.

"The McCallister family can see Mrs. McCallister now. She is in her room, 306, down the hall."

Kate and Dan hurry down the long hall. Entering the room, they see Angie holding the little one, all wrapped up in a striped nursery blanket, complete with a little knit cap.

"He's little, but he is loud and wriggly," Angie says. The cry becomes softer and more contented as she pats his little bottom. "Take a look, Grandmom."

Angie's face is shiny and red. She has pushed her sweat-drenched hair behind her ears, but she smiles from ear to ear.

She hands the infant over to Dan. Kate leans over Dan's shoulder and eyes the dark hair and ruddy complexion; the baby is already trying to suck his thumb.

"Isn't he beautiful?" Kate says.

"Yes, he is! Just beautiful! So, this is Jacob Daniel. I know his Grandfather Jake would love that too." Dan's arms gently rock back and forth as he stares down at the little bundle.

"Angie, you have had quite a day," Kate says. "Now get some rest. You are going to need it. I'll leave you two alone."

Kate hugs Dan and leans over and kisses Angie on the forehead. "I'll see you both when you get home." Kate breathes a big sigh and smiles. "He looks like he is in good hands."

She turns and heads back down the hall. She passes by the infant nursery and looks in. Six tiny babies are wrapped up tightly in their bassinets. She waves to the nurses.

This seems like such a happy place. I know Dan and Angie will make great parents. Jake would be so proud of them. They have their whole lives ahead of them.

Kate leaves the hospital, stops at the grocery store, then slowly drives wearily home. Her emotions are giving her a headache, and she longs for a quiet cup of tea.

This is turning out to be quite a memorable day!

Chapter 25

T he kitchen is quiet, and Kate sips her warm cup of tea. Her legs are propped up on the other kitchen chair.

Matt has gone to connect with his ball buddies. His knee bandage is off, and he is ready to resume his place on his ball team.

Kate tries to gather her thoughts as to what to do next. *Angie seems to be doing fine. Matt is back with his ball team. Brad is back there, planning a funeral. Poor Brad! I miss that boyish grin and that hearty laugh already. I feel like I really should fly out there. Mary was such a dear. I guess I have to begin to sort some things out so Matt can take possession of this house. Christmas will be here before I know it.*

She sips her tea. She looks around the kitchen and tries to remember all the things that have transpired since Jake brought her home from Wyoming after having been gone for that whole year. She rubs the ugly scar down the back of her head and neck.

I remember especially all the ups and downs of getting reacquainted with these two kids and being a wife to almost a complete stranger. We felt like newlyweds. It was such a transition. We talked and talked until midnight as Jake tried to bring me up to date on all that I had missed. He was so patient with me. So much has happened. My life has been such a journey. Oh, such a journey! Surprises and adventures at every turn. How did I even survive such a beating and recovery? Now I have a grandchild and a great guy to marry, who takes me as I am with all my imperfections. The Lord surely has walked beside me and given me the strength to take just one step at a time.

She feels the new ring on her finger. Kate turns and gazes out the window. She puts her cup down. It is a warm summer day. The trees branches sway in the gentle breeze in the cloudless blue sky. Her mind drifts back to Mary, then Brad. She glances down at the engagement ring again. *So much has happened in such a short time.*

She hears the crunch of car tires hitting some loose gravel in the driveway. *I wonder who that is.* Kate gets up and looks out the side window. It's her brother's pickup truck, but Joyce is driving it. The truck door slams, and soon there is a gentle knock on the door.

"Well, welcome home, Kate." There is a short girlish hug. "I hear you are a new grandmother."

"Yes, I am," Kate says proudly. "How did you know so soon?"

"News travels fast around this county. One of Angie's nurse friends brought her puppy by this morning for Richard to check over, and she told me Angie had a baby boy. I hope she and the baby are doing okay." Kate smiles, then nods. "I'm riding around in Richard's vet truck, doing errands because my car is in the garage for a tune-up. I was hoping I could catch you at home."

"Come in and have a cup of tea. Yes, Mom and baby seem to be doing fine. He's only a five pounder, and they named him Jacob Daniel. I saw them all early this morning, and now I'm sitting here, thinking about my next big undertaking."

"Your next undertaking? Kate, now what is happening?"

Kate shows Joyce the new diamond ring. Joyce's eyes widen with surprise. She steps closer. "What does this mean?"

Kate moves over to the counter and begins to prepare two cups of tea. She puts them in the microwave oven and waits. "How would you like to help me plan a little wedding and reception around Christmastime?"

Joyce pulls up a chair and slowly sits down. Kate brings over two steaming cups of hot tea. She opens a package of chocolate chip cookies and places them on the table. "How about a late morning snack?" They each reach for a cookie. Kate smiles.

"A wedding? What kind of wedding? I thought Matt would be next to get married. Just what happened out there in Wyoming? You have got to fill me in." Joyce's voice rises as she stirs sugar into her tea. "All this is a little sudden, isn't it?"

"I guess I do need to fill you and Richard in on what transpired while Matt and I were out there visiting. I never told you what I really went through that year I was gone, when I didn't know who I was or where I came from."

Joyce settles back in her chair, arms now folded across her chest. She sips her tea and crunches on her cookie.

"Well, I worked in a diner and slept in its back room for a while. The owner, Dolly, and I became good friends, and we put some mighty tasty meals together for all the ranchers and local folk. Later I was hired to take care of Mary, Brad Crawford's mother, who fell and broke her hip. I slept in a tiny room under the stairs at his ranch and then cooked for all his ranch hands while tending to her. His mother and I became great friends."

Joyce's eyebrows rise.

"It is a beautiful place, near Arlington, Wyoming. They only knew me as Rose from the diner. I still had no idea of who I was or where I came from. It was quite an experience." Kate pauses. "As time went by, I grew to love it there, and Brad and I became quite good friends. We had a lot of good times together."

Joyce leans closer, not wanting to miss anything. Her eyebrows rise.

Kate hesitates and sips her tea. She takes a deep breath. "Later, I moved into a little apartment over Doc Adams's office and went out every day to work at the ranch house. I even got a driver's license. You know the rest of the story of how Jake was contacted by Doc Adams and how he came to cart me back home with this terrible case of amnesia."

"Then what happened? How did you get this beautiful ring? There must be more to this story, Kate."

Kate takes a deep breath and pauses. "Brad wanted me to stay out there. We found we had a lot in common. He wanted to marry me, amnesia and all." She hesitates.

Joyce's mouth pops open.

Kate continues, "He has two sons, Jeff and Peter. Jeff is in medical school, and the other son suffered a bad elbow injury while he was playing pro ball. So Peter is now full-time at the ranch. They are really a nice couple of boys. Brad's wife, Rachel, died ten years ago of cancer, and his life has been tied up since then with the ranch and his two boys." She pauses.

Joyce's blinks as she glances down at Kate's sparkly ring. "So, this guy just happened to have a diamond ring stashed away for somebody?"

Kate smiled. "Well, I had a feeling he had a ring for me back then, but Doc contacted Jake, and that's when Jake came to Wyoming and brought me home. It was around Thanksgiving time. All of Brad's plans were shattered, and I never heard from him again. My feelings were in turmoil too. I had to make a big decision, and I decided I had certain responsibilities here, so I came home. I had to rebuild a marriage and try to get to know two forgotten teenagers all over again. It was really a trying time. I even got lost coming home from the grocery store one day.

"Jake was so patient and loving to me, and I found I really loved these two kids and learned to love him all over again. Angie and I really bonded, and with this latest trip out there, Matt and I really grew close. He is so much like his father. Actually, Brad's mother, Mary, and I continued to keep in touch by email, mostly about ranch news. She just passed away yesterday."

Kate stops and wipes a tear away. "She had heart trouble and never let on about how she really felt. Brad called me this morning about her passing." Her eyes water. "I'm debating flying out there for the funeral. Brad says I should stay here with Angie and the new baby and all."

"So, you really fell for this guy?"

"I guess you could say that." Kate finishes her tea. "It's a whole different way of life out there. I feel like a whole different person when I am out there. He still wants to call me Rose. I guess I'll always be Rose to his mom. Now his mother is gone." Tears begin to glisten on Kate's cheeks.

Joyce nods. "So I guess this Brad guy and you got real friendly out there." She shakes her head. "Your story and life are one for the books. Wait until your brother Richard hears this story! Now you are going to marry this guy and move out there?"

"It's not like I just met him. I was there for a year, and we shared a lot of adventures together. I guess with this last visit, we sort of picked up where we left off five years ago. He plans on coming here around Christmastime, and that's when we want to be married. Everyone can meet him then. I'm sure you all will like him. He is such a character."

She pauses. "Matt likes him, and thinks it is the right thing to do. Matt had taken on a lot of responsibility since Jake was killed. He wants to continue to live here, in this house, so I am going to see a lawyer about letting him buy it. Angie and Dan are fixed up real nice in his grandmother's farmhouse, and they seem to be doing fine. They love it there. They have done a lot of remodeling over there."

"You seem to have everything worked out in your mind. I really can't wait to meet this Brad. I am still a little shocked about your news, and I hope you know what you are doing." Joyce sounds skeptical but accepting.

"Will you help me make the wedding plans? Nothing big or elaborate, just a simple ceremony. Brad is a plain kind of guy, tall and good looking, with a little gray on top." Kate smiles. "I know you and Richard will love him too. I still have to fill Angie in on some of the details after she gets home."

"Sure. I guess so, Kate. I never expected this kind of news. I can help wherever you need me. This is a big step for you."

"Yes, I know, and I am surprised about how things turned out too. I wouldn't be doing this except my heart is really in this. I found a note that Jake wrote to me last year in my closet, and it sounds like he has actually given me permission to love again." Joyce nods. "I'll let you read it sometime. Matt read it on the way home. He thinks Angie needs to read it too. It is quite a love letter."

"Whew! And to think I just stopped in to say hi, and now I'm a wedding planner." Joyce laughs. "I still can't get over the size of that rock on your finger. He must really be a special guy, and he owns a ranch too?"

"Yes. It is a beautiful place, over a thousand acres. You and Richard will have to come out and visit."

"We would like that. Sure, why not? I guess I'm still a little speechless, but I'll help wherever I can. You know me. I love a party."

The two sit and reminisce awhile. Joyce still nods while Kate wipes tears from her cheeks. Slowly Joyce gets up; her tea and cookies are finished. "I really must be going. Richard will need this truck soon to make his house calls."

Joyce leaves, and the house is quiet again. Kate grabs a pen and pencil, and she begins to make a list of things to do for the wedding. Her thoughts are with Brad. She sniffles and stares mindlessly at her notes. Tears roll down her cheeks again.

I miss Mary so much already. I'll have to give Brad a call later and tell him the news about the new baby.

The morning passes quietly.

Chapter 26

Activities at the ranch are quite subdued as Brad and Pete go about their daily chores. Even Tom isn't whistling his merry tunes.

The funeral is planned for Friday morning at eleven o'clock at the Bible church. Word of Mary's passing has spread throughout the town and the ranches. The condolences are flooding in. Jeffery has managed to take some time off from his internship and is now home from medical school; he is seen trying to figure out how the washing machine works.

A pile of dirty clothes is heaped on the kitchen floor. Emma, the new young cook, was sent off to the grocery store to stock up on some food supplies. The house is quiet, and only an occasional bawling of some of the young calves can be heard in the distance. Jeff looks around and sees all the familiar things he remembers while growing up in this house. The large, rustic kitchen table even has a few crumbs left on it, with clumps of straw and manure left under the chairs. The tinny sound of the clock still ticks off the minutes over the kitchen cabinet. The recliner where Mary sat and snoozed still has a rumpled cushion. The missing piece is now his grandmother.

He takes a deep breath and swallows hard. A tear forms in the corner of his eye. He brushes it off and stares out the window. Jeff is now aware of the winter wedding being planned, and a little smile creeps across his lips. He shakes his head and blinks.

Some big changes are coming to the household. Maybe in a year's time, I'll be out there working with Doc, setting up my own practice. I think Kate and Dad will make a good pair. I can't wait to see her again.

He adds detergent and the clothes to the washing machine, then presses the button. *Now to see what Dad and Pete are up to.* Jeff saunters out the door and into the bright sunshine, taking in all the familiar sounds. He can hear a little commotion at the end of the box stalls.

Brad, Pete, and Tom are busy trying to separate some of the livestock into different pens. The young cowboys have herded a lot of unbranded strays and heifers in from the outlying pastures. Buyers of the beef cattle will be coming soon, and the animals need to be sorted according to weight. Jeff climbs up on the fence railing and surveys the situation.

Pete calls, "Come on over and get those lily-white hands dirty."

Jeff smiles and jumps down. "It's been a while since I wrestled with those critters." He laughs. "I guess all the rope burn and callouses have worn off. This place does keep you humble though."

Brad looks over and smiles. "Don't worry about it, son. It took a while before those baseball hands knew what to do too."

Tom looks up, nods, and shakes his head. He enjoys the gentle kidding between the boys. He wipes his forehead with his sleeve. "It seems like old times having both of you home again and under the same roof. I just wish it was under different circumstances." They all pause and look at each other.

Tom continues, "Mary is surely gonna be missed. She kept everyone in line." The guys nod in agreement. "Will Kate be coming in for the funeral?" He turns toward Brad.

"No. I told her to stay put. Her daughter is due to have a baby real soon. I'll talk with her tonight sometime. She has her hands full too. She has some official business to take care of."

The boys glance at their father and see a real faraway look. Tom steps over, pats Brad's shoulder, and nods at Jeff and Pete. An unspoken show of understanding passes between them.

Evening comes, and Emma, the young blonde and blue-eyed cook, has tidied up the kitchen and left for home. She'll return in the morning for breakfast and do the usual chores of preparing meals and running errands. Emma has been taking classes in the afternoon for a business degree at the local community college, so afternoons are quiet and less busy. She graduated with Jeff, so she is very familiar with the family. She and Jeff seem to get along really well, since she is the daughter of one of the local ranchers too. Tom teases Jeff about spending extra time helping in the kitchen when Emma is there. Jeff's face always turns crimson.

Brad is settling down in his easy chair when his cell phone rings. Looking at the phone, he can tell it is Kate. "Hello, love." He swallows. "How's it going? I really miss you." He pauses. "How's your daughter?"

"Oh Brad, she had a baby boy. They named him Jacob Daniel. He only weighs five pounds, but he's the cutest little thing. Really, a little darling. She delivered a little early, but they are fine." She pauses. "Angie was more than a little surprised about the engagement. Dan says she will come around. She will be coming home the day after tomorrow, so I'll go over and cook some meals for them, and I'm hoping she'll understand."

"Well, I guess our situation came as such a complete surprise to her. She needs some time to think things through. Maybe Matt can talk to her. She has a lot on her mind too."

"I guess you are right. I did get a chance to talk to my sister-in-law, Joyce. She was surprised, too, but I talked her into helping with the wedding plans. She and Richard, my brother, are eager to meet you. So be on your best behavior when you meet them." Kate laughs and pauses. "So, have you gotten rid of some of your herd yet? I know this is a busy time out there for you."

"Some of the buyers are coming in after the funeral. I can't concentrate on too much right now. Emma is helping me go through some of Mom's things. The house really has a different feeling without her. I miss her sitting in that old recliner, half asleep and snoring."

Kate laughs. "I know, Brad. I know what a loss like this has been for you. I feel it too. Mary was such a special lady. I can remember all the sincere talks we had while I was there. I really miss her too." Tears drip down Kate's cheeks, and she hears some sniffling from Brad too. "We'll get through this too. Mary would not want us to be crying all the time."

"Yeah, I know. She never let on just how bad she felt. I know she is in heaven, probably looking down on this poor soul. Doc says she is in a better place."

"I think he's right."

Kate and Brad chatter back and forth over the phone about the day's events and the upcoming funeral. "The ladies at the church are planning a small luncheon after the memorial service and the burial. The service is planned for eleven o'clock, and by the time we get back from the grave site, it will probably be about one o'clock. It's been great having both Jeff and Pete here at the ranch. I didn't realize how much I missed Jeff."

Brad stops. "He has such a dry sense of humor, but he's looking forward to working with Doc. He's gonna make a good doctor. Maybe when you get out here permanently, I won't be so lonely." He takes a deep breath.

"I know, Brad. I feel the same way. Maybe we should have just run off and gotten married somewhere." She can hear Brad chuckle a little. "I guess our honorable responsibilities took over."

"Yeah. I guess that saying that 'Distance makes the heart grow fonder' has some merit after all."

"I hope it's not 'Out of sight, out of mind.' Dear Charlotte would like that, I bet." Now there is laughter on both ends of the phone. "I always feel better after I talk with you. It must be that grinning cowboy smile I can imagine on your face."

"Kate, I can't wait to take you in my arms again and know you are here to stay. This place is really hollow without you. I miss your smile too. The boys miss you too. Even Tom says this place needs a woman's touch. He misses you too." He sighs.

Kate brushes away a little tear and smiles. She looks down at her little list. "Matt seems comfortable with managing the house here. I've showed him what the household bills will be like, and he thinks with his two part-time jobs he can manage things. He thinks he might be asked to fill in at the community college computer lab, help out with their Internet program, and also coach their ball games. He's hoping to continue his education so he can really teach business and computer classes full-time. I can help him out with his tuition. He seems pretty settled on what he wants to do. I've seen a real change in him. He's much more mature and ready to take on responsibilities. I'm real proud of him."

They continue to talk about future plans and all the changes coming in their lives.

Chapter 27

Kate stands in the kitchen, planning what she should cook for her and Matt for supper, when the phone rings. "Hey, Mom." It's Angie. "They are letting me go home early since I told the doctor you would be there with me. Actually, I can't leave until about five today. So Dan can bring me home after he gets done with work. Can you have a little something for us to eat when we get home? I can't stand this hospital food."

"Sure. I guess so. I've got some groceries here that I can bring over and then fix some supper for us. I can't wait to see that baby again."

"Okay, Mom. I'll see you later. Oh, by the way, Matt stopped in this morning, and we had a good conversation. Did he tell you about our little talk? He told me about Dad's love letter to you." Angie stops. Kate doesn't answer. "He can be quite persuasive when he wants to be. I've noticed a big change in him. I'll tell you about it when I get home. Okay, I'll see you later."

"Sure. I'll see you later. Bye." Angie hangs up, and Kate looks at the phone as she too hangs up. *I wonder what she is thinking.* Kate glances around the kitchen and tries to decide what to take over to Angie's house.

The hours pass, and Kate is busy fixing the fried chicken dinner at Angie's house when Dan, Angie, and little Jake arrive. Dan carries the new, little sleeping bundle while Kate is busy holding the door; Angie steps gingerly into the kitchen. She looks tired as she plops down in the nearest kitchen chair. Dan places the baby in Angie's arms and begins to retrieve the rest of the stuff from the car.

The aroma of fried chicken fills the kitchen as Kate reaches down and picks up the baby. "He sure is a cutie. How's the breastfeeding going?"

"Well, that is something I'm working on. I guess that will work out. He had already gained a couple of ounces before we left the hospital. Mom,

I feel real good, just a little tired. I'm so glad you are here. What would I do without you?" She heaves a deep sigh and pushes her hair away from her eyes.

"I'm glad too, Angie. You'll feel better in a couple of days. By the way, Matt called, and he may be stopping over for dinner too. You know he doesn't miss too many meals."

"Dan has some vacation days coming, so he wants to stay home and help out too. The doctor cautioned me about not going up and down too many steps."

"That sounds like good advice, Angie. I'll come over and prepare your meals for you for a few days. That way I can hold little Jake too." Kate and Angie share a laugh.

The fried chicken dinner is thoroughly enjoyed as they sit around the table and chatter about all the changes about to take place. Angie is eager to hear all about life on the ranch. Matt now holds the sleeping little Jake as Kate and Dan clear the table.

"Mom, Matt and I had a good conversation about this wedding of yours."

Matt looks over at Angie and his mom. Dan is quiet.

"He told me a lot of what you went through while you were in Wyoming for that year and a lot about this Brad character," Angie says. "He seems pretty convinced that this is a good thing. I mean, marriage and all."

Kate looks over at Matt and then down at Angie. Dan leans against the counter, wiping a skillet dry.

Angie swallows and looks up at Kate. "He told me about the letter you found. I mean, the one that Dad wrote to you last year. I guess I've been a little selfish, and I guess I just thought this was going to be your complete life—you know, here with us forever and ever."

Dan nods. He knows what is coming.

"I guess it will be all right if you marry this guy," Angie says. "I hope Matt is right. He seems to think that it is fine too, but I will really miss you."

"Angie, I had fully intended to keep you in the loop as to what was going on, but these last couple of days have been so busy, and now I see Matt filled you in. I know you will like Brad. Matt thinks he is a lot like your father. He is a real hard worker and just a real down-to-earth guy, a pure cowboy." Kate smiles. She sees Matt nodding. "He has a thriving thousand acre."

Matt speaks up. "Mom, I still think it would be good for you to make a flying trip out there to be with Brad and the boys during this time. You were so close to Mary."

"Matt, the funeral is Friday. This is Tuesday. I'm not sure I could get there in time for the eleven o'clock service. The ranch isn't near the airport, and it might be hard to make the right airline connections. Brad doesn't expect me to fly out there, and besides, I have never done anything like flying anywhere by myself. I would be a nervous wreck. Suppose I missed a connecting flight?"

Matt looks over at Dan. Kate casts a worried look at Matt.

"Let me see what I can work out," offers Matt. "Dan, set me up on your computer, and I'll see what I can arrange." He hands the baby to his mother as Angie looks on. Kate starts to object and stops. Little Jake begins to squirm.

"Do you really think flying out there is a good idea? It is such short notice. This would really be a spur-of-the-moment decision." Kate looks after Matt as he strides into their living room. Dan looks down at Angie and winks.

He whispers into Angie's ear, "I think I can take care of things here for a few days. What do you think, Angie?"

"I guess we could manage this new little one by ourselves." She looks up at Dan. "Go ahead, Mom, and fly out there. We will be fine."

Kate looks up, surprised. She hands the baby down to Angie and takes a deep breath. "I'm not really sure about this. I'm a little hesitant about flying anywhere. I don't remember ever getting on an airplane. I would be by myself. Do you really think it would be okay to leave you and the baby and fly out there?"

Angie nods. There is a call from Matt to Dan.

"Hey, Dan. Come look at these plane connections. What do you think? These are all minor airports and smaller planes." Dan looks over Matt's shoulder. "She could land there at that small airport and rent a car and be there by Friday morning. That's cutting it kind of close. We can even make a car reservation for her today." Matt hits a few keys. "Hey, Mom. Come look at this. What do you think?"

Kate walks over and peers over Matt's shoulder. "I don't know, son. I've never done anything like this before. That looks like a lot of airline schedules to meet across the country. I hope all of those planes are on time and there are no delays. Are you sure you can manage while I am gone?" Kate straightens and looks at Matt and Dan.

"Don't worry about us back here," Matt says. "Dan and I can handle things while you are gone."

Kate sighs. "I guess I should get used to some spur-of-the-moment actions because Brad is full of those kinds of decisions too." She smiles. "I can call him and tell him the change of plans." She takes a deep breath as Matt is busy punching the computer keys. She goes and gets her credit card. "It looks like I will be leaving late Thursday afternoon. Maybe I can sleep on the plane going out there."

Chapter 28

The next few days pass slowly for Brad and the boys. There is a little crispness in the air. The penning of the livestock is almost finished, and the big job now is the feeding and fattening up of all the animals until the buyers come. The young cowhands are slowly drifting back to their homes and back to school, and they are eager to sign up for the local rodeo.

The phone calls have continued each night between Brad and Kate. She informs him of her pending trip out there for the funeral but that she won't be arriving before Friday. Matt and Dan have arranged for Kate to fly into a small private airport near Laramie. She will be doing some night flying on the red-eye express. The smaller airlines have tricky connecting flights.

Friday morning comes, and the daily chores must be done before ten thirty. Brad looks at his watch, wondering how Kate is navigating the flying experience. He seems worried. He sees storm clouds in the distance.

Kate looks at her watch too through sleepy eyes. It is almost ten o'clock in the morning. She has been flying all night. This is a much smaller jet, a "puddle jumper" as Matt called it. She has not slept much. She is nervous about getting there on time. So far the connections Matt set up have been good, with a two-hour delay at the last airport. It is raining with thunder and lightning, complete with a tornado warning.

She nervously looks around. She counts only twelve passengers, and several have slept the entire time. The snoring of the men and the turbulence of the wind hitting the plane have kept her from sleeping through the dark early-morning hours. There is no smiling stewardess on this plane. Her stomach churns as she grips the armrests with each little dip of the plane. She can barely see the ground below. Her mind sends up little prayers for her safety.

I'll be so glad to put my feet on firm ground. I can't wait to get out of this plane. I am so tired.

She hears a little *ding* as a reminder to fasten seat belts securely. They will be landing soon, but the plane seems to be flying in circles. A voice comes over the intercom. explaining the delay. "A couple of loose cows are running across the open runway, and two cowboys are trying to round them up."

She peers out the small window and sees some dust being kicked up. Kate looks at her watch. *Great! Just what I need. Another delay!*

Finally, she hears the wheels being released, and the ground seems to be rising to meet them. Soon she feels a gentle bump and knows she is on the ground. *Finally! Now to get a car! Matt said this airport was only about two hours away from the ranch. I hope so!*

Kate stretches and yawns, then grabs her carry-on bag and proceeds to step out of the plane and into a cool cloudy day. The airport is small, so finding the rental car area is easy. It's right by the front entrance. She walks up to the counter and waits.

She taps her foot against the tile floor. There is no one behind the desk. *Where is everybody?* She looks around. Slowly a little gray-haired lady returns to the desk. She smiles. "May I help you?" She has a slow western drawl.

"Yes, I believe I have a reservation to rent a car. My name is Kate Remington."

"Let me see. Yes, here it is. You were supposed to arrive two hours ago. Your car has been rented to someone else. That was our last one."

"Really? But I need a car." Kate shows her irritation. She is too tired to argue. "How do I go about getting one?"

"If you can wait about an hour, one of our cars should be returning soon."

Kate sighs and looks at her watch. It is almost ten thirty. She will have to adjust her watch for the time change. There is a two-hour time difference.

"You could have a bite to eat while you wait, miss. The coffee counter is over there." The lady points behind Kate.

Maybe a warm cup of tea and a soft bagel would taste good right now. She takes a deep breath. "Thank you." She turns and heads toward the beverage counter. She checks her watch again. *This is turning out to be quite a trip. Maybe I should have stayed home. Everybody seems to be running in low gear around here.*

Kate orders her tea and cinnamon bun. They are fresh out of bagels. She dials Matt's number and leaves him a quick message. She settles down at one of the small tables with a booth and a soft cushion, and she sips her tea. She holds her weary head in her hands. Her eyes begin to close. *I need a good nap.* She takes a deep breath and begins to doze off.

A half hour passes. Suddenly, there is a light tap on her shoulder. Startled, Kate almost falls from her seat. She sits up straight. Her eyes blink open wide. It is Dolly.

"What are you doing here?" Kate says. "I must have fallen asleep."

"Brad called me. He was a little worried when he heard your plane was delayed because of the storm, and he asked me if I could pick you up. I just got here."

"Oh, Dolly. You are a sight for sore eyes. I am so tired. They rented my car to someone else. I have had quite a trip, and then there was that storm delay."

"Come on. The car is parked out back. We may be a little late for the memorial service, but I'll get you there. Brad is quite worried about you. He has been watching the weather forecasts."

Kate nods as she picks up her carry-on and follows Dolly to her car. "I am so tired. I didn't sleep a wink on that plane. Two men snored loudly the whole time. It was the only plane Matt could find to get me here by Friday. So here I am!"

"Maybe you can catch a little nap while I drive. The sun looks like it is trying to peep through the clouds. It looks like it may be a decent day after all." Dolly starts the car. Kate's bag is in the back seat. "Brad will be glad to see you. I don't think he has been sleeping much either." Dolly pauses. "It's been over a week since you were just here. I hear you have a new grandson. I hope everything is all right back home." Dolly looks over at Kate.

"Yes. He is a real cutie, but he only weighed five pounds. They named him Jacob Daniel. Dan is taking a few days off to help Angie, so I think they can handle things."

"We didn't really expect to see you again this soon, but I'm glad you are here." Dolly smiles. "I know Mary was very special to you."

"I had to explain everything to Angie and Matt, and they are the ones who encouraged me to fly out here. Matt made all the arrangements. He has been taking care of everything." Kate yawns. "He is a very special son. I am so lucky to have those two."

The ride with Dolly is long but uneventful. The storm clouds pass behind the mountains as Kate leans back and closes her eyes. The two hours pass quickly before Dolly turns into the little country church yard. Kate awakens when she hears the crunching of the gravel beneath the car's tires. Pickup trucks are parked haphazardly across the stony driveway.

"It looks like the whole town is here," Dolly says.

The memorial service has started. Organ music can be heard through the open windows. Dolly parks the car. Kate and Dolly hurry up the steps and quietly take a seat on the back row. The church is nearly full. The backs of gray heads can be seen scattered throughout the entire congregation. Kate can see Brad's tall head up front with the boys beside him. She glances over and sees the Simpson sisters sitting off to one side with Charlotte.

Dolly nudges her arm. Kate grins. "Dolly, do you think she is toting a gun? I'm surprised she is even here."

Dolly nods and whispers, "Maybe she is trying to make amends with Brad. Don't turn your back on her." Kate smiles.

They direct their attention to Pastor Taylor, who listens to the lighthearted comments of some of Mary's friends. There are a few chuckles, and heads nod in agreement. Pastor Taylor clears his throat and begins a little sermon on the richness of heaven. His voice is loud and booming. All eyes and ears are on him. The fans whirl overhead. The women sit quietly and listen intently.

"I know our dear sister, Mary, is in heaven. She was a true prayer warrior for Christ and was deeply loved by all those who were close to her. She will be missed. She gave her heart to the Lord when she and her husband first arrived here and helped settle this area. She and her husband helped to build this very church."

Heads nod in agreement throughout the church. Kate can see the back of Brad's head as he too nods in agreement. The pastor continues by reflecting on the importance of living the Christian life. He ends by adding a small prayer for the ones left behind. Tears fill Kate's eyes. Dolly puts her arms around Kate's shoulders The organist takes her cue and begins a soft, moving verse of "Amazing Grace."

Jeff and Peter stand up and help to maneuver the closed casket to the side door. Brad rises and nonchalantly gazes around behind him, unable to find Kate and Dolly. He sees only the very tops of the blue-haired Simpson sisters. He takes his seat again.

The young cowboys from the ranch line up as pallbearers. They carry the casket to the waiting hearse as Kate and Dolly quickly rise and hurry out of the church unnoticed. They head straight to her car and wait. The young cowhands now pile into two of the dusty pickups and line up next behind the hearse. The hearse begins to head out of the churchyard in front of the cars that will follow.

Brad and the two boys follow in Jeff's car. The pastor follows Brad. Only a few more cars file out behind them. Kate can see Doc in his car with Dolly's dad, Dave. Sue, with some friends from the beauty shop, is next in line. Dolly and Kate are next.

The ride is just a few miles around a winding country road and then up to the little mountain ridge speckled with old granite tombstones. The clouds have parted, and the sun begins to shed its rays across the wide Wyoming grasslands. It is a warm, peaceful sight, but Brad is restless, looking at his watch. Jeff and Peter watch their dad's nervousness as they approach the cemetery.

The line of cars stops as the young ranch hands carry the casket to its final resting place. There is a small green canopy tent covering the grave site. Brad looks over the small party and spies Dolly and Kate coming up the hill. He finally relaxes, smiles, and waves. Jeff and Peter see their Dad wave, and both breathe a sigh of relief.

Kate and Dolly step under the tent as Brad closes in on Kate. He puts his arm around her waist and nods to Dolly. Jeff leans over and gives Kate a little hug as Peter stands nearby. There is a quiet rustling of a gentle breeze filling the tent. The air is warm.

The pastor looks about and begins a short closing prayer as the casket is lowered into the ground. Flowers slide from the casket's top and fall into the grave. No one speaks as one by one friends approach Brad and the boys.

Cheeks are shiny with moist tears as hugs are exchanged. Doc reaches out to Kate and welcomes her back. He grabs Jeff and gently pulls him aside.

Sue and Dolly, with Dave, her dad, stand off to the side. Peter watches the small band of close friends as they say goodbye. Slowly the group disperses at the grave site as they head back to the church for some light refreshments.

Brad and Kate remain under the tent with the boys. "I was really worried about you when I got word that there was a tornado watch where you were landing," Brad says. "I'm so relieved Dolly offered to pick you up. I'm glad this day is finally over." His weary eyes look down at her as he pushes a few stray gray hairs from his forehead. "It has been a long week. We are really going to miss Mom." He sighs. "But I am so glad to see you. How was your flight?" He takes a deep breath.

"Don't ask. It was nerve wracking. We had several delays and a stretch of bad weather. I hardly slept a wink. Lots of snorers on board!" She shrugs. "Dolly has offered for me to stay with her for a few days before I fly back. I hope that trip will be a little less exciting. Matt scheduled this whole trip with all the right connections. I don't know how he did it. The kids really encouraged me to fly out here. I was really hesitant about leaving Angie and the new baby. I guess I have never flown before, and I really don't want to fly again like that." She sounds adamant.

Brad gives her a little peck on the cheek and hugs her tightly. Doc and Jeff move closer since their deep conversation is over.

Doc puts his hat back on and turns to Brad. "I can take the boys with me and drop them off at the church if you would like. You two can stay here awhile if you like and get caught up."

"Thanks, Doc. I appreciate that." Brad looks over at his sons. They nod. "Sure. I'll see you all later." He pulls Kate closer. "We need to talk." He pulls Kate over to the vacant folding chairs, and they sit down. The breeze causes the canopy to flutter up and down.

"Why don't you cancel your flight back to Maryland?" he says. "We can just get married here, this week. There is no waiting period in Wyoming."

"But, but Brad. I thought we agreed on a winter wedding. I've got Joyce planning it back home. Do you think now is the time to be thinking about this? We just had Mary's funeral, and our emotions are on edge. What would people think? So soon after all this?" She looks directly into those big blue eyes. "Your spur-of-the-moment decisions really make me nervous." She catches her breath and pauses.

He grins. His arm is around her shoulder.

She smiles, gulps, and blinks. "I don't even have a wedding dress with me!"

"My mother wouldn't care how or when we get married, and besides, who cares about a wedding dress? I'm all for boots and jeans. We can contact the pastor and a few close friends for the ceremony and then drive back to Maryland for our honeymoon and surprise your kids. How about it?"

"I don't know what to say. Well, I am all for avoiding another flight like the last one." Kate smiles and nods. "I never expected this. Brad Crawford, if I didn't love you, I would think you were crazy. I think I am even crazier for listening to you." She laughs aloud." What about all the business dealings of yours with the selling your livestock? Aren't the buyers coming this week to haul them away?"

"Peter and Tom can handle most anything. In fact, most everything should be done by next Wednesday morning. How about an early Wednesday evening wedding? I'll have some of my money from the buyers by then. Afterward, a few of us can go to that new restaurant out of town for a little celebration, and then we can take off after that. I'll talk with Pastor Taylor on Sunday and see if he can perform the ceremony this Wednesday evening. How's that?"

"I don't know." Kate stops. "I'll need to go shopping. Maybe Dolly can go with me and help me pick something out. This is all so sudden. I need to call the kids. What will they think?"

"Let's just surprise them and show up married. Call Joyce about our plans. She can get a little reception ready for us to meet all your friends in about a week." Brad grins his broad smile. "We're not teenagers, and we don't need a big fuss. We can do this. Why wait?"

Kate is speechless and trying to think. Her thoughts are spinning around in her head.

"We can get a marriage license on Monday morning at the courthouse."

"I guess I am just not a spur-of-the-moment type person. I like to plan things out."

"Then it is settled. Let's head back to the church for some light refreshments. I promised the church ladies I would come back for a few minutes. We can tell Jeff and Pete later about our plans." They stand and embrace each other after a long, lingering kiss. He smiles down at her.

"You always knock me off my feet," she says. "I'm still speechless."

"Just say yes, and let's do it."

Chapter 29

It is six o'clock Friday evening, and Jeff is sprawled out on the brown leather couch. Peter is hunkered down in Mary's old recliner, his feet hanging over the footstool. Brad rests comfortably in his worn, dark leather recliner. His arms hang loosely over the chair's arms. A few snores are heard.

The funeral is over, and everyone seems ready for a nap. The tension of the day is relieved, and everyone seems to be more relaxed now. It has turned out to be a perfect cloudless day with a gentle breeze and lots of sunshine. Doc, Dolly, and Kate are at the kitchen table, talking in low whispering tones. Coffee mugs sit between them.

Kate yawns between her sips of tea. It has been a long day. She begins with announcing the wedding plans Brad and she discussed under the canopy. Doc and Dolly nod and smile. "You know, Brad surprised me with this idea of getting married while I am here. He wants to spring it on Matt and Angie when we honeymoon back to Maryland. I told him I didn't even bring a wedding dress. He laughed and said boots and jeans would be fine."

Dolly and Doc laugh. Dolly speaks up. "Kate, stay with me at my house, and in the morning you and I can go shopping. There is a little dress shop at the end of Main Street where we might find something suitable. What do you think?"

Doc nods, smiles, and adds, "I think the plan is coming together. Just do it, Kate. I think your kids will understand."

Kate looks over at Doc and Dolly. "My thoughts are going round and round in my head. I really think I should let the kids know what is going on." She looks at them directly. "You two seem all for this wedding. I feel like there is a conspiracy going on. Did Brad talk to you both about this plan? Is this the way things are done out here? The next thing will be you will have us getting married on horseback!"

Doc and Dolly let out some loud chuckles. "No. Brad has said nothing to us. But I had a feeling something was going on. Brad is like a smitten teenager. When he comes into the diner, the only thing he talks about is you, Kate."

Doc nods in agreement. He glances around and sees Brad getting up and approaching the table. Brad smiles and puts his arms around Kate as he leans over and plants a gentle kiss on her cheek. Kate is surprised but accepts the strong, gentle arms around her and the quick kiss.

She readily smiles up at him. "So, you're done with your quick nap. Have a seat. I see the boys over there are still asleep." Brad pulls out a chair and sits down. "Dolly has offered for me stay with her and to help me go shopping for some things. I'll need to cancel my returning flight back to Maryland. I hope I can get a refund."

"Sounds good to me. I'll speak to the pastor on Sunday and see what he has to say. He may want us to come in and meet with him before the ceremony. What do you think?"

Kate yawns and nods. "Right now, I am so tired I could be talked into anything."

"Let's see, who would we invite?" He stops and looks around the table. "It would be everybody here plus Dave. Also Sue from the beauty shop and Doc's receptionist, Mrs. Murray, and my two boys, Tom and his wife, and the young guys who worked with us all summer. That would be about fifteen, counting us. We could all go out to dinner after the ceremony to that new restaurant out on the highway. What do you think?"

Dolly winks at Brad. "You mean, the Simpson sisters and Charlotte are not invited? Who is going to spread the news around town? She may want to give you all a real shot-gun wedding."

They all laugh heartily as Kate wearily rises from the table. Kate picks up two coffee mugs and places them in the dishwasher. Doc rises and hands his mug to Kate too. He pats Kate on the shoulder and smiles.

He puts his hat under his arm. "I think it is time for me to leave. I need a short nap too. This has been a long day. I've got to see a few patients on my way home. Hopefully, it will just be to renew their prescriptions."

Dolly also nods and stands while picking up her purse and looks over at Brad. "You can bring Kate by the house later if you wish. Dad will be there while Sally and I finish up at the diner. I'll see you later, and then we can go shopping for that special dress in the morning." Kate is still yawning as she nods to Dolly. Dolly hurries out the door and leaves Brad and Kate alone. Pete and Jeff begin to stir out of their naps.

"It looks like we are almost alone again," Brad says. "Let's go out on the porch swing, where we can talk." They quietly open the screen door and settle down on the soft cushion of the porch swing. He pulls her close, and she rests her head on his shoulder. "I have been miserable without you. All my dreams have you in them. I'll be so glad when these cattle buyers are gone and I can concentrate on something else. First it was Mom's passing. Then it was the funeral. Now it is the moving of all this cattle. I guess this wedding should be a piece of cake." He breathes a sigh of relief. "I think I need a vacation."

"Your vacation will be a slow-driving honeymoon trip back east." Kate yawns while resting against Brad's shoulder. "Everything will turn out, but I still need to call the kids and tell them I won't be home next Tuesday. They might think I got lost in some airport. I'll phone them in the morning from Dolly's house."

Brad nods in agreement. He yawns. "They are going to wonder what is going on."

The swing continues to creak with each little push of Brad's foot. The evening clouds begin to roll in, and the cool breeze brings a hint of a possible storm. Kate's eyes close as the swing sways back and forth. The distant howl of a coyote can be heard in the far-off valley. The western sun begins its slow descent, dipping behind the far-off mountains. There is a peaceful quiet around the homestead as Brad's strong, tan arms pull Kate closer.

Chapter 30

It is Saturday morning, and all is quiet in Dolly and Dave's quaint mountain home. Kate rolls over and looks at the clock. It is eight o'clock as she glances out the window. The lawn is glistening from a nighttime rain, but the sun is already high up in the sky. Such a beautiful morning!

Kate dresses and heads to the kitchen. She hears the clicking of a coffee cup. Dave is settled in his favorite chair and reading the morning paper. He looks up. "Good morning, sleepyhead. I hope you slept well. Dolly and Sally are at the diner. I have breakfast fixed here if you want something to eat."

"Maybe just some tea and toast. I'm not really hungry." Kate yawns. "I've got a phone call to make, and then I guess when Dolly gets back, we can go shopping." She flops down in the chair. "My life has really taken some surprising twists and turns. I feel like I am on some kind of adventurous and unreal but loving journey. Maybe it is this crazy amnesia and not remembering just how things used to be." She yawns and sighs. "I feel like with every step I take, I just have to trust the Lord that much more."

Dave looks up and gives an approving nod. He puts the newspaper down.

"I am beginning to realize what Mary told me about my life is true and that my life is in the Lord's hands," she says. "Sometimes I feel like my faith is like an innocent child's." She pauses. "Dave, do you think I am doing the right thing? You know, marrying Brad now and surprising the two kids?"

"I know one thing is for sure. Brad loves you and thinks the world of you. I think this match was made in heaven." He laughs. "You two will have many happy years ahead of you, and you have the blessings of both your families too." Dave fixes Kate a hot cup of tea and pushes a tasty cinnamon bun in front of her. "Here, eat up. I'll go relieve Dolly so you two can spend the day shopping. Sally and I can watch the diner for a while."

Kate begins to munch and sip her tea when she hears her cell phone ring. She quickly leaves the table, finds her purse, and answers the call. "Hello."

It's Matt. "Hey, Mom. I got your message that you arrived okay. I hope everything is all right."

"Matt, I'm glad you called." Kate takes a deep breath.

"Are you sure you are all right? You sound a little tired."

"Well, Matt. It's this way." She takes a deep breath and walks back to the living room with the phone. "Brad wants to surprise you and Angie." She pauses. "He wants us to show up in Maryland next week as newlyweds."

"Really, Mom?" He stops. "Really? That would be quite a surprise all right, a real shocker. But Mom, does Angie and Aunt Joyce know about this?" He sounds flabbergasted and breathless.

"Not yet. Just you so far. Brad wants to have the livestock sold and then get married this next Wednesday at six o'clock by Pastor Taylor. What do you think?"

"Really, Mom?" He hesitates. "I don't know." He takes a deep breath. "Well, I guess so. I guess whatever you and Brad want to do." He pauses. "You two are just full of surprises." He laughs again and pauses.

Kate stares at the ceiling and nervously paces. She can feel his hesitation. "Well, I guess so. Sure, why not? I can fill Angie and Aunt Joyce in. They are going to be really surprised."

He laughs some more.

Kate takes a deep breath and smiles.

"When should Aunt Joyce plan for your little wedding reception?"

Kate relaxes. "How about a week from this Saturday? Knowing your Aunt Joyce, she can put a party together at a minute's notice. I can just hear her now." They both laugh aloud.

"Mom, you are really falling into Brad's spur-of-the-moment lifestyle, but you sound real happy. I think Angie will be okay with it too. I'll talk to her and Dan again."

The two talk on for a few minutes about future plans and then hang up. Kate returns to the kitchen and sees Dave smiling. "I just talked with Matt."

"I heard part of your conversation. Is Matt okay with the new plans?"

"He was really surprised but seems accepting of the idea. He likes Brad, and on our way home, he read that special love note that Jake wrote to me. I think he understands."

"He's a good young man. You can be real proud of him. I like the way he has stepped in and helped you through all of the your ups and downs. You and Brad are going to have quite a blended family." Dave rises and clears the table. "I'm going to go on down to the diner and work with Sally so her mother and you can go shopping. I'll see you later." He grabs his hat and heads out the door to his old pickup truck.

The house is quiet again as Kate washes up the few dishes and gazes out the window over the sink. She sends up a silent prayer. *Oh Lord. I feel very happy and blessed. All through this mysterious amnesic journey of my life, I have felt your presence and your guiding hand. Thank you for your protection and for surrounding me with loving and gracious people. The prayers of your people have carried me through rough waters. You are giving me two very loving families and some very special friends. My cup is running over.*

Tears stream down Kate's cheeks as she sniffles and wipes at her face with a soapy finger. She grabs a towel and wipes off the tears as she hears the back door open. It's Dolly.

"Well, are you ready for our shopping spree? The stores will be opening soon, and Dad and Sally are watching the diner. Kate, I need to change my clothes and take a quick shower, and then I should be ready. I think I have scrambled eggs all over me. Sally dropped a whole plate of bacon and eggs on the floor, and we spent half the morning slipping around on the tile. At least the floor is scrubbed now."

Dolly laughs as she takes off her apron. "It's never a dull moment in that place. Oh, yes, one more thing. Word is spreading about your wedding. Sally let the cat out of the bag this morning when she served coffee to some of the ranchers." She glances over at Kate's surprised look. "You may have the whole town show up at the church on Wednesday. Brad is very well respected around these parts, and these people love weddings and celebrations. They don't need a special invitation."

"Oh no. Do you think Charlotte and the Simpson sisters will show up too? Do you think they will bring the sheriff?"

Kate and Dolly start giggling.

"I have no idea, but let's concentrate on getting you to look like a real bride. This is going to be fun. I know just where I need to take you." Dolly pushes her blonde hair behind her ears. "Kate, I remember the day you stepped into my diner that very first time. You were with that old truck driver, and you looked scared to death. You told me that unbelievable story about what you had been through and that you weren't even sure of who you were. 'Just call me Rose,' you said."

"You're right. I was scared to death, but you gave me a job in the diner and a place to lay my head. Those days I can still remember." Kate shakes her head. "We cooked a lot of meals together and had plenty of laughs too. It was your idea for me to go and care for Brad's mother, Mary, when she broke her hip. I would have never met Brad if it was not for you." Kate steps over and hugs Dolly. "You know, I would like you to stand for me when we get married. Brad may have his sons stand for him. How about it?"

"Why sure. I'd love to. Well, I'd be honored." She steps back, hands on her hips. "Now I guess I need a new dress too." They both laugh as Dolly heads for the shower.

Soon Dolly and Kate are walking down Main Street and looking in all the windows. "Here's the store I told you about. Let's go in."

A plump little lady approaches them with pins still lined up on her sleeve. She has high-arched penciled eyebrows and twinkling blue eyes. Her gray-tinted hair is teased high up on her head. Her stubby little fingers reach out to offer a friendly handshake.

"Good morning, ladies. I'm Annabelle Wayne, but you all can call me Belle. I'm just finishing up some alterations. What can I do for you?"

"We're looking for a wedding dress and a maid of honor dress." Dolly states it so matter-of-factly. She smiles at Kate and winks.

"Who is getting married?" Her arched eyebrows rise again, almost reaching her forehead.

"This is my friend Kate, and she's planning her wedding on Wednesday. We would like to look at some special dresses. I don't think Kate here will be hard to fit."

"Come this way. I think I have just the thing." Kate and Dolly are led over to a special rack with dresses all enclosed in plastic bags. "Here is a darling, creamy light-pink dress with some lace around the neck and bodice. Try this on." She removes the dress and hands it to Kate.

Kate's can't take her eyes off the beautiful, long dress.

Dolly nods. "Look. It's a size eight. Wow, Kate. It looks like it will fit perfectly. Try it on."

Kate looks it over and smiles. She heads into the dressing room. Dolly continues to look over some of the other dresses and tries on several. The morning passes with the two women trying on lots of outfits and finally settling on their first choices. Kate seems happy with her pale-pink dress. It fit perfectly with no alterations needed. Dolly settles for a pale-blue two-piece outfit. Their next stop is the shoe store; then they head to the florist and then finally to lunch.

"You know, Dolly, I feel like I have put in a full day's work. I am tired out."

"Yeah. Me too. Let's drop these packages off in the car and then stop in at the luncheonette for a quick bite. I think that dress looks beautiful on you. Now, we will have to convince Brad to shed his jeans and plaid shirt for the big day. He might even shave." The two laugh and giggle as they head down the street.

Chapter 31

Sunday morning arrives, and Brad, Kate, Jeff, and Peter are found on the very last pew of the Bible church. Off to the right and a few pews ahead are the Simpsons and Charlotte. Brad quietly nudges Kate in the ribs and whispers, "Don't you think we should invite Charlotte and the Simpsons to the wedding?" He grins. "I have a feeling the whole town will show up, so why not three more?"

Kate gives him a surprised look and whispers back, "Are you kidding?" She pokes him in the ribs. "After the gossip they have passed around town about me? Are you crazy?"

The boys look over and wonder about all the whispering. Jeff frowns at his father. Kate catches Jeff's frown and tries not to giggle.

Jeff whispers to Peter. "Those two are acting like smitten teenagers."

Peter just smiles and whispers, "Yeah. I've not seen Dad so happy in a long while."

Before long the last hymn is sung, and the parishioners begin to file out of the church. Pastor Taylor shakes hands at the doorway as the church continues to empty. Kate and Brad hang back and shake a few hands as he introduces Kate to some of his long-time ranch friends. Kate catches a glimpse of Charlotte and the Simpson sisters making their way over in their direction. She gently nudges Brad in the ribs for him to look around.

Charlotte stomps toward them, swinging her purse, while every little bleached-blonde hair on her head never moves out of place. Her eyes are mere slits. Hannah and Harriet suddenly stop. Charlotte sashays over and says quite loudly, "Well, if it isn't Brad Crawford and little Miss Kate." Her shrill voice makes Brad turn in her direction. "I hear there is a wedding being planned. Well, isn't that nice?" There is sarcasm in her voice. "Brad Crawford is marrying a murderer." Her arms are folded across her chest.

There is perfect quiet in the now-empty church as the last of the old-timers hurry out the door. Pastor Taylor hears part of the conversation and walks toward them, smiling as he extends his hand.

"Glad to see you all in church this fine day." He shakes Brad's and Kate's hands, then nods toward Charlotte and the sisters. "This sounds like quite a lively discussion." He glances back at Charlotte.

Brad speaks up. "Pastor, I need to speak with you about some wedding plans if you have the time. And Charlotte, as for that last comment, you are not being fair. Kate shot that guy in self-defense, and I don't appreciate you spreading some insane story around town. You don't know all the facts." Brad's voice is very definite.

Charlotte's eyes pierce through Kate as Kate steps behind Brad's shoulder. Pete and Jeff stand off to the right within earshot, nodding and rolling their eyes. Things are a little tense. There is an uneasy quiet. The pastor scratches his head and tries to smile. He steps back and notices Charlotte is feverishly looking for something in her purse. She sniffles. She nervously snaps open and closes several compartments.

Brad steps in front of Kate. "Charlotte, now calm down. We don't need a scene in church." Tears fill her eyes as she yanks out a handful of tissues. She snaps her purse shut.

Pastor Taylor takes a deep breath and even looks relieved as he steps back. He is aware of the stories floating around town, especially the fact that Charlotte is toting a gun, her hot temper, and the friction between her and Brad.

Jeff and Peter move closer to their dad as Peter whispers to Jeff, "Whew! I thought dear old Charlotte had a pistol hiding in there. Can you just imagine her as our stepmother?"

Brad steps over to Charlotte. "Look, Charlotte. I'm sorry the real estate deal fell through, and as I said before, I'm not ready to sell the ranch, at least not now or anytime soon. As for a future with me, I've made up my mind. My future belongs to Kate here."

Charlotte wipes her eyes and sniffles again. She looks back and forth from Kate to Brad. Kate grabs Brad's hand and looks around from behind his shoulder. Kate takes a deep breath as Pastor Taylor speaks up.

"Look, Charlotte. I can see you are upset." His voice is soothing, always the peacemaker. "Let's talk about this. We can all still get along.

We don't need these spiteful and angry feelings." Kate nods. "Brad, why don't you and Kate head back to my office. I'll be there in a few minutes. You boys can have a seat here for a few minutes."

He then addresses Charlotte. "Charlotte, he has made his decision, and I am sorry your feelings are hurt, but let's try to calm down."

She continues to whimper and wipe her eyes. She stares at Brad as he and Kate turn to head to the pastor's office. She dabs her eyes.

"But, but, I had some great ideas for us. We were going to travel and …" She is now sobbing. She gasps for a breath. "You don't understand. I was planning a great future for Brad and me, until Missy here showed up from some long-lost place in Maryland. I feel like a woman scorned. My feelings are more than hurt. I have been crushed! It has been a low blow!"

She blows her nose. Pastor Taylor puts his arm around her shoulders as she wipes her reddened face and taps her shoe against the wooden floor. Harriet and Hannah step closer to Charlotte, and Harriet gently pats her on her shoulder. Charlotte turns around as she is gently led to the church door. Charlotte's sobs can be heard as she passes Jeff and Peter while leaving the church.

Peter leans over and whispers to Jeff, "Whew. I really thought we were in for a showdown. I'm glad the pastor stepped in. Charlotte is a force to be reckoned with. I hope she doesn't cause any more trouble for Dad and Kate. I wonder if she will show up for the wedding."

"Let's go out and wait in the car. They head outside. Dad shouldn't be much longer." They watch as the women drive away.

Jeff's stomach begins to growl. "Maybe we can convince Dad to stop off at that new restaurant outside of town for a bite to eat. I hear it has great beef barbecue."

"Yeah. I could eat something too. As for you Jeff, you look like you have missed a few meals. How much weight have you lost?"

"Oh, with all my crazy hours of on duty and off duty at the hospital, I hardly have time even to sleep, let alone to eat. I might be down a few pounds. Actually, being home this week has been like a little vacation, especially with all the good food Emma has been cooking up. I just wish my time home here was not for a funeral."

"Okay, here they come. They look happy. They are both smiling. They look good together."

Brad and Kate approach the car. "Okay, boys. The date is set for six o'clock Wednesday. The pastor has cleared his schedule. Kate and I are to meet with him on Monday evening to go over a few things." He looks at the two. "How about a Sunday dinner?" They nod as he grabs Kate's hands. "Let's head out to that new restaurant. I hear their beef barbecue is good. We can arrange for a little wedding reception there too. I hear they have quite a special menu. What do you say?"

The boys grin and look at each other. Jeff chuckles. "That sounds good. Hmmm." He looks back at Pete. "Good old Dad. I think he can still read our minds. Let's go."

Chapter 32

Monday morning comes early. It is barely light at the Crawford ranch, and already three long empty semis are rumbling down the lane. The barn and corral lights are on as they park near the loading ramp. Tom, Brad, and Pete greet the drivers and help them maneuver the big trucks into place. The loading of the livestock begins. There is a lot of bawling and mooing as the steers are prodded up on the loading dock and into the trailers. After one truck is loaded, the next one backs in and fills up with the lively Black Angus steers and cows. It is a noisy scene. Soon the third truck is loaded, and then it too heads out the lane and down to the feed lots, and later the cattle will be transported to the slaughter houses. Tom, Brad, and Pete now head to the house for a quick breakfast before the next wave of trucks come. The busy day passes with other semis rolling in and hauling out loads of bawling black cattle.

It is now almost six o'clock in the evening, and Kate and Brad nervously sit in Pastor Taylor's office. The pastor begins to review some papers on his desk and looks up at Brad. "It looks like everything is in order. I guess this is just going to be a small family wedding."

"Well, Pastor, we only invited a few of our closest friends, but from what I am hearing, the whole town may show up." He clears his throat and looks over at Kate. He pushes the hair back from his forehead. "Our plans are to have my sons, Jeff and Pete, stand for me. And Dolly will stand for Kate here. We plan on a leisurely trip back to Maryland for a honeymoon. Jeff will have to hurry back for his internship at the hospital, and Pete and Tom will hold the fort down at the ranch while I am away. Most of the livestock will be gone by then, so things should be fine while I am away."

"Brad, I remember how your wife, Rachel, died, but you need to fill me in on how Kate's husband was killed. I know Charlotte has her own version."

Kate speaks up. "Yes, dear Charlotte. She even sent the sheriff out to question Brad about the episode." She nods and continues. "Pastor, Jake, my husband, was run down by some maniac at work and was killed. Then, to make a long story short, the guy came gunning for me to kill me too." She pauses and looks over at Brad. "This crazy guy set fire to some buildings at the plant where Jake worked and then tracked me down at my brother's vet clinic. He shot my brother, Richard, in the leg. Luckily enough, though, Richard had his pistol with him and with only one bullet in it. I grabbed it and fired and actually shot the guy. Boom! He fell over dead!"

Kate swallows. Brad nods and smiles.

"It was quite a sudden reflex action," she says. "I had never fired a gun before in my life, so it was purely an act of self-defense. I was exonerated by the police and the judge, and no charges were filed against me."

Pastor Taylor leans back in his office chair, nods, and smiles. His glasses are pushed high on his forehead. "That is some story, a little different from Charlotte's version. I assume the sheriff can back you up with your account. I believe he contacted the state police about the incident when Charlotte approached him."

"Pastor, yes, he did look into the incident and seems satisfied with the report," Brad said. "I know that I talked to you also about Kate's history before and all about her amnesia, so as for any other history, she has two children and one new grandchild back in Maryland. They all seem agreeable to this wedding."

"I guess I just want to make sure everything is legal and that no one shows up at the wedding to cause a commotion." He stops and smiles. "Brad, I've known you for a long time and also your whole family, and I have come to respect you very much, and I wish the best for you both. I think Charlotte will calm down," he says, taking a deep breath, "and not cause any trouble."

The meeting ends after a few papers are signed, and Kate and Brad head out to make the final reservations for the after-wedding dinner party.

Two days pass, and hundreds of beefy livestock are now gone and sold to the highest bidder. Tom, Pete, and Brad have been busy cleaning out box stalls and mending broken gates. The wedding hour is fast approaching. Back at Dolly's, she and Kate are busy with their hair and nails as Kate nervously looks at the clock.

"Oh my goodness, Dolly! In two hours, I'll be Mrs. Bradford Crawford. I can hardly believe it." She takes a deep breath. "I wish Matt and Angie could be here. I miss seeing them and that new baby, little Jake."

"You'll see all of them and more too at the reception they are planning for you back home real soon. I know they will all like Brad too. It should be quite a party."

"Oh, Dolly. I guess I'm just getting nervous. I wonder if I was this nervous when I married Jake." Kate laughs.

"It's a big step for both of you, but I know Brad has been flying around here on cloud nine. I think you two are meant for each other. Things will settle down after the wedding. You two are the talk of this town."

Chapter 33

I t's a perfect cool autumn evening, and the wedding music can be heard streaming out the open church door. The gravel parking area is full of a variety of pickups and family cars. Brad, Jeff, and Pete wait impatiently in the pastor's study. Their tall western boots are shined, and their bola ties are tied tight under their stiff white collars. Their yoked western jackets are embroidered with curly lines up and down their sleeves.

Jeff nervously fingers the gold band in his pocket. He looks at his father and smiles. "I've never seen you so nervous before, Dad." Pete glances over and smiles.

"Boys, I'll just be glad when this is all over. I'm not used to being this dressed up. This stiff collar will rub my neck raw." Brad shifts from one foot to the other. He takes a deep breath and cracks his knuckles. Pete opens the door a crack. He peers out.

"Hey, Dad! The whole town is showing up. I thought it was just going to be us with Doc and Tom with his wife, Sue, and Dolly, Dave, and some of the young cowhands. It's no wonder you are nervous. I think I'm getting nervous too."

"I was afraid the news would spread like a wildfire. I hope they aren't all going to show up at the restaurant and expect me to feed everybody." He laughs.

The wedding march begins, and they slowly walk out to the rustic altar single file. The congregation stands, and Brad sees Dolly, dressed in blue, coming down the aisle. Her hair is curled on top of her head. Her silvery dangling earrings twinkle as they catch the glow of the church lights. She nods and winks to several friends as she passes by.

Brad swallows hard when he sees Kate step out in the aisle behind her. Beads of cold perspiration dot his forehead.

The soft church lights cast a bright glow off Kate's auburn hair. She smiles and nervously holds a bouquet of white roses. She looks radiant. She sees Brad grinning up at the altar as he nervously pushes his graying hair off his forehead.

The wedding music plays a little louder now. Her soft, pink, lacy gown gently touches the floor as she makes her way down the aisle. There is a little creak under foot in the church's floorboards and a low murmur as she passes the smiling faces. Pastor Taylor glances at Brad and grins.

Kate beams. Her hazel eyes are sparkling. She sees Brad's toothy grin as he steps closer to her side. He takes her arm and pulls her close. There is a hush in the church as the music finishes and the congregation takes their seats.

Pastor Taylor begins with a solemn prayer as all heads are bowed. There is a hush in the church. He asks a special blessing for this couple, and as he ends, the congregation agrees with a loud "amen." He begins again with "Dearly beloved, we are gathered here to witness the marriage of this couple" when a loud *boom* is heard.

Suddenly everyone is startled. All heads turn and gape at the back of the church. The front door of the church has slammed shut, and there stands Charlotte, looking a little disheveled. Her clothes are wrinkled, smudged, and barely matching. She stalks up the aisle on blue wobbly heels and looks past Kate and Brad to the pastor. Her makeup is smeared, and her eyes are red.

"Have you got to the part where you ask if anyone objects to this marriage yet?" she says and hiccups.

There is silence.

Brad and Kate have turned and now stare at the spectacle in the aisle. Pastor Taylor breaks the silence. "What is it, Charlotte?"

"I just want to congratulate this fine couple on their wed-wedding," she stutters. She is clearly inebriated. She is a little wobbly and tries to maintain her balance.

There is murmuring from the pews as all eyes are on Charlotte. A few chuckles can be heard.

"I have no more objections to this wedding since I know that this day will be forever remembered by everyone in this town and this church, because the upright Brad Crawford is marrying a murderer." She stares with an evil sneer and points a shaky finger at Kate.

There is a sudden hush in the congregation. She awkwardly turns and staggers out as a broken heel is left in the aisle. The church door slams behind her. There is now a slight murmuring in the congregation.

The pastor turns to Brad, shakes his head, and says, "You now have a very memorable wedding. Shall we continue?"

Kate and Brad nod, hardly able to contain themselves. Brad moves closer to Kate. Dolly giggles and shakes all over.

The congregation chuckles as the wedding proceeds. Jeff grins as he hands over the ring to his father while Dolly hands a shiny gold band to Kate. The ceremony ends with a long, loving kiss. Then men throw their hats in the air, and the women clap, ready to welcome Kate into their ranch families.

Brad and Kate march down the aisle, arm in arm. There are warm handshakes, hugs, and lots of congratulations as their friends and neighbors greet them at the church door. Dolly, Jeff, and Pete stand outside, greeting friendly faces as the crowd lingers nearby. The new red Chevy is decorated with streamers and a "Just Married" sign with a long line of tin cans tied to the rear of the car.

As Kate and Brad take a step down the church steps, Kate hesitates. She looks over and sees Dolly waving. As a barrage of white rice is showered over their heads, Kate throws her rose bouquet to Dolly. Dolly reaches up and grabs the flowers as Kate and Brad duck away from the rice and head for the car.

Jeff and Peter rush to the front seat as the newlyweds slide into the back seat. Jeff starts the car, revs the motor, and takes off with gravel spinning beneath the wheels. The crowd begins to break up as a few cars and some beat-up pickup trucks follow them out of town, tooting their horns as they go. The clatter of the tin cans and the honking of the horns follow them to the new Beef and Barbecue Restaurant.

A room has been reserved, and the group heads to the banquet room for a feast of steak, ribs, and all the trimmings. After the guests have been seated and there is a quiet over the crowd, Jeff stands with a glass of champagne.

"I would like to make a toast to the newlyweds." Everyone picks up his or her goblet and holds it high in the air. "To Kate and Dad. Here's to a long life of health and happiness and to many years of rich blessings. We love you both." There are smiles all around as the champagne goblets are clicked together and sipped.

Brad stands and clears his throat. "I just want to thank all of our dear friends for sharing this remarkable day with Kate and me. It has truly been a real journey down life's path for both of us, and now we have two great families blended together to share our lives with. This is really a special day for us as we start our new life together." He looks down at Kate. "I actually thought at one time that this day would never come." He winks at Kate as she blushes. "When Charlotte came down the church aisle, I wasn't sure what she had in mind."

There is laughter and smiles all around. He hesitates and takes a deep breath. He brushes a tear from his eye, leans over, and gives Kate a tender kiss. There are some oohs and aahs from the young cowhands. Friends smile and nod as the dinner is about to be served.

Chapter 34

The weather has turned warm with just a hint of an autumn breeze approaching. Some leaves have turned a golden yellow while others along the roadside are still a deep green. Brad and Kate have been on the road a few days and have enjoyed visiting a few historic areas.

They drive north to Yellowstone National Park and see bison and waterfalls, then through mountain passes rich with mountain goats and bears. They travel south through Colorado and view Pike's Peak. Every day is a relaxing cruise through a territory of sights only read about in history books. Next, they travel through the Great Plains of the Midwest and on to Missouri.

They visit Nashville and the Grand Ole Opry and even hear some of their favorite country singers on its stage. Next, they head north for Maryland through the hills of Kentucky and West Virginia. They spend their nights in cozy bed-and-breakfasts while dining at little wayside eateries. Soon signs point to Washington, DC, and to all the great museums and memorial statues.

Traveling north on I-95, they soon come to the exit for Elkton, Maryland. Kate begins to recognize familiar landmarks. This is all new territory for Brad as she directs him to her familiar brick Cape Cod house. It looks the same as when she left, with Matt's car parked in the driveway. Their new red Chevy comes to a halt, and Brad toots the horn.

The kitchen door opens, and out strolls Matt, a sandwich in his hand. "It's about time you two newlyweds got here." He grins from ear to ear. "You two sure took your time getting here. The reception party is scheduled for tomorrow night at Uncle Richard's house. I was beginning to worry something had happened to you." Brad and Matt shake hands, and then Matt gives his mother a long, embracing hug.

"We are fine." Brad glances down at Kate. "We just took the long way to get here. We saw a lot of pretty sights but not half as pretty as your mother here." Kate blushes and puts her arms around Brad's and Matt's waists as they walk to the kitchen door.

"Is everything okay with the house and with you since I've been gone?" she asks.

"Mom, everything is fine. There are a lot of people anxious to see you and meet Brad. Angie and Dan will be over later tonight. I think Aunt Joyce has everything under control. Angie has been helping her."

"Oh, good. I can't wait to see little Jake again."

"Mom, I even had the cleaning lady come and give the house a thorough going over. I'm sleeping in your old bedroom, and you and Brad can use my room at the top of the stairs, if that is all right with you two."

Kate looks a little surprised at Matt and then looks at Brad. She shrugs. "I guess that is okay. I am a little surprised though. Are there any other changes I should know about?" Kate's voice is a little troubled.

"I moved Dad's chair over to the corner of the living room and put my favorite one in front of the TV." He looks pleased.

Kate lets out a big sigh. "You seem to have taken over this business of being in charge quite well." She looks around and relaxes. "At least the kitchen is the same."

"Yeah, but I don't have much food in the house. We might have to eat out tonight." He laughs. "I can take a quick ride into town and pick up a pizza to go and get back here before Angie and Dan arrive."

"So how does pizza sound?" asks Matt.

Kate looks at Brad. "You know, son. That is one thing Brad and I have not had during our entire trip back here." Kate smiles. "Pizza will be fine. You may want to pick up some bacon and eggs too while you are in town for breakfast in the morning."

Brad steps closer to Kate and puts a reassuring arm around her shoulders. He nods at Matt. "Don't worry about him, Kate. He will survive. He's just like Peter and Jeff. If it wasn't for Emma, we would probably still be eating chicken five times a week."

Matt picks up his jacket and hurries out the door to his car. Brad follows him to his car and begins to haul their suitcase in. He looks around at the tall oak trees and neatly mowed lawn. He sees a birdhouse in an old pin oak tree and the worn basketball net hanging from the pole in the backyard.

He turns and carries the bags into the kitchen. Kate stares out the window.

"Kate, I can see Jake's and your influence all over this place. There is a certain quietness and peacefulness here. I'm sure Matt will take care of this home just like you and Jake did. Maybe someday he can raise a family here too."

"Brad, I know from all the stories Jake and the kids have told me, we did a lot of living here. I just don't remember any of them. So maybe, just maybe, starting a new life with you will bring some cherished memories too. We already have quite a few." Kate winks. "It's a new chapter in my life as well as for you too. I know Matt and Angie with Dan and the baby will come and visit us, but I really feel like a stranger in my old house already. Maybe it's the changes Matt made with my old bedroom." She sighs. "Maybe it is all for the best. I guess it's a little nostalgia creeping in."

Brad steps over and turns Kate around. "Look, Kate. It's a new beginning for all of us. Life's journey can bring a few twists and turns, but we all have to look beyond our journey's curves and dead ends. We are looking forward to a great life together, knowing that our children will share in it too. Come on. Help me up the stairs with these suitcases. Matt will be back before we know it."

In no time at all, Matt returns with two large pizzas—one pepperoni and one loaded with extra cheese, mushrooms, sausage, and peppers. There is fresh-baked hard bread and good old french fries. The kitchen is filled with the glorious aroma of the steaming hot Italian toppings.

The trio sit down around the table and fills their paper plates. Matt wants to know all about the happenings at the ranch and what Peter is doing. Kate sits back and listens as Brad brings Matt up to date with all the ranch news and the selling of the livestock.

Suddenly, there is a slight knock at the door, and before anyone can answer it, in come Angie and Dan. Dan carries a tiny bundle, with pink cheeks and a few strands of dark hair peeking out beneath a little knit cap.

"Oh, look who is here!" Kate rises quickly and hurries to Angie. She gets a great big hug as Brad stands to meet them. "Dan and Angie, this is Brad, and Brad this is little Jake." Kate steps to Dan and gently reaches for the baby.

Brad shakes hands all around and peers over Kate's shoulder. Little Jake is wide awake and begins to squirm. Large brown eyes peek out from under his little skullcap. Kate pats his back as little Jake begins to smile and coo. "Look, Brad. Isn't he beautiful?"

Brad peeks around her shoulder and takes the little cap off. "Yep. He looks just like his daddy." Dan laughs. "Congratulations to you two. You have a good-looking boy there. I guess I never thought about this before, but I am the new grandfather!"

Everyone laughs.

"Kate has told me so much about you and Dan," Brad says. "I feel like you have always been part of my family too. As for Matt here, Peter and I tried to make him a real cowboy at the ranch." Brad pauses. "He had a little trouble after he got dunked in the horse trough, but I think he passed the test."

Everyone laughs.

"Okay, Brad, you don't need to go into the whole story," Matt says. "I never told them about the horse trough ordeal." He laughs. "So let's finish this pizza and catch up on the rest of the news with the newlyweds."

The last piece of the pizza is devoured, and the talk around the table is casual and lively. Angie smiles at her mom and looks at Brad. An accepting nod lets Kate know all is well and that Brad is a welcome addition. Kate fills the kids in on all the sites they saw on their leisurely honeymoon trip there. Brad sits back and enjoys the interaction between the kids and their mother.

The evening passes quickly, and Angie pulls her mother aside to review what Aunt Joyce has planned for the Saturday night reception party. Angie explains, "It will be a very casual affair with some homemade hors d'oeuvres, a wedding cake, and ice cream. Everyone seems excited to meet Brad, especially Uncle Richard."

"I think Richard will put Brad at ease once they get together," Kate says. "Brad is not awkward around anyone. He just gets a little antsy when he is away from the ranch for a while. He knows that Peter and his foreman, Tom, can handle just about anything while he is away. He keeps in touch with his cell phone. He has never had much of a vacation before.

He was always too involved in his ranch work to go anywhere. You and Dan will have to make a real effort to come out and spend some time with us. I'll need to see that baby too."

Angie nods as Dan approaches with a sleeping baby. "It's time for us to go, Mom. I'll see you tomorrow night at seven o'clock at Uncle Richard's." Kate and Angie give goodbye hugs, and Kate gives a little peck on little Jake's warm cheek.

Early Saturday morning, Kate is busy packing up all the little essentials she wants to take back to the ranch with her. Clothes and trinkets are sorted and packed in boxes. She reviews special instructions on all the appliances and details of the house with Matt.

Matt stands back and gently answers, "Yes, Mother. Yes, Mother."

Brad is busy maneuvering all the things around in the car for the trip home. The special chest Dolly's dad made for Kate when she worked at the diner will have to be sent later. The official transfer of the property and the signing of the papers can all be done long distance through the mail. Things are being carefully checked off her list and are finally coming together for Kate and Brad's final departure. Now, for the final farewell party for old friends and family.

The evening is cool, and Kate's mood is a little reserved. Brad is quiet. She knows this will be hard, especially saying goodbye to all the friends who have helped her through Jake's tragic death. It is almost seven o'clock.

They reach Richard's house in Matt's car, and the parking area is comfortably filled. All the lights are on, and some lighthearted chatter can be heard coming through the open windows. Richard and Joyce are at the open front door, greeting the guests. Brad and Matt follow and step back, allowing Kate to enter first.

Richard grabs Kate for a lingering hug, then steps back and offers a hand to Brad. The two men shake heartily. Tears creep into Joyce's eyes as she and Kate share an embrace.

Introductions are quickly shared between them as they head into the decorated living room and out to the crowded backyard. Brad tightly holds Kate's hand as they mingle and greet the friendly faces.

The night is exhausting for Kate. Soon Brad finds comfort in spending time with Richard and Dan. The threesome seems to bond immediately. Compliments are shared for all the good food with cake and ice cream.

Joyce and Angie, while holding little Jake, talk quietly as the evening slowly comes to an end. The guests slowly gather around Kate and Brad for a final goodbye and express their wishes for a safe trip back to Wyoming.

Later, Richard and Joyce sit down with Kate and Brad, and reminisce about some old times and all the changes taking place around them. They promise to take a trip to Wyoming for a visit, probably next summer.

Finally, the weary Kate, Brad, and Matt arrive home, tired but content that all the goodbyes are finally over. Kate is tired as she and Brad climb the stairs together. Tomorrow they will head home to the ranch to make a new life together, leaving behind some very special memories.

Kate pushes back the curtains and peeks out the upstairs window. The stars twinkle brightly, and the moon has a silvery glow around it. Kate remembers her other journey back home several years ago with Jake, when he drove her home from Wyoming. She remembers her amnesic days as Rose.

Now there is a new journey facing her. It's her future life in Wyoming as Mrs. Bradford Crawford. She takes a deep breath. She feels content and settled now. She can still sense that unseen but guiding and protective hand, leading and carrying her through this special life's journey.

A little tear appears on her cheek. She flinches as she feels another set of protective hands around her shoulders. She turns and sees Brad's face and broad smile. His hands are warm and a bit calloused but loving and protective.

A warm kiss is felt on her neck. "Come to bed, Mrs. Crawford. We have a long trip ahead of us in the morning."

Printed in the United States
By Bookmasters